John Mella

TRANSFORMATIONS

Chicago Review Press

ISBN: 0-914090-16-X
Library of Congress Catalog Card Number: 75-18961

Parts of this work have appeared, in altered form, in *Chicago Review*. Brief portions of *Transformations* appear in the prose of W.B. Yeats.

Chicago Review Press Books are published by Curt Matthews and Alexander Besher, and are distributed by The Swallow Press, 1139 S. Wabash Avenue, Chicago, Illinois 60605.

Chicago Review Press, Inc., 172 East Walton Place, Chicago, Illinois 60611.

1

n 1906 the actress Lena Ray, for the past season the rage of England's theatres and music halls, disappeared. The manner of her vanishing was characteristic; during her celebrated performance of Jonson's most famous masque—with its intricate cloud-machinery and wave-machinery and authentic thunder-claps—she managed to appear in a cunningly disguised mirror which, upon being abruptly tilted, erased her image in a dazzling flash of light. As the witty reviewer in *Punch* quipped: she went out in a Ray of light. No one, however, was chuckling. Her manager pleaded total ignorance, as did the director at the Savoy, her fellow actors, everyone down to the blue-and-gold uniformed usherettes, with their cute page-boy hair-dos. It was rumoured, though, that she slipped out through a trap-door deceptively marked "Entrance" (decorated in each of its four corners with winged Cupids) to join, down an obscure back alley, a playwright who was infatuated with her. There Dame Gossip stopped, bumped her long nose against a blank wall. She left behind a bankrupt company, a famous theatre suddenly destitute of its primary source of revenue, and innumerable stage-struck hearts fractured by her most melodramatic exit.

It was not known (it being a carefully guarded secret) that she was one of the most flagrant transvestites of her age. Female dramatic parts were, of course, in those times, often taken by pre-adolescent boys, whose clarity of delivery and aesthetic detachment made for greater control (not to mention stability in the company; the Italian travelling troupes, despite their great fire and bravura performances, were notoriously unreliable; I recall a performance of some *commedia dell' arte* in Naples which kept a full house waiting a full two hours while the prima donna sulked in the wings). She, however (habit and devotion are irresistable), managed from the inception of her career (at the age of 9) to project the image of a totally natural female of our species. Over the next several years after her début her young body swelled normally and magnificently—perhaps blinding the scores of thronged admirers from noticing the straight and symmetrical frame upon which it was hung. That girlish treble did not deepen, crack and break; it merely mellowed into a rich and creamy contralto. The cheek which blushed or paled under the duress of stage emotions, far from roughening with a summer stubble, actually seemed to grow smoother as the blood rose or subsided. Perhaps it was due to the talents of her stage-manager, the late Will Sly, perhaps to her own strange genius (who can forget—but I am looking ahead—those eerily effective Chinese eyebrows, blackly curving in their chalk-white face, on the very eve of the Manchurian conflict?), but she had critics, an adulate public, the make-up men themselves, completely enter into her illusion.

It was to be my part to move behind that illusion.

2

I recall the first time I glimpsed that fatal creature, who was to imprint so deeply the texture of my existence. We had gone, a group of us, to attend the premier of *Beauty's Rose,* then opening at the Globe. The spring weather was somewhat melancholy and mistily English; it aureolaed, with a post-impressionist palette, the gas-lamps along the deserted squares. The hansom cab moved smoothly behind the glossy posteriors of its quadruped engine; the curtains rustled, revealing snapshots of scenes which were later to become famous—the Bridge, the River itself with its hurrying life, the Liberty of the Clink, with its picturesque taverns and innumerable ditches in which garbage, dead canine and rodent life, and the bilgewater of the Thames sloshed; then green-mildewed patches (an early version of suburbia), a venerable chapel or two (this was of course before the extensive bombings of the Civil War), and the theatre itself, the focal point of countless streams of citizens, some coming muddily over the fields, other (as ourselves) elegantly in hired transportation, and still others by water. The black-and-gold banner had been hung out, with its asses' ears—signifying a public entertainment was in the offing. The year was 1897—the year of so many changes at home and abroad. Lord Kitchener was investing the Soudan with fire and sword (supported, incidentally, by a fine phalanx of newly minted howitzers just bought from Germany). Australia had declared independence, provoking a declaration of war on the parts of both England and its oversized colony America. Liberal Gladstone had been succeeded by war minister Pitt. The "micro-mini" skirt which was, along with its acid-rock music, to make England internationally famous, had not yet revealed its gleaming flank in the distant tunnel of time—the style now being the "maxi," with its hoops and long graceful trailing skirts, a style far more congenial to my own tastes, despite my avowed propensity as a "leg man." In three years the Queen was to celebrate her Golden Jubilee following fifty resplendent years on the throne; preparations were already being made; the River was being dredged to allow the royal barges passage, costumes were being designed in the extravagantly exclusive boutiques along Threadneedle Street, plays and odes were labouring in the overheated brains of Grub Street, and the backdrops and props for enormously expensive masques, some of which transplanted "real" objects and artifacts into their weighty canvases, were secreting in the vast studios of East End. And the invention which was, a scant eight or nine years later, to lead to the utter transformation of the subject of these pages, was but a mere glimmer (I almost said "lightbulb") in the brain of its impoverished originator who lived (hibernated, holed up) in a deteriorated portion of abjectly misnamed Regent Street: the Magic Lantern which, when exposed to moving slips of celluliod imprinted with various images, was able to produce the most transcendent illusion of motion, grace, life and, yes, Time itself, and the illusionary triumph over Time.

But of those ghosts, and their exorcism, more will be spoken anon.

3

While that venerable vehicle—which seems, in retrospect, as slow as the slowest of stage machines pulled across the bare platform by creaking ropes and pulleys—draws up to the private entrance of the great Globe (burnt down, alas, during a Christmas pageant some years later), we may visit those early scenes of flickering illumination; and, even as the reigning star of that constellation undergoes her laborious toillette, surrounded by harpyish lesbians, gaping mechanics, homosexual cosmeticians (of her cosmetics more will have to be appended in a later note; one remembers not only Max Beerbohm's solemnly witty put-on in that famous issue of the *Yellow Book* but also the prophetic poetic essay of the divine Charles "Eloge du Maquillage"), and the usual perfumed and wigged assortment of *poetes maudits, dilettantes,* and general hangers-on, we may safely withdraw into an entirely different quarter to inspect the artifacts gathered therein. That inventor's workshop, or laboratory, was of a spartan simplicity (his name, curiously enough, was "Image," and it is as such, in a different rôle, that he appears in Yeats's memoirs); at one end were shelves anchored at varying heights on which were placed, and rotated, lanterns of different sizes which had, attached to their muzzles, the most outlandish shutters (cranks, slots, pinholes); at the other, a blank whitewashed wall which he kept religiously scrubbed. The other walls were comfortably lined with books, works on theology in Greek and Latin. That room was always a pleasure to me, with its curtains of grey corduroy over door and window and book case, and its side-walls covered, where not with books, by brown paper, a fashion invented, I think, by his occasional room-mate Horne, that was soon to spread; and talking there by candlelight it never seemed very difficult to murmur Villiers de L'Isle Adam's proud words, "As for living—our servants will do that for us." It was in that isolated chamber that the inventor Image carried on his imaginary life, and there alone. I was often puzzled as to when and where he could have met the famous men or beautiful women whose conversation, often wise, and always appropriate, he quoted so often, and it was not till a little after his death that I discovered that these conversations were but figments. He never altered a detail of speech, and would quote what he had invented for Gladstone or Newman for years without amplification or amendment, with what seemed a scholar's accuracy. His favourite quotations were from Newman, whom, I believe, he had never met, though I can remember nothing now but Newman's greeting to him, "I have always considered the profession of a man of letters a third order of the priesthood!" (the *litterateur* was the inventor's alternate ego), and these quotations became so well known that at Newman's death the editor of *The Nineteenth Century* asked them for publication.

It was, though, in his so-called "relations" with famous faraway beauties of the day (and I can still recall the solemn caressing way he had of intoning that pontifical word) that his dreams brushed against the rough fibre of "reality" to produce, as if that solitary frottage, that onanist's discreet manipulation, could make a true being, slender, two-dimensional pictures which gave the illusion of depth. Alas, it was only after the poor man's ignoble death—over, of all things, an Italian restaurant owner's plebian daughter—that I realized the source of these supposedly private sittings: the transference, transformation, of mezzotints, tintypes, incredibly detailed lithographs, to his magic squares of celluloid. There was, first, the "divine Sarah," a large, dramatic woman to whom the charitable among us might apply the epithets "statuesque" and "stately"—none of whose languishing poses, which look merely awkward or grotesque in their frozen stationary quality, suggest the remarkable fire and force of her delivery—one that had, I must be honest, too much "soul" (and that is to say not enough heart and intelligence) to suit my tastes. Then the great facial and structural qualities, which suggest motion as the other suggests stasis, of the incomparable Isodora Duncan and Cléo de Mirode—recall, if you are old enough, or, if you are not, look, look for one moment, which will quickly eternize itself, into a photographic album of those faces: the halfclosed eyelid drooped and faintly yellowed, like old vellum, but incredibly smooth, a chalkwhite expanse of cheek, breathtaking butterfly wings of eyebrows, and the eye, immense, liquid, suggesting depths but with a totally surface, or hermetic, expression that was inexpressive, meaning devoid of meaning. Vaguely androgynous—am I saying too much already?—they resembled large graceful birds of prey mating in some distant azure that folded, enfolded them in its perspective, so that one could not tell male from female.

As if one wanted to: for the effect these strange half-human creatures had (especially when subjected to my inventor's process) was not, really, that of a *femme fatal* (a curvaceous cutie, a svelte starlet), but that of a being at once encompassing and transcending the male and female spheres; a master-mistress of all men's passions; an eye in which the meaning of the sexes was gathered and quintessentialized, then released (the smoky dingy lantern suddenly flooding its store of light) to gild the object whereupon it gazed. That evening of strange slow shadows comes back upon me now—now that I have another darkness to contend with; we had just returned from our tour of the provinces, with their ill-lighted, draughty playhouses, yokels reeking of garlic and grease, and goodwives whose oleaginous stench was always overlaid with strong doses of cheap perfume. The host at whose chambers we dined, a sometime partner in real estate named Burbage (no relation to the great actor and theatre-manager) invited us, over brandy and cigars, to visit what he called a "labyrinth-maker" in whom was contained "the wave of the future" (he used an odious French phrase later to become a standard cliché at cocktail parties). We went without a murmur.

The new King that year (1905) was undergoing his somewhat lengthy coronation, despite threats of plague (a red star in the East; riot; mutterings of sedition); the playhouses were threatened with closing, and a new faction in Parliament, the Puritans, had arisen. Never anything but a weak minority hitherto, they had trebled their power through alliance with the new merchant class and, grown bold with successes in the military campaign against the Spanish-Australian Alliance, they were beginning to move with increasing confidence into what our lawyer (former representative of the Ploughboy Clubs) called "legislating public morality"—which in our case meant banning all dramatic productions. For the time, though, our forces stood firm, mainly because the new King (late of Scotland), like his predecessor, was an avid theatre-goer, had indeed written a learned essay on the subject in Latin (replete with quotations from Aristotle, Longinus, and Boileau). A sickly man, he was enamoured not only of scholarly subjects but scholarly plays as well; it is from the opening of his reign that the star of our great theatrical rival, whose *forte* was a rigorous muscular prose, "realistic" detail, and a close adherence to the "unities," became ascendent, to finally merge into the period of the great journalistic novel which followed. That scholiastic passion extended, surprisingly, not only to dry-as-dust Latin commentaries but included (such was his largeness of spirit) his three picturebook children as well (two princes and a ravishing princess—whom, despite their apparent boundless good health, he was to outlive). The last years of his reign, as we all know now, were troubled by the first stirring of the internecine conflict that was not only to divide the country into warring classes, but the civilized world behind those classes—to culminate by that action no native Englishman would dare perpetrate: the bombing of London, its landmarks, its historical buildings and the quarter which caused its greatest friendly critic (Holland) to call it the "architectural museum of the world." Other effects were less obvious but further-reaching. The class (and I use that word as the biologist does when attempting to name a new species, or mutation) against which all free-breathing Englishmen were arrayed (and these included gentry, artists of all degrees, and the whole motley crew of "Royalists") was to emerge solidified and, finally, triumphant, their leader (called by Yeats "that warted, opinionated head") firmly entrenched as the Lord Protector—

a cheap euphemism for the first, and last, dictator this country has ever tolerated.

But in the days of which I speak that *bouche noire* was but the darkest inkling in a few diseased brains. The lingering trace of our Queen was still felt on the trembling corpus of a grateful country—and by a cluster of awed foreign powers, humbled by the might of her navy. Art, although we knew it not, was at its highest pitch, its living tap-root bedded deep in the foul mire of its origins—not in the Court which was to appropriate its bloom by amputating its pistil, stamen, shaft, and earthy fertility. The City was divided by that dramatic art which included Poesy as its finest breath in the shape of the three great rival theatres, the Rose, the Swan, the Globe; for as yet that sense of comedy, which was soon to mould the very fashion plates, and, in the eyes of men of my generation, to destroy at last the sense of beauty itself, had scarce begun to show here and there, in slight subordinate touches among the designs of great painters, dramatists, craftsmen. And what, after all, remains now of that sense? A flicker of light on an empty wall. A mask turned face down in its crushed black velvet. The voluptuous vanishing buttocks of a Cupid's nude cheeks. The sigh, the swish of wet departing tyres. A blurring tear. A darkened window.

4

Yet hear me, o ray of departed light! If I write less of you than of the stage upon which you appeared—and less of that stage than the larger, sordid, banal and beautiful stage in which *it* was anchored—is not that because you are, indeed, that very elusive something, a sunbeam in a dirty test-tube, an image suggesting depths and deliriums but, in itself, no more substantial than the screen upon which it dances, the skin of vision with which it is fleshed? Thus it was that I, a pedant and a scholar, an obscure bibliographer labouring in the innermost recesses of the British Museum, turned popular playwright (and thus incurring the wrath of the redoubtable Shaw—but of that more anon), so as to make that same wall liven with vivid colours, take on the hues and tints of a deeply felt emotion, one felt in solitude and thus cast on the screen of one's solipsism. Did I say I first saw her at the opening of *Beauty's Rose?* That is a mis-statement of sorts; for I, I alone, am the author of that aery nothing, that fancy fleshed out faintly, that "something consumed with naught", along with the 60 or so librettos, skitlets, masques which she redeemed by her presence—among which were (think back, oldsters) *Music To Hear, The Darling Buds Of May, Bare Ruined Choirs* and *Nothing Like The Sun.*

At that first production—the single radiant cell which was to multiply so promiscuously later—I entered with the others, an obscure, doubly obscure author who, in the recesses of some arcane research, had spun a slight golden web that was to catch, briefly, and only long enough to irradiate and immortalize, a rare species, the only member, in fact, of that species. We entered swiftly and withdrew to our box. The new gas-jets provided a ghostly, even illumination; the scroll-work glowed with gilt paint, cupids peeped, cherubs pouted, and, between the apexes of the pseudo-Doric columns on which leered stylized masks of Tragedy and Comedy, limpid pools of sapphire floated. Below, the pit crawled with its myriad life; fishmongers competed with perfume distillers for reek, goldsmiths' apprentices maneuvered for the best positions with their natural rivals, the silversmiths' lads; and over all, hung a cloud of thick grey smoke produced by the incineration of tobacco, a habit newly introduced from the Colonies, and one the King of Scotland (later of England) was to diatribe against; but here, above the moil and garboils, all was serene as, with superior perspective, we overlooked all.

This was the play, remember, in which, after the sport with the moonstruck poet that the leading Athenian citizens have, the spirit-queen Gloriana appears in gauzy filaments that diaphanously divide and multiply her sex: at once Dionysus and Diana, the creature, young limbs akimbo, hovered on crude black threads in a perfect wash of wondering applause. I had sat silent, struck dumb by the apparition. On my left sat my escort for the evening, a furry-headed nubian graduate student of African studies, whose slender columns of legs were chiaroscuroed with white net stockings in a baroque design of scroll and leaf; on my right the bulldogjowled female professor of English whose speciality was the Irish Literary Revival (dissertation: A. E. Russell). I myself was rendered immobile, even as the machinery creaked, the giggling goddess lowered, ankle and elbow and shadowy torso clasped by invisible strings, the cloud machine pushed clouds across the streaked enamel heavens, and there, in the foreground, a gentle nubile stream purled and creakled and rippled, its sinuous length inflected by hidden gears—immobile as there moved the visible incarnation, only hinted at in what I had written. The masque proceeded in its jeweled deliberate pace; the goddess tempted, the poet fell into song, betrayed by that stinging honey; she vanished; and that queer transformation, that "cobbler's apprentice" entered from the wings, more correctly, from the still-glowing, still-palpitating residual impression that yet haunted the roomful of dazed retinas—entered in his boyish smock with the work-pockets from which obtrude the handles of a hammer and an adze. This sudden juxtaposition of images, the goddess with the fair grobian, the muse with the deaf-mute, produced in me a strange constriction, a peculiar tightness in the chest, a loss of breath, as if I were watching the incredibly distant action from under water. That miniature action ground imperturbably forward, found its tiny denouement (cobbler crowned queen, poet king; delicate intercalation of recorders and lutes). The imaginative director of this ornate and stately pageant left us with an enchanting last image: the sylvan glade filled with flowers and its spring, in the centre of which, humming with sweetness, the hive (like Othello's handkerchief a catalyst to the action, the maneuvering of the lovers together) dripping with its accumulated store of amber syrup and around which dance, to a stately marriage division, some furry bejewelled hymenoptera, magnificently striped in bold black and gold, antennae aquiver, multifaceted eyes catching the torchlight and taperlight in flashes, gleams, hints of deeper richness. He, we, I, heard nothing of the breakers of loud applause (mothers, nephews, cuckolds); the exit is there, crowned with lurid fire; to the right must be a backstage—that way (excuse me; excuse excuse excuse), smoking couples wreathed in tendrils, programs leaving the steps, a dead restraining limb in batesian tuxedo, a door, one more door, propped buttocks, stools, and there, multiplied by mirrors, magnified in the apprehending, framed with—with postcards, or pansies, or pale God knows what flowers (plastic, my dear, but true gold still), I saw what I had thought I saw. There was a half turn, a half smile. With a gasp of recognition I entered.

5

he cylinder holds tape: and as a human being does, stores impressions, brightly coloured, hazy or clear, on innumerable squares of blank fibre that, upon being combined and recombined, produce the illusion—it is only an illusion!—of motion and life—

"That figure, now—milkwhite limbs against a pattern of roses, blushing and damasked—lovely, but only as an object of contemplation—see how it flushes into breath and spirit when subjected to my process—the eyelids start and flutter—the pulse quickens—the blood blooms on its field of snow—all that is needful is for some thoughtful demiurge to place human speech in that lovely distended pouting mouth, now only a pitted cherry capped with a bubble of saliva—

"Or here—surely you recognize that building—well what would you say if I told you that is no simple model or architect's mock-up—but the original in-scale drawing of the great Inigo Jones himself—you see he has put his initials under the east portico (disguised, it is true, as a couple of emaciated sight-seers)—as well as a thumbprint mimicried as an amorphous school of doves in flight—

"Or . . . "

He had changed his lodgings but you would never guess that from sitting in this darkened room, as we were, aware only of empty gloom and of the bright images that chased themselves across the blank wall opposite. He reminded me of a notorious uncle of mine who delighted, with the aid of a lump of tallow and a prestidigitating hand (which seemed to possess at least a dozen flying fingers), to throw a group of mesmerized children into delightful hysterics by the monsters he conjured from our tediously empty wall—the same wall which, on long bright endless afternoons, I would turn my face to, as white and featureless as the visage that stared back. This room was, it is true, larger than the previous one, but if anything it was more bare and uncluttered than ever, with only the intangible flickerings of light gaining in detail and richness. In the darkness I could see his tousled head—a halo of silk with something darker at the centre—hunched over the controls of his machine which was purring and disgorging from its seemingless endless reel a fountain of disconnected images. To my right the burly Burbage loomed in the inky gloom (I mean the actor; that other, with the cigar and insurance portfolio, had mysteriously disappeared, though eventually he turned up again as an importer of foreign films and pornography); to my left, loosely crossed legs elegantly garbed in dove-grey piping, lounged the slender figure of Will Sly (whose initials are, now that I think of it, the same as my own); I could faintly see the tapered fingertips of one hand holding up the mirror-image of the other. The room, indeed, with which we were blindfolded, needed to be only slightly larger to be that of a miniature theatre, a tiny jewelled point, pulsing with light, in the darkness that now shrouded the City. That year (the spring of 1906—exactly six months since her abrupt desertion of our Company)—we had, after some weary wrangling, become the King's Men after the accession of James—marked the first of the series of scurrilities that came to be known as the War of the Theatres, and a small group of us had retreated to the becalmed eye of that storm to wash off, in bathings of luminence, its vitriol and the smoky flashbulbs of reporters. Who sat in the darkness there with me?—not unlike, now that I come to think of it, the darkness I am now situated in, or, for that matter, other darknesses (all night is identical) wherein I watched lovely images of light which made me a part of the blackness that gazed. Well, there was, first of all, Burbage and Sly, who shared a row of chairs with me; Ralph Barnes, one of the newer publishers, who specialized in translations from the Italian and French (*Orlando Furioso* and a stylization of the *Romaunt of the Rose* were two of his more successful titles); Leo de Forêt, an inventor-associate who occasionally collaborated with Image; Henry Condell, a fellow actor; a few tarts, all wig and wistaria and wink, that had worked as "extras" in a recent production; on the other side of the humming projector, Image's in-and-out friend Robert Horne, who had recently become one of the prominent young interior designers of East End (he had, indeed, designed several of our more successful sets, one of which was picked out for praise by, oddly enough, Shaw in the *Saturday Review*). Over the ceiling, in time with the internal combustion of the iron cranium to our rear, luminous shadows floated, some shaped like whales, others like camels, cormorants, or figures out of mythology, still others like the fingers of an enormous hand. Outside, the fog enclosed us further in its thick, crawling scalp; we could hear muffled reports of cannon firing over the River, an exercise performed, I believe, to reassure the paranoid fears of tradesmen and toilers that something was being done about an imagined invasion of swarthy Spaniards and grim pale-faced renegade Australians.

That literary skirmish, with its stacks of mock bodies—Dekker was later to call it "the merry murdering"—seems now to belong more to the 18th century than to our own day, but it was associated with two new developments in the London theatre: the rise of companies of boy-actors (the Children of the Chapel Royal and Paul's Boys were the two most prominent), and the rapid growth of satiric comedy, especially as practised by the team of Jonson and Shaw (called by Wilde the "Beaumont and Fletcher of the modern age"), Chapman, and Marston (the latter known today largely because of an undistinguished, but influential, essay by Mr. T. S. Eliot). The one, of course, led to the other: in the mouths of towheaded striplings the invective and venom these self-styled reformers and critics oozed sounded merely striking and arresting, and the Royal Censor who attended opening night could be counted on, especially if well-plied with solid or liquid gold, to be chuckling instead of choleric at those key passages which anatomized, with dull blade and duller brain, so-called "evils of the time." Our Queen, I believe, would never have tolerated such vendective pomposities, which erred not so much from the side of poor politics as poor taste, but the new King not only permitted but actually encouraged such efforts, no doubt because they had a somewhat hoary tradition (Aristophanes, Plautus, and that old stand-by of ancient and modern mediocrities senile Seneca, whose name makes one think of a tall Red Indian glistening with bear fat rather than the stumpy gnarled Roman farmer he undoubtedly was, reeking of garlic and cheap red wine). From the boys' companies this thin watery gruel spread to the two other major adult companies of the City, the Lord Chamberlain's Men and the Admiral's Men, which seemed, in the process, to shrink from a former spaciousness and luminosity: from the noble blank verse of Marlowe, honey of vowels fenced in with the membrane-thin comb of consonants, to the almost-prose of Webster's and Eliot's verse dramas, which sound like nothing so much as the *Times Literary Supplement* chopped up into arbitrary lines. The newly literate audience that daily packed these houses was, of course, enthusiastic (the enthusiasm of the chicken upon discovering that it can operate quite well without a head) to view their lives, if one can call them that, paraded before the public eye; I can still recall the gasps and exclamations as now a landmark ("There's St. Paul's! There's Westminster! I can see London Bridge!") and now a familiar domestic scene (a prose pudding bubbling in the background, baby's diapers coagulating in a corner) was conjured up by some sordid Soho sorcerer or Aldwych alchemist. From these depressingly intimate scenes it was, obviously, the merest child's hop to live "porno" shows (which depended upon the skillful use of lightings and shadings to avoid censorship); the advantage of these rudimentary entertainments was, of course, that they eliminated the playwright altogether, depending as they did upon the free improvisation of the glistening and grunting "actors." And very soon—sooner than any of us realized—the last of the formal distinctions that cramp, compress, and release the energies of our art had vanished: the "audience" forced its way onto the stage to join what clearly required so little talent, and the room needed only the transformation of a few fixtures to eerily resemble a Roman coliseum of the 1st Century A.D. or a German "delousing" station (the last stop before the cremation ovens) some nineteen-odd centuries later.

The drama our Company produced, while unabashedly popular, never pandered to the boundless public appetite for banality and sensationalism (bread and circuses) that our rivals, gradually and unwittingly, did; being less concerned with the brute prose of modern urban life than in its transformations into the poesy of the past, the pulse of the present. That poesy, even then, at the height of its prodigious development, was in its decay; for the forces which its brilliance held in abeyance were even then gathering, like the dripping of an immense stalagtite, into the uniform petrifaction we know today.

What relief, then, it was, to withdraw to this delightful retreat, where the mind might find, among those images, its own resemblance, and from it create other worlds, other seas, weaving, from those skeins of fire, garlands of repose! I had no way of knowing how the others felt, but it was as if I wandered solitary there, noting, in those faces that flickered on the bare wall, and that were as if carved from stone, the solid stately flow that was the earmark of the divinity I followed. The encounter, then, was all the more rude for being totally unexpected. The previous series had followed, over Attic furrows, their dry, crumbling soil planted with corn and groves of olive trees, a local image of fertility, broad and heavy and elusive, some incarnation of Ceres or Cybele, from temple to shrine to grotto (that soil—dry yet glistening, grainy yet rich—reminds me of nothing so much as the mist-swept fertile valley by the ocean that is the state of California), and there, in the midst of all that increase (cattle heavy with young, the fields yellow with shimmering ears of corn), by a freak of montage, or merely a scissors' absentminded snip at the wrong moment, the scene abruptly shifted to a London music hall filled with smoke and abrasive gas-lights. The hand that had held the *lumière-cueilleuse* ("light-gatherer") had not been steady, and at first there was only an impression of plaster seraphs dancing a jerky jig, incarnadined petals exfoliating with impossible celerity (like those marvellous Disney "speed-ups" in *The Living Desert* and *The Walking Forest,* the cacti or columbine, compressing days and weeks into minutes and seconds, budding and blooming before our eyes)—except that here the motion was in the beholder, not the beheld. Finally the blurs solidified and shaped themselves, and I could see a stage decorated in a pseudo-Oriental manner: an Eastern shah or sheik, surrounded by opulent retainers, gazed with rapt attention at a vacant portion of the stage (rear) where a curtain inhaled, exhaled to the obvious susurrus of a bellows or wind-machine. There was a sound of heavy breathing which could not have come from the film, since "talkies" had not yet been developed. I waited impatiently: that gilded interior was too well known to me to elicit much interest (was, indeed, just around the corner, sandwiched between a butcher's shop and a small Dissenter chapel, which used its neighbor as a topic for some unneighborly sermons); the play or musical I did not recognize, although the style was familiar to me (an ornateness, a softness, a sensuality, that a Russian translator of Yeats has called "the minor poetry of the flesh"). The curtain abruptly bellied inward, as if someone had attempted to thrust a rapier through it. A brief soft struggle ensued; a vague anatomy was gradually emerging, was evolving arms, legs, and what looked like a rudimentary tail. It was like watching some lowly organism attempting to struggle up the ladder of evolution, assert its claim to a structure that yet surpassed, eluded it. Then a limb freed itself from the fleshlike veil that encumbered it; slender phalanges separated, floresced into a milky corolla and began plucking at the gauzy skin that, without warning, shockingly proceeded to split down its protuberant belly revealing the naked trembling protoplasm beneath.

She was, in fact, not naked at all; that blinding impression of whiteness (the whiteness of mirrors and transparent things) was the effect of her clinging secondary skin, a wondrous substance that cleaved to the very articulation of her form, and yet, despite the soft lunescence of its radiance, could not steadily be looked upon. Of her face, her eyes alone were visible; these were darkened and deepened, as if with belladonna. They looked straight before at nothing I could see. With a sudden heart-lurching abruptness the Eastern king clapped his hands and she broke into a barbarous dance I seemed to have seen before, a thing of veils and velocity and violence. With a gasp I noted, in the background, a severed head being borne in on a salver, stuck in a pool of its own coagulated blood. A veil shivered before its features: I recognized a mock likeness to an Irish gentleman who had recently been involved in a scandalous lawsuit and public trial. The dancer spun; the eyes alone seemed motionless, and looked out past me with a certain mocking impassivity. I strove against them for a moment. Then two things happened at once: I recognized that spurious king—a notorious lesbian with a moustache and dark silky hair between her breasts—and, to my left, from a black oval that must have been a face, a high-pitched giggle rippled.

6

Toward dusk on the first day we came into the little village of St. Melarc in the west of Cornwall, and at the inn where we engaged for rooms we began to set up, in the spacious central courtyard, our simple equipment—an elevated platform erected, at that time, by extending four broad wings from each of the sides of our largest wagon, and propping them with beams underneath. A single star stood luminous over one dusky gable; the air seemed violet, and so heavily textured that one was almost nourished as one deeply breathed. From the surrounding fields wafted the scent of new-mown hay, and, across the gentle rivulet that local commoners dignified with the name of stream, a tinkling and lowing of returning cows drifted, their stomachs filled with mulch and their udders weighty with milk. A solitary bell tolled vespers. With a peculiarly suffocating emotion I watched a darkened pane of glass across the courtyard grow flickering lighter as a candle was borne inward with invisible hand. That pinpoint of luminence pulsed, as if in communication with the even star that hung amorously in the empurpled heavens, shedding its radiance over the pregnant velvet gloomy curve of earth below. The others had removed to their rooms; I alone remained watching, as the night grew greater, and the constellations began to light their ancient fire.

That first tour, undertaken almost immediately after my conscription into her Company—there was a threat of plague and, rather than risk the forced closing of the playhouses, we decided to replenish our drained coffers in the provinces—remains in my memory as something absolutely tiny, pregnant and removed, as distant and illuminated as a landscape viewed through the large end of a telescope. Those minor productions on those minor stages—situated, as it were, in the darkest rear rows of the vast theatre known as Renaissance Europe—are memorable only in that they are the connecting link that lets us down, by an easy transition, from the highest pomp and proudest display of the Thespian art, to its first rudiments and helpless infancy. With conscious happy retrospect, they lead the eye back, along the vista of the imagination, to the village barn, or travelling booth, or old-fashioned town-hall, or more genteel assembly-room, in which Momus first unmasked to us his fairy revels, and introduced us, for the first time in our lives, to that strange anomoly in existence, that fanciful reality, that gay waking dream, *a company of strolling players!* It was thus that I was privileged to be present, if not at the very inception, then at the gestation and radiant birth of the dramatic art that was to be England's chiefest and crowning glory—present, I say, at that brutal crude fertilization, which was to breed out of country manners courtly ways, out of dung a stately delirium, a controlled, ornate dream; present, but yet absent of the presence I craved; for the sole moments I had any contact with her were those during which she appeared on our various makeshift stages, illuminated with a pale afternoon light, or with the smoky torches of some moonlight revel; thus, the only way I was able to keep her at all was to spin words of capture, golden webs of poesy in which she would, unwittingly, be snared. The history of the solitary passion in which I was entangled is, then, in a very real sense, the history of English drama, for it is only by tracing the one—by following, that is, the very lines which she uttered and which held her to one point—that I am able to glimpse, faintly, and as if through a series of rippled glasses (the symmetry reversing and double-reversing itself in the process) the outlines of the other.

It now, of course, seems strange that I had no knowledge of her existence save on the stage I created for her with my words: but at the time it seemed, I daresay, the most obvious thing in the world. She became for me a trick of vision, a thing to do with the way that innumerable eyes focused, and it was my task, increasingly, to contain within that single elusive shape all the varied drama of a multitude. That multitude comes out of the wings, converses, makes love, murders, vows, expostulates, withdraws, leaving, as always, a solitary figure illuminated at the central focus of the surrounding forest of eyes—a figure which those infinitely varied stares multiplies into an infinite procession of being.

I think, now, from a considerable vantage of retrospect, that it was an unconscious decision on the parts of all of us that I should be separated from the central emblem in the rich tapestry I wove; as if, by mutual consent, a number of otherwise unrelated people should happen to dream a common dream, and so produce a different world than the one they inhabit. And thus, from a mixture of clay and saliva—of dirt and my own fluid substance—I moulded and shaped a fair body of poesy that had not yet been seen in the common light of day. In one bare rented room after another, in a daisy-chain of hamlets that criss-crossed the rural England of those days (the fields unenclosed and open to the naked eye of the heavens), I educed that body, from ordinary materials that lay ignored around me—rooms that, somehow, through the odd system of seniority which obtained in our Company, were always situated either at the subterranean bowels of the inn or private manor we lodged at, or in an aery attic, its wide dormer windows open to wind and weather and the distant melting azure. There I would sit, while the day shaped in the fields outside, and make, within the even tinier room of my skull, my brain the female to my soul, making it the womb for my still-breeding fancy, giving to aery nothing a local habitation and a name while, without, those others carried on the actual business of living, albeit I at times provided the lines. Thus I shaped for her new countries, new geographies, since, due to the lighting, the climate, or the time, she could not inhabit the one I occupied. As soft spring rains turned the roads to mud, and mist rolled in over the downs and tumps, transforming everything to outline and making of sticky yellow-green leaves liquid amber jewels, I penned those early romantic comedies, lifted from penny-dreadfuls and bestsellers on crumbling yellowed pages I found in one attic or another, or one coffee-table or another, but in limpid metres that made of their banality still pools reflecting the deeps of man's imagined heaven, those which, no doubt because of their despised popular origins (the earth and excrement clinging to the milkwhite hair of some uprooted exotic plant), Shaw was later to call "frothy nothings," "insipid saccharinities," "sugarspun concoctions consisting mainly of air." In Ilyria, in Verona, in Elsinore—those mythical and melting countrysides—I would have her appear, a page-girl on a deserted strand, feeding the rapt audience with an excess of vowel-music till, it seemed, the appetite would sicken and so die; or, on a balcony aswarm with voluptuous vulva-shaped roses, each with its corona of thorns, she would lean over, inclining her gaze to the moon-filled garden with its clumps of darkly stirring bushes, where her corsetted and cosmeticked beloved awaited, like their audience, for those notorious and numbing words that seemed, as if by magic, to narcotize all critical opinion—and that heartclogged audience, without waiting to hear them, breaks irresistably into a syrup fountain of applause. I cannot begin to describe the effect such moments had on me, trembling in backstage blackness, or in the obscurity of a shameful balcony; it was as though I were draining a strong potion of eisell, or as if my nature, most fresh and pure in its regard, were almost subdued to what it worked in, like the dyer's hand; for, be it to my sorrow, the only way I was able to keep her was by making a spectacle of her. And when, as occurred too often in my accursed art, some hirsute opposite would enfold that fair slip of light in his boorish exulting footballer's arms, then, as those tight curls on the thick and empty skull (empty but for the words I injected) blocked my imploring vision, and I execrated myself for those too, too explicit stage-directions, then what blackness consumed the miserable rind of my heart! But things base and vile, holding no quantity, love can transpose to form and dignity. Those moonlight revels that I looked upon—what were they but the feast I spread for myself, that I was starving for, and that I yet could not partake of? jewels fetched from the deep of some trance that, on being grasped greedily, faded into the common light of day. Those bushes, those wandering woods, those entranced and transformed beasts and lovestruck faeries caught in an evening's lightspun web of enchantment, eyes darkened and delirious, as mine were, with Cupid's corrosive juice, were contrived that I might see that same young Cupid's fiery shaft quenched in the chaste beams of the watery moon. After such an orgy—and that was exactly how I thought of it—I would return to my room, drained, exhausted, and, reviving a taste of India ink, lower the gas-jets, throw myself on the straw-stuffed pallet, and turn my face toward the fertile blackness. In the morning, wakened by the passing of slippered feet, or the sun's ruddy wick firing through the mists, my mouth would taste as though it had been surfeited with sweets, a hollow dripping with honey that flies had feasted upon and that had coagulated into pale amber bile.

During that first tour we must have, by my computation, travelled some 2,000 miles, along a skein of muddy pocked roads that spiderwebbed all the southern portion of our isle and the Midlands (where later Blake's "satanic mills" would vomit their aerial sewage), yet of that bumping, bone-wearying, vision-jolting pilgrimage I remember only a series of blurred snapshots: hedgerows bobbing up and down to the tuneful derisive whistling of blackbirds and chaffinches, muddy ponds raising themselves on the narrow circumscribed horizon, half-naked brats staring moonfaced at our topheavy passage, bellybuttons white, half-hidden by folds of dingy skin, destitute monks, their tonsures sunburned, their legs showing bony and hairy and filthy through the remains of rich broadcloth (they had, within my father's generation, been stripped of their extensive and fertile properties) and dwindled to but shadows of their former well-fleshed Boccacian profiles, hairy-legged sluts squatting by the roadside to relieve themselves—a brown trickle oozing from under their smocks—and, once, a shepherd and his lass, as in the elegant poem by the courtier, but how dirtier, how infinitely more faded and futile than that perfect cameo, in slow and serpentine copulation by a crystal stream bedded with smooth quartz pebbles, the neglected flock moaning and raising great clouds of white dust by the wayside which, mercifully, cloaked their activity so that we passed without incident.

At that time, the extensive system of "motels" had not yet begun their transatlantic migration (although in not a great number of years that scandalous best-seller was due to appear which would describe, from the inside out, as it were, their organization and peculiar "new world" morality); we thus often lodged, when not at one of the primitive but hospitable inns with which our country was blessed, at a private manor of one of the local gentry, and there took our simple repast, amid the bayings of our squire's kennel or the twitterings of his aviary, before issuing out to a rented field surrounded by fragrant clover or alfalfa, and under some stately grove of laurel or linden trees, or the more gnarled and massive oak, erect our makeshift eminence before a steadily increasing trickle of gaping yokels. We relied, in fact, upon these same bumpkins to rapidly spread the word of our arrival, and in that regard we were rarely disappointed: we almost never had to resort to the tactics we used at larger towns, the printing, usually at an exorbitant price, of posters to which lurid colours were added by hand. Then, next day, immediately after the noon meal, criers would be sent through the poor few streets of the hamlet scrannel-piping the name of the entertainment and those of the principal actors, Burbage and Kemp, of course, leading this list; and, the wind and weather notwithstanding, the street rapidly packed itself with exclaiming, expectorating humanity, some from the shops and smithies along the main thoroughfare, others from neighboring farms or even distant ones, those having begun their trip the evening before; I can recall standing in a fine misting April rain watching windows flung open and heads, like those of flowers, thrust out to soak in moisture and the melody of that approaching voice. By the time the afternoon had reached its midpoint our black flags, denoting tragedy, or gaily-coloured ones, telling of some more popular entertainment, had been flown, and the field, already, began, if the weather were even slightly inclement, to be churned into thick creamy soup, with additions of moles and hummocks of turf, under the clogs and hobnails of an eager populace. I, as befitted my position in the Company, customarily collected the pennies and ha' pennies at a gate formed by two wooden horses. The crowd would accrete noisily and smellily, bringing with them all the fragrance of their daily occupations (fish might predominate in one burg, sheep in another) till, it seemed, the little field, barren till now, budded with a heavier and more dolorous harvest, that stood bareheaded under the gentle spray of an April rain, or the pale steaming gold of an English midsummer sun. By the time I had finished with the last of the stragglers the action would already have begun, and I would lean back against one of those wooden quadrupeds as, at the centre of the field, our stranger hybrid would begin to unfold its petals.

The sky, often, would bend down so closely, with its load of fine combed lamb's wool, that it would seem to enclose the rondure of the earth, and the small segment of it we stood on, as tightly as a helmet or a skull—one of those emblems you have seen when they plow up a forgotten graveyard to make room for new tenants.

The sun would trim its wick against the advance of earth's shadow. I see, now, people restlessly waiting the withdrawing of an imaginary curtain. A light seems to fill one spot. There is the general effect of a squint.

The words that rise in a pure crystal fountain are, gradually, muddied and lost in layers of earth, clay, gravel, and viscous standing water. The burgeoning fields, fertilized by that prodigious seed, await their harvest-time. The sun's yolk breaks through the mist, spreading long streaks of golden nourishment that hang tremulously dripping from stalk and shaft and bowed head bending over from their own pregnant weight.

The gracious canopy clings to the earth's four corners. Birds and insects are caught in its fabric.

The great globe itself tilts. A shadow eats the curve of living earth. Stars consume themselves. The entrails of beasts quiver as constellations move into conjunction.

The voices, in the distance, would rise and fall limpidly; the words themselves could not be distinguished but their tone, their deep vibrant timbre of meaning, was unmistakable. That of Burbage was most prominent; his range was remarkable, especially in the declamatory parts of our more sombre tragedies, and I can remember distinctly several times a covey of partridges, startled out of tall grass or lilac bush by the booming resonances he projected, flying straight into the sun overhead; or the shyer skylark, once, interrupting his full-throated flight in pure astonishment at the deeper echo the earth's curvature reflected below. Then—as if all this had been but prelude—the central corolla lifted its white stamen and fertilized itself. Partaking of both natures, its own and that I bestowed, that figure would return to the tiny unseeing eye of the thing I dreamed. When I closed my eyes I could see it even more clearly: a blank spot at the centre of the fabric that was yet alive with substance and with a meaning I could not as yet fathom, the invisible nucleus of a dancing atomie, holding all together and still not apprehensible. When I open my eyes (I remember thinking) I will wake from a dream to a dream.

7

Reports and reviews of our fledgling efforts (the efforts of a new species in struggling through the stages of gestation) were not slow in trickling back to us from London; as far away as Wenlock or Cardiff or Swansea (our travels taking us in a kind of elongated egg north, then west and south along the coast) we would find, in dusty wayside posthouses, in the back rooms of lending or circulating libraries, month-old copies of the *Times, Mirror, Century Magazine, Tatler, Country Gentleman, Saturday Review*, and other more recondite publications, and read of the dull reverberations in the City our pellucid provincial explosion had caused. It was, as I told the other members of our Company, inevitable, given the somewhat sterile classical education of most of these correspondents, and the growing utilitarian philosophy of a burgeoning middle class, that these Oxford and inner Temple gentlemen, whose virgin Latin tongue was as yet unimpregnated with the Saxonisms that make it the fertile breeding ground it is, should react against the world we had artificed out of common materials—including a simple classical strain, not overly-laboured, that wove its golden thread through the pewter and clay of our baser fabric. Thus Shaw, from the pulpit of the *Saturday Review* (26 Sept. 1898) wielding his Olympian thunderbolts (which, oddly enough, despite their "intellectual" hue, are tipped with the Cockney scorn of one of his most famous characters): ". . . stagy trash of the lowest melodramatic order . . . in parts abominably written, throughout intellectually vulgar . . . judged in point of thought by modern intellectual standards, vulgar, foolish, offensive, indecent, and exasperating beyond all tolerance." That suspending of tolerance, hypothetical though it is here, was to become increasingly significant in years to come. Or the indigent Greene, poverty-stricken despite his Classics degree from Oxford, goaded beyond fury by what to him were no doubt easy successes, penning, in the *Apollo Review* of that year, the famous diatribe about the "upstart Crow, beautified with our feathers" (a tavern in Southwark later named itself with this gibe). We were in Bath, situated on the Nova Avon, with its isolated groves most rich of shade hanging above that mild flood, taking, as the Romans did before us, those restoring waters, when we read this last sorry piece of dementia which, in its way, was perfectly true, our wit and fancy ranging freely, like Ovid's bee, plundering those golden stores only to release their hidden sweetness. The villa where we were pleasantly situated was surrounded with green willow trees whose roots, thrusting powerfully into the compact loam of the region, drank deeply of those same waters which vivified us.

The production we were staging that evening was of a rather newer kind: on a spacious unenclosed balcony overlooking the sweet waters of the Avon, which connected, not many miles hence, with the wider billow of the Ocean himself, we arranged, for a group of local aristocratic "swells" who must remain anonymous, a mute tableau of the Birth of Venus, on a scungille shell made of reinforced plaster-of-paris, clad only in her long cornyellow waterfall of tresses, surrounded by balloons representing attendant cupids, in a transplanted Mediterranean from whose sapphire navel she issued. The air was filled with the aroma of fresh crustacea, mussels, shellfish (an early attempt at "kinetic drama"). Doves fluttered about her. In the background, salty mariners chanted some old ditty. The over-educated dandies in the adjacent room were enchanted, and pattered their feet delicately on the floor, as was the fashion, to indicate approval. One limb covered the shadowy groin; the other floated free, disclosing the tender inward of its hand. Below, someone belched. Tired of holding the one position, she shifted; the taperlight, struck by a moist wind, revealed the ivory abdomen, all cream and crimson, which seemed to soften and glow, as if it were a lodestone that sucked all illumination to itself, leaving the surrounding area in shadow. The fish smell lingered on our clothes for at least a fortnight (until, in fact, we reached Bristol and the ocean). Although we were not aware of it, the room contained more nobility than we suspected; a dark and veiled figure in the rear of that inner chamber was later whispered of as being no less person than the Queen herself in disguise, accompanied by George Carey, later Lord Hunsdon. It was her habit, so rumour said, to travel thus unguessed-at, so as to be able to indulge her appetite for gaming, fox-hunting, hawking, and local theatrics. That arrogant silhouette, however, said nothing on that occasion, although she must have been pleased, due to the classical antecedents of the slight miniature we sketched. It was from that time, I think, that we began to rise in Dame Fortune's eyes, for shortly after our return to the City we were appointed the acting servants of the Lord Chamberlain himself

—next to that of the royal favour, the most coveted position in our profession. The City greeted us with a thick fog in which were suspended the fine cinders of squat warted chimneys surrounding Southwark and the theatrical district (later, when transplanted to Los Angeles, then a small mission overlooking the Pacific, this would be known as "smog"). This fog was a greasy, cold, clinging, almost animate thing, that made of mute passers-by dirty white outlines, bubbles of gross corporeality; and it was not difficult, as we made our slow and painful way across a serpentine River into the gas-lit recesses of the "night-life" district, to imagine that the bulk of an alien beast possessed the City and we, tiny moving specks of life, but loose matter so slowly and so surely being digested and transformed into different shapes. Under the brown fog of that winter noon the City seemed unreal, and the hurrying, wordless pedestrians, the bodies of newly-made corpses washed in a lethean mist to attain forgetfulness.

In the evening hour, the violet hour, at our temporary lodgings in Puttenham Square I noticed, on a newspaper covering my window, the headline: PARLIAMENT DECLARES WAR. Universal conscription for all males to be . . . Another, smaller, pane gave the variations of a list of twenty "industrials." A third, the current permutations of Cap'n Kidd, a popular cartoon character based on a bloody but beloved melodrama then setting attendance-records at a Spanish theatre called the Aragon. A fourth was empty; the breeze whispered wetly and dolorously through its opening, bringing with it the queerly sad odours of evening meals being prepared. The Chapel of the Sacred Heart, a scant three blocks east, struck six o'clock. I could hear the others unpacking on either side of my room; above, an acrobat practised his echoing falls endlessly, and through the empty window I could see, across the courtyard, a long shapely shadow, perhaps that of my heroine, trying on a pair of ballerina tights. A necklace lay in a dish on the dresser; its yellow eyes looked unseeing at the invisible scene unfolding in the hidden recesses of the room. One floor above a disembodied arm, lightly dusted with fine brown hair, arranged a chessboard with careless precision: white was clear, almost transparent glass, black an army of shadows. A pipe held in an unseen hand sent up a thin grey column which curled around black knight and white bishop—a loose alliance of sorts. Someday (I thought) I shall have to compose this scene, or re-compose it, adding only—and at that moment an invisible door opened and someone entered: the figure-8 the smoke had been forming lazily transformed into a naught. The light one floor below had been extinguished and, after the space of about an hour, that of the upper room followed suit.

Upon our return to the City several of us, together with a number of Irish expatriates, formed the Rhymers Club, and met regularly above a little tavern in Cheapside called (after its patrons) "The Amusing Actors" (later it became the private club of that name, of which Wilde was briefly president), and there I first made contact with the members of what Yeats was to call "the tragic generation"—Dowson, Johnson, Lady Gregory, Wilde, Nashe, Synge, Madame Blavatsky, Swinburne (once), and others too numerous to itirate. There we would test our finer productions upon each other, and it was from these meetings, indeed, that our Company's first witty Ovidian fruit was plucked and given to an adulate, if somewhat cliqueish, public. As the City daily became more "industrialized," and slums spread, cancer-like, from one parish to another, bringing with them the artifacts of urbanization—prostitutes, gin, and ugliness—and the now-famous London fog, immortalized by Dickens and Hogarth, was brewing in its foul Stygian cave, we artists and poets came more and more to look upon our little room, lit with tiny hanging spirit-lamps, as a kind of fortress against an indifferent, nay, a hostile and alien world, upon whose iron fetters we would try the veils and gauzes of Poesy and Art. That society, like the later, more theosophical Brotherhood of the Golden Dawn, which included the infamous "Beast 666," Aleister Crowley, produced little but talk (and in the latter case an occasional spurious Black Mass or two: a whimpering goat, a naked woman—skinny waitress or dimestore clerk—and bad Latin muttered with equally bad breath), yet from those overly-refined interiors were to issue the noble periods and iron-veined rhetoric of the author of *A Vision* and *Areopagitica*—the greatest lyric poet our century has yet seen, and the staunchest apologist of human liberty. It is, I think, equally significant, that this onetime senator from Ireland should, in the midst of his most ambitious poetical project, abandon it, hammer his flowing quill into an iron-tipped barb, and take to the composition of those fiery embattled pamphlets that were to lead him to imprisonment and a premature grave. It was, in fact, in gaol that I saw him for the first and last time—the same gaol that had held Oscar Wilde for two years at the beginning of the century. His head was of the type generally known as "leonine," and his hair fell shockingly white in long waves over his shoulders. The spartanly furnished room was very nearly in shadow; he was virtually blind from his incessant literary efforts (even during his incarceration he laboured mightily, not only for the cause to which he had devoted his powers, but to deliver his family from the debt with which it was burdened), and one hand shaded his eyes, as if even this dim light were too much for them. There were, I believe, few words between us; the ostensible reason for my visit was to give him the bound proofs for the 1939 edition of the so-called "First Folio," which originally had been issued in 1923, that he had, for this edition, contributed prefatory material to—although there was little reason to do so since, first, he could barely make out the relative shape of the book, much less its contents, and, besides that, the world-wide war which was to be precipitated but a week later was to completely obliterate any interest the volume might have held. A single opening in the wall, the size, perhaps, of a small postcard—at the distance I was standing it looked as large as a pinhole—admitted a weak trickle of pallid muddied light. The walls were inscribed round and round as with a piece of charcoal held by desperate fingers, but the words were of course illegible. If we consider how our light is spent, in works, too frequently, of darkness, wasting the sun's life-giving radiance to create a hall of shadows in the heart, will we not sit in darkness, as this poet of light did, to let his inner fire illuminate the world with his vision? Alas, I too, I too—I found myself thinking, as I gazed on those blind and capable fingers—I too have sought out the darker portions of the universe, that I might see the light more clearly, albeit I was perishing of that oblivion; to trace with hopeless clarity the patterns, the messages, the symmetry, which were filling the void with solid light, and making of my seeing blackness an abomination; I too . . . But as I looked at his bent head, which almost sleepily propped itself on his left hand, I noticed with a start that his right hand, poised over the volume I had brought, was doing something very wide-awake—tap-tapping against the cover with a rhythmic, almost iambic staccato, thump-*thump* - thump-*thump* - thump-*thump* - thump-*thump* - thump-*thump*, as if that finger were a blind worm attempting to communicate with higher organisms. I froze in surprise, staring uncomprehendingly at the mad little dance below. Then I saw his rheum-covered eyes flash upward and to his left: the narrow slit in the door held suspended in its diameter a pair of beady gaoler's eyes; without difficulty I could imagine the rest of his gross bulk, and I looked downward again, trying to comprehend the code that mutely flashed its signals at me. To this day I have not managed to crack that enigmatic dance of digets; it was, as I said, almost unvaryingly iambic in metre; it came in small groups or spurts of three, intermediate groups of twelve, and large sections of twenty-four and forty-eight almost inaudible tappings. Was it a last poem? A last message to his third (and last) wife? A last message to the universe, that the cap of black imprisonment which oppressed him did not permit him to commit to paper? We shall never know, because I shall never know. The sombre, ochre-suffused parting remains blurred in retrospect—an impression of fingers, a lowered head, a final mute appeal before the pseudo-efficient young Notzi, in brown belt and brown shirt, closed and locked the door between us; and a series of interconnecting corridors assured me that not even in dream would I be able to find that oppressed and secretive room. Next week a newly resurgent Teutonia precipitated the late worldwide hostility, whose effects we still see in the bombed cathedrals and abandoned air-raid shelters, by the so-called "blitzkreig" of Poland, and I was not to hear of him for some twenty years when, shortly after the "Glorious Revolution," I read in the *Los Angeles Times* a two-inch obituary describing, in a horribly skeletal fashion, his accomplishments and final demise (shortly after being released from prison he died, in a hotel room not unlike the cell he had just quitted, of coronary thrombosis). One can well imagine, I thought at the time, that microscopic bit of print calling up for me the London we had both known together, though separately—the gas lamps coming flickeringly alive in the purple gloaming, along the Strand, up Queen Victoria Street, down King William Street, to where Saint Mary Woolnoth kept the hours—imagine that grey imprisoned ghost creeping out and into the landscapes he knew and loved and evoked, now no longer existing, but alive in his verse, the meadows and groves, the smooth enamelled green spangled with forget-me-nots, and nymphs and shepherds pirouetting to his stately measure in shade and sun, and the voice, to whom he gave utterance in the majestic rhythm he knew best, saying, "Toilest thou? Suffer to enter this your kingdom. For I am the Word you made flesh."

The landscape, though, of which he proved to be the final celebrant, was, during that first year of our tour, and triumphant return to London, just emerging sketchily from our combined efforts. Drayton had undertaken his 15,000-couplet ingestion of England's countryside, county by county, hill by rolling hill; that same country was receiving slighter but more piercing transformations in scattered flowering lyrics in masque and miscellany. The stars that year (or so my astrologer tells me) were in particularly fertile conjunction; triumphant Mars was atop glowing Venus, which stood out large and green each evening over the melting thread of horizon, showering abundantly her rays over the sleeping fields, which seemed to groan and glisten, as if in the grip of a moist sweet dream; the threat of plague (the ostensible reason for our tour) had been dispelled, and the house of the healer was once again ascendant. Lion and archer mated distantly, fed by bright arrows of desire, and Orion, surrounded by the beasts of the heavens, loosed swarms of stardust into their milky paths. Inanimate nature, it seemed, received an animus, a shaping breath; dull earth and inert water, impregnated with air and fire, filled their wombs with wonderful forms. The roads running into the City that autumn were choked with creaking wains stuffed to fullness with their golden harvest of nuts, corn, fruits; the barmaids seemed more buxom, their breasts heavy and ripe, their haunches full to bursting with sweet love's lubrication; a fine haze or dust, as of powdered gold, seemed to cover everything we looked at till we thought the alchemist's words would be revealed and the age turned to gold. The many streams and springs that decorated the surrounding countryside for pureness seemed rare, brighter than sun-shine; no molten crystal, but a richer mine, even Nature's rarest alchemy ran there; diamonds resolved, and substance more divine, through whose bright-gliding current might appear a thousand naked nymphs. A richer shade, too, cooled those banks, upon whose brims the eglantine and rose, the tamarisk, olive, and almond tree, grew, as kind companions, in one union, folding their turning arms, slowly, in vegetable love.

Then too, it seems to me, those landscapes—so easily acquired, so quickly lost—are virtually inextricable from their description; one remembers not merely a tree, say, but the shape and colour of its shadow as it falls softly upon the resilient sward; and not simply its shadow, but the hue of its reflection in the faces of those who sat underneath. This, as I have said, was before the modern system of farming by enclosure had been initiated; and except for winding hedgerows, aflower with sportive blooms, the fields lay open to the heavens in all their pied beauty, yellows and greens mixed with the more sombre browns and furzed greys, and Virgilian stands of trees accumulating the weight of days in the richly textured shadings beneath their boughs. Not long, indeed, till the forcible rape of that most fertile landscape, the loam, with its glistening sillion, bladed by the brute shovels of snorting bulldozers, paved with unending rivers of concrete, and the sticky yellow petalcups of the thorny hedge replaced by squat rows of brick tenement houses—all the mediocre artifacts, in short, of the mediocre author of *1984*. From the single slightly elliptical oval that the staring heavens shaped it was transformed—as if all that rhythmic poesy were to be bound in hoops of iron—into a mirror of the earth it overlooked: a cluttered scape of warted brick and concrete in which fat rubber sausages floated, only minutely distorted from the smoke-emitting exhausts of the so-called "horseless-carriages" below that the inventor Ford, now tinkering in obscure oily basements, was to loose from his belching factories.

The change from the one to the other had, I think, already begun, as we made our slow way back into the City that fall, though we were then at the height of our collective powers. Our first act as a Company was to complete the purchase of our first theatrical property; this we found ready to hand in the dilapidated structure which the bankrupt elder Burbage, James, was only too glad to exchange for a generous settlement, although he retained a keen interest in its operation, and never was known to miss an opening. It was this theatre which, after undergoing several radical transformations (from the Theatre, to the Curtain, to the Globe, and finally the Savoy) emerged as the first large motion-picture palace, the prototype of all those gingerbreaded ghostly gaslit houses of illusion which were wildly to spread through the realm at the beginning of the next century, to reach their apotheosis across the wide river of the Atlantic, in sundrenched California. As it chanced, I was present at the initial screening, the "baptism of light" in which the edifice was immersed, late in the fall of 1906. Autumn had taken on a peculiar character that year, at once unbearably bright and heartlessly empty. The skies were of an utter blueness I had not noticed before, a bare rubbed unplumbed surface that the unadorned lacery of twig and branch only accentuated in its emptiness; the spires of cathedrals, the distant winding snake of a retreating River, the very bricks of the warehouses lining its dolorous banks, were illuminated, with a curious kind of interior clarity, as if mysteriously lit up from within. It was as though I were watching the beauteous desolation of the declining year from an incredibly remote viewpoint: trees bare of their foliage, their bark loose with the flesh showing through rubbed portions of the fabric, glowing in the full radiance of a slanting late-afternoon sun, that clarified but gave no heat, appeared to me as removed and impossible of possession as the veined depth of a rare stone under a jeweller's screwed-on eye, or the transparently-paned structure of a hollow insect's wing under the thick and dispassionate cornea of a microscope's gaze. I had at that time given up all hope of possessing her; she had abandoned our Company since 1905, and although occasionally rumours and reports trickled back, carrying with them unpleasantly odious and ominous undertones and undertows of insinuation, we were not favoured with any more than a glimpse here, a glance there, the partly hidden oval of a face palely fluttering behind a Japanese fan at one "espresso" bar or another, a boulevard of rain-glazed elms catching and releasing her slender hurrying form, leaning slightly forward in its haste, in the shifting prison of its boles; or at one matinée or another soirée, behind a crush of what seemed the entire population of London, the heartcatching unmistakable symmetry of bone and balance and pivot would materialize, making, in the sudden inrush of breath, the packed room empty. She had gone, I say; and London that season never seemed more unpopulated as I loitered in the deserted lanes of this or that district, hands in pockets and whistling a hollow tune to myself. In the parks, the lawns were covered with fallen gold; the windows of the apartments opposite glinted steadily, shedding long drooping tear-like jewels of fire through the naked boughs. I walked north, along the River that swam cold and blue obliquely to the rays of the westering sun, and in the distance, between the buildings that rose to my left, thin tendrils of smoke floated and were slowly dispersed in the sky's sapphire depth. It was gradually, and by unnoticeable stages, that I surrounded myself with the old theatrical district in which I had first come to know her, in my earliest productions—the so-called "Gold Coast," named, by some unexplainable quirk of association, after the great ivory and gold-mining region on the west coast of Africa. This had undergone drastic changes since those early days, a combination of urban blight and municipal neglect. To the east, along the spacious elegant curve of the River, stood the impregnable bastions of "high-rises"—rectangular slabs of concrete and glass inhabited by hordes of *nouveau riche*; although between these might be glimpsed the smaller and more solid structures of older buildings, fabulous mouldings of pale yellow brick, fences of black iron filagree, lawns of the most incredible springy turf, and leaded wavy-glassed windows from which stray sun-beams might glance on such a day as this. From this exclusive district, protected by a newly mounted police, small lanes twisted westward, named, as was the fashion, after tribes of American Indians—Seminole, Ottawa, Delaware, Huron; on these were located small and exorbitantly expensive *boutiques*, mens' hair-dressing salons, and parlours for the meticulous grooming of poodles, pekinese, pismires, pugs—not to mention an odd item or so, such as the Episcopal bishop's manor, an old polished relic from pre-Reformation days, kept in absolutely top-notch condition by an annual Masked Ball which no self-respecting member of the *beau monde* would dream of not attending, and, a knight's move opposite, the "Ploughboy Mansion" inhabited by its middleageing millionaire founder Hugh Henfer, his "hen hutch"—a bevy of plastic-coated beauties in a specially-designed uniform that thrust the mammae up and out, an uncomfortable lopsided effect, and the glutaei down and in, which must have produced an army of hemorrhoid-sufferers—and a stupendous assortment of electronic gadgetry. Perhaps three blocks further the theatrical district proper began. Originally these large somewhat baroque buildings, constructed on the strictly utilitarian principle of getting as many people as possible into their interiors (providing, of course, an unobstructed view in the process), had been kept in good repair by the considerable revenues that flowed into their box-offices; but with the moving of two of our competitors to the newly affluent suburbs, our remaining Company, at the Globe, felt a slackening-off in the daily attendance; and it was not long before we were forced to place it under a long lease to a French company who wanted it for some inexplicable purpose. "Theatre Row," as it was called, was subsequently to metamorphose even more radically into a line, first, of strip-tease joints and burlesque houses (Whisky-A-Go-Go, Disco, etc.), later into a series of notorious pornographic movie-houses, littered with dried semen, empty wine bottles, and the sticky coagulum of stale buttered popcorn. At the time I took my unexpected tour, however, this row of beautiful old buildings stood in excellent repair, and detailing of moulding and cornice (finestranded angel hair, flat demon nose) drawn with exquisite clarity by the sun's delicate pencil against a background of luminous moving shadow, and the stained-glass insets—a ram's twisting horn tipped with silver, a ewe's golden fleece—glowing with hidden fire as the radiance on the other side of the building sought and then found a tenuous corridor for its overflow. The intermediate buildings were of weathered brownstone and limestone, the latter a crumbling honey-coloured substance that gave the impression of great antiquity, although they could not have been erected much earlier than the reign of the last Henry. An occasional tiny triangular mall, planted with a laurel tree and a few stately shrubs, a small private school for the preparation of pre-seminarian boys that guarded its grounds with walls of impassive granite slabs and ornamental grilles in the shape of various sacred insignia, completed this elegant yet lusty and life-filled promenade, down which, at the height of its popularity, might be seen, swaggering or mincing or languidly strolling, the entire heterogenous strata of London, from dowagers in full train, bewigged dandies affecting the currently fashionable widebrimmed black hat, Spanish cape and white frothy ruff eructate with starch, to the "theatre-crowd" from the industrial central portion of the City, dressed even more extravagantly in high laced boots and pointed collars, and the boot-blacks and beggars who lived off the superfluity of this gay and glittering district. It straggled out, however, rather quickly, into the main concourse that ran into the heart of the City, along whose grey widely-spaced flagstones I now approached. Further west, to the left of my slow progress, the lanes narrowed rapidly and ran, with a kind of muted sigh, into the noisome crowded clangorous slums of Cheapside.

My approach was, as I said, gradual and unconscious, the old surroundings accreting around me with much the same insidious crepitation, the sense of "layering" that we get when waking in a strange house, the slowly rousing consciousness picking out an artifact here, a detail there, to weave into its life-sustaining cocoon, as we, or mother Dana, weave and unweave our bodies from day to day, the molecules shuttled to and fro ceaselessly and sighingly; it was with a strange ripple of surprise, then, that I found myself approaching through the vacant luminous streets the disparate cluster of buildings standing in the mild wash of late afternoon sunlight, like the faces of ones we have known intimately but lost, come back to disturb the placid surface of a dream. I found myself unwittingly at the entrance of the old Globe before I realized where I was. The long beams of solid sunlight had reached a row of oval windows in the building opposite, and were bent back waveringly to the marquée I loitered under. A small poorly-printed sign was pasted in one corner of the ticket-dispenser's cage (now thickly curtained in mahogany and dust); it announced "the initial screening of the immortal myth of Pasiphaë—Attendance by invitation only." The word "screening" meant nothing to me yet, but I noted, in the list of subscribers at the bottom, several familiar names, and without hesitation I pushed at a door I had handled many times. Unquestioningly it yielded softly, and I entered the empty echoing interior.

As those who are frequenters of daytime entertainments will know, my light-gathering eyes did not immediately adjust to the gloomy interior from the world-washed luminence without; dazed residual images lingered, swimming sun-spots of oily radiance, red and yellow and bleeding orange, behind which the darker and more ambiguous inner shapes lurked. At length objects began to knit together. The gloom divided into a mirror-backed corridor, with all the ornate scrolls, curlicues and involutions I had followed so intricately and often with my practised eye duplicated in reverse fashion, giving a false impression of spaciousness. With a queer sense of a split—or, rather, not merely being in two places at once, but even more of being extended hugely beyond one's true dimensions—I watched myself walk uncertainly down the long empty familiar passage-way. A glass case, now darkened, held rows of small bars wrapped in silver and gold foil. A curve in the long looping hall extended it in the other direction, and I had the eerie sense of meeting myself as I approached—as in that marvelous story by Chesterton where the man in the darkened passageway sees himself reflected at the other end, and fails to recognize the enigmatic figure standing there.

The interior of the amphitheatre proper was so hollow and so unpopulated that I was several minutes locating the few inhabitants scattered here and there among the newly-installed "reclining seats," an invention allowing a seated person a variety of postures, from a perpendicular 90° to almost a slumbrous 180° angle. The high walls were draped with a rich closely-woven tapestry in which browns, reds and greens predominated, that depicted a hunting scene over and over (a stag transfixed with Diana's keen arrows, the little god of love reclining in one foliaged corner, a beautiful youth averting his face half-stretched upon the flank of his hunting courser); the ceilings were newly-painted in a deeper, more cerulean hue, in which small suns and moons were floated, and the dust of innumerable stars; bright indistinct figures could be described among their shadowy groupings, a throne, a harp, a crown. An immense luminously blank sheet rippled at the far end, where the circular stage was wont to stand; below it the "prompting pit" had been widened and deepened to form what was to be called the "orchestra pit," an invention contrived to allow for the lack of sound in those early experiments. A three-piece band muttered and rumbled in its interior now—cello, kettledrum, rebec. High oval stained-glass windows let through their apertures coruscations of sapphire and diamond. To the rear, on a raised dais, a pyramid-shaped object stood upon a draped eminence. A figure in a black robe or djelleba, that had an almost priestly effect, bent over it in thoughtful concentration.

Thunder leaped from the pit as I lowered myself in the last row, and the lights, already dim, were extinguished, leaving a buzzing blackness—but not before I impressed upon my sensitive retinas the lingering image of three figures to the front, dressed in conservative business suits, one of whom, if my vision did not deceive me, was *entrepreneur* Burbage, clad in a French pearl-grey suiting. One hand was draped loosely over the seat to his left; on it a signet ring flashed briefly, then was extinguished as the inky tide of blackness rolled through the vast reaches of the hall, resembling, in its sensuous eclipse of the rapidly dimming light, the daily and deadly nightfall of the mind. A finger of radiance fired in the gloom, a beastlike image appeared on the screen—a general impression of hairiness and bulk that focused into a bull or bellerophon (I never have been able to keep these semi-divine creatures distinct in my mind): black grizzled carapace, obsidian eyes with a shockingly brutal effect of consciousness lurking in their impassive depths, and immense weaponlike fifth limb extending itself gradually from the lower apex of the leathery massive nether thighs. Elegant throat-clearing from somewhere in the interior. Earthly thunder from the pit.

Although murky darkness possessed the entire lower portion of the hall, faint trickles of the pale radiance that bathed the world outside penetrated the gloomy upper area, bleeding inward with a furry velvety insinuation watery almost colourless washes of light through the oval openings above; in one of these a large fly, leftover of the preceding summer's fullness, hummed and bumbled, outlined perfectly, in antennae and bulging faceted eyes, against the upper depth of that distant blue. The screen had melted into shadows which were rived by a stonewhite bolt from the louring cloudchoked heavens. In the electric flash of its illumination the figures scattered throughout the theatre formed a large loose D, or perhaps an even looser O. A whitely tremulous blur formed on the screen, fluttered, scurried into the tangled interior of what proved to be a rankly overgrown garden aswarm with creeping vines, burdock, thistles, fat with larded nameless vegetation in which assorted jeweled toads blinked, adders hissed and slithered. "An allegory of the state," I heard someone whisper in the emptiness to my left—why is it that I always seem to perceive things from the sinister side? Now the pale blur solidified into the trembling nakedness of an albino bitch (dog or human), udders swinging from side to side as she loped toward the bulking statue of a quadruped hooved beast. Its belly shockingly fell open, and from a tangled clump of lilac the woman—though almost on all fours—dragged a small step-ladder, erected it under the gently swinging trap door and, to the lurid flashes of distant heat-lightning, ascended uncertainly into the invisible interior above—an eerie impression of a caesarean operation in reverse. One ankle dangled in the nemoral vine-entangled gloom like a pale bait on a dark summer stream, then was jerked abruptly upward in a white streak.

The fly sang in the autumn stillness, fell silent, sang.

The columns of sunlight angled gradually upward, as if being levered over the edges of the hermetically sealed windows. Dustmotes hung suspended in their viscous golden fluid.

Through one window, miraculously clear as molten crystal, I could see one luminously silver cloud floating free, almost dissolved in light, glowing as if stamped hot from a fiery forge, so irradiated that the retina seemed etched with its breathing outline. As slowly as a school of dream-fish it eased through the liquid azure of the fading autumn sky, blue as with some immortal indigo dye; slowly, slowly, as if being erased by the dying sun, its burning edges eroded, then offered up the moist interior of their substance in an almost audible sigh of expiration.

Then the sky lost its colour all at once, all at once the light died from the heavens, and all the chamber was emptied of everything but the close preternatural darkness and those bestial silvery images moving apart and mingling on the screen. There was a rustling around me as of dry leathery leaves—a rhythmic susurrus as of breathing when, during the long night of illness, the patient in the critical ward moves the sheet of the steam-tent with his irregular inhalations and exhalations, so that the nurse can tell, in her midnight rounds, exactly at what stage of sickness he floats. Two images I transcribe from the pinpoint end of that ancient telescope (the surrounding tubular nothingness, the bright and tiny speck of existence hovering in the distance): the hairy beast of the heavens descending along the plinth of an ornate lightning-bolt, and a white petal-like plasma holding itself motionless, momently visible through the wooden slit the intelligent monster inexorably obscured with his immense and, at the terminal "shot," total, bulk.

8

had a parakeet that fall of 1906, a creature of blue and gold she had kept in one corner of her current apartment—a basement affair near the River which cost a small ransom and which the sun visited just once daily, squeezed in between two monolithic buildings and a horizon of slate roofing—and which she had, as with so many other sensate and insensate things, abandoned. It had no mate, and as I was loth to see it pine in mute solitude, I bought it a mirror, a small oval mock door into the world beyond, a bit of reflected brightness for its drab surroundings. Except for feeding times, which gradually became briefer and briefer, it would perch before that inanimate piece of glass by the hour, fretting and preening its silvery underfeathers, entranced with its image, the shadow of its species working as if from within, billing and moaning and winking, and, as the afternoon light would gather and then flow from the interior of the glass, waving in its plumes the various light. As that shaft of sunlight would slant athwart its cage, falling upon the breast and wings of ruffled gold, it would sing momentarily; then, as the glass would darken and gather shadows to itself, fall silent, and peer more closely and intently at the darkening image fading within. Little dunce, I would whisper, as it lay, beak against reflected beak, its tiny nostril-specks dilating in the intensity of its emotion, wide eyes clouding over with a milky substance and the pulse in its soft throat fluttering at what seemed an impossible rate, a snowy thud-thudding below the red ruff around the beak; little fool, as in what, for him, must have been a totally empty universe, he chirped and twittered, filling the void with his alien language.

My apartment that year looked east toward the distant invisibly inflected River, that had held, a scant six years earlier, the glorious burden of the Queen's flotilla, passing with purple embroidered sails the embankments packed with crowds gathered in honor of her Jubilee, but whose waterway was now empty of all but the brilliance of that autumn sky. More adjacently, the Water Tower (which was virtually the only building of note to survive the Great Fire of 1868) rose pale and yellow into the frame of my dormer window. It was built from a rarely-found kind of limestone (the quarry was exhausted of its rich store all too quickly), and, as the day waned, gathering layers of light in a ripple of glass or the rough shadowy texture of brick, it seemed to transmute the square old-fashioned weathered face of the tower into a precious, almost white, wealth of gold. Four floors below my tiny apartment began Rushlight Street—so called because of the innumerable glass-enclosed tapers that were the emblems of its flickering insubstantial life. There it was, along that glittering crowded boulevard, that I began my long fruitless search for her, which was to end only when she deigned to manifest her presence once again—in the play of my most adamant rival.

That search, begun merely as a matter to occupy an empty heart and hand, soon took on a definite structure of its own—as we imagine a string of genes, linked randomly at its genesis, creating and recreating its own unique combination with a rigour and necessity utterly lacking in its free-floating synthesis; so here; as I followed through those twisting streets, bright with autumn's desolation, a vague and nameless impulse (seeing hints only in a bottomless square of glass shaken in a sudden gust, in the feathery pattern of branch and twig thrown against the ruddy brick face of a westward-fronting building), I found myself gripped, as it were, with the very emptiness and rush that filled the streets by day and night, the vagrant aery impulse which like an animal stalked over the cobblestones, sucking into spirals dry leaves and the torn wings of newspapers. One of those sheets, pasted against a high iron paling by the ceaseless wind, announced the formation of a new "Parliamentarian Party." Behind it long grass, deeply and richly shaded by the oblique rays of an early October sun, stretched to the mild limestone visage of an old retired bordello. The newspaper was three weeks old. A portrait of a stern figure in a vaguely clerical black uniform, complete with Sam Browne belt and short clipped moustache, stared impassively from one fluttering corner. On the other side (how did I manage to get over that fence?) the pale face of the current reigning music-hall queen gazed ambiguously past a minister (war, munitions) in the act of kissing her extended hand. The fingernails were dyed a deep, almost black, crimson, and gave the impression of being filled with blood.

One year earlier (1905) was marked by the unprecedented closing of the theatres—unprecedented because there was not the usual excuse of the plague, or even that of alleged sedition, behind that unexpected and brutal shut-down. We had, in fact, for several years, following the celebration of the Queen's jubilee in 1900, entered upon a peculiarly rich, fertile, and a-political field of dramatic endeavor, fenced in, as it were, by the productions, in 1900 and 1904, of that drama of reconciliation and marriage which takes place on an imaginary jewel of the deep—although, toward the end, when she was so abruptly to desert our flourishing Company, our dramatic themes were to become somewhat overclouded by an inexplicable shadow, a hint or threat of loss, that crept into the gaily painted banquet hall where the marriage-feast was spread, the wedding-guests disported in loving attire, the harp struck by skillful tapering fingers (one of which might be decorated by black unreflecting onyx), the clown pirouetting in a spiral of vibrant melting colour, while, without, against the leaded rippled glass that separated us from the vast and dingy areas backstage, a white and twitching face would suddenly be pressed, with the emptiness and darkness stretching behind acting as an insubstantial backdrop. Thus, as unimagined and unexpected, did our bloom slowly wither. Mounted "storm troopers," in pairs and threes, soon grew to be a common sight on the erstwhile peaceful streets of our villages and cities, and soon the ugly head of repression was raised as more and more power passed into the hands of the military. I remember distinctly—how could I forget?—the dreary and drizzling morning when we arrived at the massive doors of the Globe to find them sealed by the huge leaden padlocks of the State.

That evening I went out early, having, now, nothing to occupy the long hours of darkness, just as the large empty globes of milky radiance were coming alive on the boulevards. The crowds that thronged these thoroughfares seemed thinner than usual, I noticed, and this sparse effect was only accentuated by the darkened marquées where the numerous creatures of the street were wont to gather. A moon, rubbed thin and almost transparent, floated fishlike and silvery above the spire of an adjacent cathedral, and my footsteps, as I leisurely picked my way among the passers-by, sounded hollowly against the cobblestones. From pure aimlessness my route evolved into a definite hurrying progression that ended in a tiny cramped terminus, her darkened apartment on East Wilton Street just off the River (and just down the street, by the way, from the tall monolithic slab that was to become the headquarters of Ploughboy Clubs International). I stood across the street trying unsuccessfully to focus through the opaque waterlike depths of the half-windows that looked out from her basement rooms. The foyer itself that led into the building was lighted, but its walls, brocaded in red and gold, stared back at me as impassively as the stony face of a gaoler. The floor immediately above was also lighted, although the shades were partly drawn, and against their luminous surfaces, moving slightly in a draught, I could see the shadows of the insubstantial inhabitants moving here and there, meeting, merging, and drifting apart. Through a slit in one aperture I could see, distantly, an arm lightly dusted with golden hair arranging something on a table. A silhouette floated toward where that appendage terminated in an invisible torso. To my left, down the gentle arboreal incline of the street, I could hear the strong insistent current of the River as it passed its flanks along the insinuating curve of the embankment. The moon had cushioned one bonewhite arm against the silver of a slate roof. From the position of the shadows—faint columns and cornices of deeper pitch dropping soundlessly along the length of this involuted street—it must have been between nine and ten. As I stood uncomfortably shifting from one foot to another, needles prickling the calves in somnolent waves, hypnotized by the display of blackness and secretive light yonder, an officer on an inky steed accosted me, and as I groped for some kind of answer to his forgotten interrogative, those lights opposite abruptly went out—leaving, however, residual stars floating fishlike in the current that now rolled through the entire artery of this portion of the City's corpus.

Although I did not know it at the time, she had already taken her leave, and as I gazed for one last time at those darkened and sightless sockets of windows staring out into emptiness, I was reminded of nothing so much as the stage after the last act has rung the curtain down—that sudden change upon the instant which fills or empties the heart so radically, and by which the heart is nourished, for it is by the perception of a change, like the sudden "blacking out" of the lights of the stage, that passion creates its most violent sensation.

The tour which we embarked on shortly after the abrupt cessation of theatrical activities in the City proper (foreshadowing the more permanent closure some thirty years later under the aegis of the so-called Protectorate) was marked with the absence of what was so luminously present on the first tour; indeed, as our caravan made its slow and painful progress out of a suddenly indifferent City, we were surprised and shocked by the changes that were already apparent over the once pregnant and unbounded countryside. The rills and crystalline network of glittering streams, that had unwound luxuriously and leisurely throughout the greening fields and swards, shaded in delicious counterpoint with sleepy spangles of sunlight by the overhanging willow or water-loving linden, had muddied that brightness imperceptibly, until naught could be seen in those moving depths save the poisonous jade of unprocessed sewage, or the milky bellies of dead fish floating in an uneasy backwater, taut with corruption. The almost feminine undulation of field and weathered hill, variegated with that pied beauty which an obscure Jesuit had celebrated in the late years of the last century, was now disturbed rudely by the verticality of smoke-stack and factory tower, and was already beginning to be covered by rows of uniform bungalows; and the earth itself, hitherto unmarked by any tool more nocuous than the common plow, now revealed its naked defenseless flesh under the scoops and dredges of horrendous machines. Our repertoire, too, gradually took on a similar faded quality, as the flow of new material lessened to a tiny trickle, and then to a series of slowly falling droplets catching, in the prism of their gently distended orbs, all the spectrum of an increasingly distant rainbow. A satiric streak, a vein of iron, found its way into the mother-lode of our finer poetic passages, until they came to resemble the masques and comedies of our most famous rival; and in the historical plays and tragedies that came to take up the bulk of our performances the prose speeches, as if they were cancerous organisms, proliferated until they overweighed the poesy of which they were the mere appendage. The fields where we were wont to spread our humbler entertainments became increasingly inaccessable; time after time, upon being directed to a remote plot of ground, we were stopped short by barbed-wire fences, newly introduced from the western plains of America, or, more frequently, a rude excavation half-filled with muddy water, signifying that real-estate development was not far behind. Even the unenclosed courtyards we found were, more often than not, boarded up or filled with new farming implements that had become popular with the younger members of the gentry, and we were, often, forced to resort to the unoccupied town hall, or the spacious dining room of one of the more affluent of our patrons, or even the bare echoing tiles of an old Benedictan refectory, now empty of nourishment for these—let me see—seventy-five years.

The weather itself, as we made our halting progress through the strangely transformed countryside, was filmed over with an indeterminate and dingy haze, that made of objects discrete and fragmented images, much the same effect as the celluloid squares of my inventor were to have upon an unsuspecting and passive world a few years hence. The sun, in my recollection at any rate, muffled his fiery head in layer after layer of obscuring atmosphere, until aught that could be seen of his presence was, at best, an oily lighter grey against the unchanging monochromatic wrack; and our speeches, accordingly, took on an appropriately "indoors" quality—even when spoken under no less elevated a ceiling than that of the clouds themselves—as if the circumference of the world-stage upon which we strode had contracted to that of, say, our skulls.

Our route now took us north and west into the rapidly developing Midlands, skirting easily and delicately the desolate unpopulated Yorkshire moors that the Brontë sisters were to immortalize some years hence, where, to crowds of newly created factory workers, we staged what can only be termed "historical farces"—crude intermixtures of low comedy (which yet had a venerable, indeed almost senile, history, stretching back to Plautus and beyond) and stately blank verse dealing with the presumably lofty machinations of state which was to find its popular level of stagnation in the historical fantasies of an entire generation of hacks (the favourite era stretching from the reign of the last Henry to that of the last—and first—Elizabeth) and those films filled with fox-hunting scenes and Wolsey or Richelieu standing around uncomfortably in thick ermine and chains and medallions. The popularity we effortlessly drew upon was, this time, due to radically different circumstances than those that operated in our initial tour. An entirely new literate class awaited our laggard arrival, the product of a system of universal compulsory education which was, in turn, made possible by the prodigious affluence that flowed from the colonies and from the handful of scientific discoveries made during the last century producing in this, our inharmonious twentieth, the so-called "Industrial Revolution." The invention, though, which probably had the greatest single effect in producing this large and growing class, was that of movable type, and with it all the organs for the rapid, indeed thoughtless, transmission of information, the periodicals, newspapers, and journals of the modern world.

We played in unused football fields, muddy and malodorous, with one of the crossbars dangling in a wet wind. We played in newly-made "parking lots" deeply ridged with the iron wheels of wagons and charabancs. A factory whistle would indicate the division between acts. Below, in an adjacent valley, a neighboring stream might flow sluggishly, bearing its freight of detritus in its sewer-brown colon toward, as it were, the anus of some distant estuary. We played under skies that were empty of everything save a fine grey ash suspended in a semi-liquid mist. Although the dramas we staged involved more sheer physical activity than ever before, what I remember of our labours on that tour are not the duels, battles, and sorties with which they are interspersed, but a peculiar emptiness and sense of being abandoned—perhaps induced by the infertility of the fallow earth itself that lay uncultivated all around, waiting for the magic touch of some real estate tycoon to be developed into a shopping centre, an outdoor movie theatre, or the flushing pink stucco of a neon-rimmed motel. Migrating birds flew through these grey and dreary fields that autumn, through the unharvested hay and stray stalks of corn, casting no shadows as they flittered southward, carrying with them, as they merged into the deepening dusk, the faint and fading memory of all the increase they had, unwitting, witnessed. Against the fences that spiderwebbed these fields in long looping strands of barbed wire (supplanting the natural and flowering hedgerows with which they were once decorated) small but growing heaps of rubbish raised their mounds, speckled with glittering metallic waste. And, through meadows once unimpeded by any grove of tree or bush, spangled, in their lush spring-fed grass, only with pale blue asters and the grotto-gold of clumps of swaying sunflowers, the naked unliving peeled boles of telegraph poles (former pines, cedars, laurels; sacred to Diana, Demeter, Apollo) lifted into the unadorned heavens their sad unchanging phalloi.

Betimes, in one factory town or another, or in the series of straggling clapboard hovels that limped up the side of some mammae-like hillock being divested of its inner riches, I might see, outlined against a heap of slag, a child in a smudged white pinafore picking some wild flowering weeds, who spoke only the dialect of the region, so that, try as we would, we could never discover her antecedents, or explain her strange presence in that most unlikely place. We followed the deepening autumn north along the Severn River for awhile (through lanes where once that young, now immortal, athlete was carried aloft, his garland briefer than a girl's), wending our way under cloud-driven skies, past deserted villages, chilled by sudden squalls, until we reached, at our most northern point, not many miles distant from the Scottish border, an isolated asylum run (as we discovered) by an extreme offshoot of some Dissenter sect, whose grey rough granite face frowned inhospitably from the midst of louring hills which seemed, as we peered through a light clinging mist, to be formed of denser coagulations of cloud. These were covered, we found upon drawing nearer, with a deep discoloured purplish furze, through which the November wind sighed disconsolately—a springy blanket that was to become reminiscent, retrospectively, as I was to discover, of the almost surreal scrub which covers the desolate foothills and mountains that rise, gradually and threateningly, as one passes over the parched plains of Nevada westward to California, with all the morose and mammoth inflections of derangement. These hills, while lower, and not as overpowering in their effect, had yet the same outlines as their more sinister copy; and as we painfully picked our way over the pitted cowpath that dignified itself with the name of road, huge black crows released themselves from a dark and stirring cornfield to our left, that glowed preternaturally in the early autumn twilight, while, from the battlements that bulked directly ahead, storm-coloured rooks rose like flakes of aery ash into the thickening and lowering air. In the rear of the wagon I manned, fitfully and jerkily, I could hear the rustle and rasp of costumes and accoutrements of our profession—crowns, swords, shields—as they were mingled together by our uneven advance. To my left and rear, in one blurred corner, the bulky form of Burbage (an affair of rags and bellies) snored stentoriously; further back, his head propped up by a sack of dirty laundry, our new clown, Robert Armin, dozed gently, adding his more musical intonation to the *a capella* strains of nasal viol and esophigal bass that rose from the darkened interior of the small Conestoga we rocked and swayed in. As the massive gate gradually solidified at our approach, one of us noticed that it had the same iron ribbing in its oaken slab as did the Marshalsea Prison, the Tower of London, the National Guard building just off Rushlight Street, and other official edifices—ones, at any rate, under the direct or indirect control of Parliament. I roused Burbage, who applied a meaty set of fists to the solid-seeming gate, which, however, echoed hollowly at his energetic knuckling. After some few minutes, during which the only sounds we were aware of were those of the ceaseless wind and our own more uneven breathing, a smaller door, hitherto invisible, opened in the larger gate, and in its narrow frame a sharp white face appeared unexpectedly, framed itself by a black rough-woven material; this twitched at us, and inquired, in a gutteral dialect (Northumbrian or Gutnish) that was barely understandable, our names and business. We were left standing for an unconscionable length of time, I remember, the darkness growing around us with all the implacability and insinuation of the approach of nightly unconsciousness, and were, indeed, expecting that the night now upon us would have to be spent on the open road, when the entire gate moved noiselessly inward, and, with a sigh of relief, our conveyance slid effortlessly within the gloomy and overshadowing walls.

From what I later was able to reconstruct, this building in former times had been a monastery, devoted to the preparation of pre-university lads for holy orders; but this was appropriated when the edict of 1834 took effect under Henry VIII that divested all orders of their extensive properties. Its original usage was still noticeable in the long tiled waxed corridors which echoed reminiscently under the pensive slap of slippered feet, in the cool and cavernous kitchens, ventilated by their well-planned exposure to the north, in the chapel, now, of course, stripped of its sacred images, but still possessing the same effects of light and shade with its highly-placed narrow vertical stained-glass windows which shed blue and crimson light into the upper regions of the room, formed as a cross with short rounded arms, in the sensuous cold odour of wax intermingled with that of incense whose vapour, rising in a thin quiet stream, smouldered in a brazier to the rear of the nave (this latter, I now realize, is an impossibly anachronistic detail; but let it rest, let it rest). There was, in that place, a certain pleasing asceticism, having to do, as I discovered, less with the moral tenor of the lives of its inhabitants, than with the sheerly physical texture of its solid construction, the way the light fell along the white plastered walls, for example, collecting a sensuous stipple of shadow in its meditative gaze, or, on winter mornings, chill with the obliquity of the sun's retreating rays, the skin of ice on the water-ewers as, overhead, the bells tolled for matins. On such mornings, too, in the pre-dawn stillness, if one were to arise and remove himself to the lofty bell-tower that overlooked an even loftier range of mountains to the east, one would see, framed by noble spare pediment over which the red-tiled shell of roof arched, a pure light welling upward through deepening layers of sapphire, peacock green, burnt orange, crimson, and almost inky violet, in which Hesperus, the morning star, pulsed distantly, so large and solid it seemed almost detachable from its luminous background. As one stood, chilled almost to immobility by the utterly transparent cold surrounding one as if in atmospheres of clear ice, a tendril of smoke might be seen to rise, straight as a plumb, from one of the outhouses below, dissolving itself pungently and aromatically, without a visible trace, into the silky texture flushing throughout the entire hemisphere. Then, the crystal air freezing the lungs until they seemed to light up the entire interior of one's body icily and lacily, the huge bell overhead would break the single immense crystal that formed itself around one's numbed perception, and shatter into ringing fragments the oneness of that solemn scene.

Such, at any rate, were my impressions, as I loitered around the well-kept grounds, always under the watchful eye of some unassigned "frater" ostensibly telling his beads (another oddly Papist custom that had managed to live through the fire of Reformation in this curiously isolated backwater of English Protestantism); as I would walk through a shaded arcade connecting two buildings, or the natural grassy alley meandering between a stand of hazelnut trees and an orchard of gnarled crabapple, I would hear, to one side or to the rear, the monotonous hypnotic *click-click* of those endless watchful beads (who knows what huge ever-open eye existed in his heaven, never extinguishing its fire, or lidding its ever-watchful malevolence!) Within that well-ordered, almost monastic cosmos, however, unexplained pockets of ruin, neglect, and disorder remained, the stranger for that the inhabitants, or custodians, of the place (called, now that I think of it, "New Bethlehem") took no notice of them, seemed indeed to be oblivious of their very presence: gardens over-run with fat snake-like creepers, upon which a small poisonous berry sprouted smelling most vilely when burst, and silvery with mildew and dry-rot; arbours so compact of shade that, under their tightly-woven foliage, at broadest noon it seemed the darkest midnight; streams choked with the rich black acid-smelling excrement of nocturnal animals; and, within the building itself, broom-closets stuffed with a foul assortment of rubbish—sheets stained with a brownish fluid, pinking shears that had tufts of uprooted hair adhering to the edges, dolls with the most human-like features and skin I have ever seen brutally eviscerated and dismembered, broomsticks fashioned into immense phalloi, wooden shoes with rust-coloured stains around the tips, old ledgers in Gaelic or Gutnish, their columns spidered with figures in unknown currencies. I heard a rustle, once, as of a rat, deeper behind one such cluttered corner, but I did not investigate. Elsewhere, in the sub-basement, a field of trunks and packing-cases extended into the gloom, dispelled only slightly by the mounds of phosphorescent wood, mildly rotting away into lightlessness, that were heaped at intervals in the hollows of the dank and dripping pillars which supported the immense edifice overhead; these, however, as far as I could tell, were all securely locked; and so whether they held the sacred implements I was told they did, or some crueller collection of tools—pincers, thumb-screws, slender-handled scoops for the deoculation of the more impatient patients—I will never know.

Indeed, now that I think back on it, it seems strange that we were allowed within those precincts in the first place; for, considering our profession, we must have been anathema to their unforgiving eyes. I can only conjecture that the superiors of the institution wished, in their devious, almost Jesuitical, way, to mortify and edify such of those among us who were, according to their way of thinking, not beyond salvation; though the shape and texture such salvation must have taken in their most secret interior visions I shudder to think of, when I consider the use to which that venerable, mossy, friendly old building was put to. If I have seemed to digress from that function in the weaving of these impressions, it is no accident, for I am hard put to it to explain, plainly and without subterfuge, exactly what went on within, partly because of the distastefulness of that activity to me professionally (thrusting crudely into actuality the monsters and mutations that should remain in the imagination), but also, and mainly, because the place seemed populated less with corporal bodies, than with what might best be described as philosophical abstractions, in the sense that their presence here was not so much due to those disorders which are found in any standard text on the subject, than a common understanding which undeniably worked among both inmates and keepers, though in what subterranean fashion I could not as yet fathom. There is, it seemed to me at the time, as I moved through this alien, almost subaqueous world, with all the naked feeling of a solitary fish in an illuminated bowl, a peculiar string in the harmony of human understanding, which in several individuals is exactly of the same tuning: this, if you can dexterously screw up to its right key, and then strike gently upon it; whenever you have the good fortune to light among those of the same pitch, they will by a secret necessary understanding strike exactly at the same time, causing, in those that are thus magically allied, a hum, a quiver, a vibration of response and relief, almost a shudder, except that this is purely an internal phenomenon, not related to any physical process, being in fact an undiluted and (as far as I know) solitary example of an epistemological event, all the more marvellous in that it occurs among more than one of those floating particles of disparateness that Leibniz calls monads. Windows of the soul indeed, these magic apertures, in that otherwise hermetic cage called human consciousness, lead out to those others, and from their intermingled invisible beams, weave worlds that silently advance, silently pass. Such was the world I was now immersed in, related to the larger one without by only the most tenuous of threads; and it is my belief that were our Company not known to be under the royal patronage, it would have disappeared as quietly and unnoticeably as nutritive matter being ingested and transmuted, so slowly and so surely, into other forms.

Moving through that many-eyed place, as evanescently and immaterially as an image floating through a mirror, I was struck by the queer thought that its founder might have been that most Irish of philosophers Bishop Berkeley, whose ghostly idealism remained fallow and unformed until, in the more bitter spiritual and mental climate of England, he found the opposite that stung his thought into expression and made it lucid; for the inmates of this place, far from suffering from any organic disorder, were victims of a rare strain of schizophrenia, one that had long defied classification and cure, and which might best be described as "referential mania," or, even more exactly, "historical disorientation." In this form of the sickness, the patient is, to all ordinary observation, normal, but reveals a chronic dislocation as to temporal perception: the single flowering present (the result of an uneasy alliance between perceiver and perceived) is split, in his flawed vision, into an indeterminate, remote, and romantic past, while the "present" in which he feels himself bound, as in a strait-jacket or a nutshell, he perceives from the classical "realist" stance: the everyday pragmatic modern world which latter-day novelists are so fond of gruesomely dissecting (forgetting as they always do that "realism" is as much an image, an idea, as "idealism"—both words in any man's pocket dictionary). To this enclave of fellow-sufferers the evolving Present which, like the River that encircles and establishes our earthly City, changes, moves onward, and yet retains its identity (in a peculiarly anti-Heraclitean sense) has its life in a distant Past; the age we know as Elizabethan, thus—the flower-gemmed Present of this account—existed to these lost wayfarers in Time some three hundred years earlier, in a mist-shrouded land that is virtually mythological; while the time in which they feel themselves trapped, the late eighteen-hundreds and early nineteen-hundreds, they termed the "Victorian" era (after an obscure though brilliant Indian queen). This remarkable split was similarly applied to all fields of human endeavor, and indeed to the affairs of the entire biosphere; thus the present age, which we know as one of great lyric and dramatic achievement (at least in its ascending arc and starry zenith) they have placed, by a kind of literary psychosis, in that remote time, while their illusionary and fragmentary "now" is, to them, one of commerce, industrialism, empire, and all the crude and simple-minded machinery that goes to make up the modern novel (which outdated engines, I hope, this literal account in no way resembles). In similar fashion, the era that immediately followed, the long, peaceful, almost scholarly Jacobean one, was twisted and perceived as the "Edwardian" Age—after, insofar as I am able to gather, a handsome, dissolute playboy under whose lurid shadow England was to enter her bloody War of 1914 (like the Civil War some twenty years later, generated by internecine conflict at home). Alas, so fickle is the Muse of History, with her impassive three faces, that this relatively isolated disease was to break out of its confinement and, as the years of the present century accumulated like so many stones at the bottom of a dry well, so spread over the face of the once-living earth that the relatively sane majority was soon to find itself at a distinct numerical disadvantage, as witnessed by the rapid dominance of Dissenter sects in England, with the narrowly Biblical interpretation of history which made them congenial to such splits, and, throughout the navigable world, their peculiar spiritual mutation appearing under many guises and garbs (the most lethal of these being, of course, the spectre of National Socialism in Germany). This queer crossbreed of fantasy and fact was nowhere more apparent than here, at a primitive stage in its evolution, in the strains of a virtually imperceptible, incredibly rare epistemological disease, close by a range of disturbing dark hills that march north into the Scotland that is both of the gentle and believing James, our ruler at the time, and the wry agnostic Hume, who was to turn, with his pragmatic wand, the entire perceptible universe into image and illusion; here, in these shaded walks, and long echoing intertwining corridors, from which abutted the widely-spaced isolated cells in which the various members of this community passed their lives; in the regular pacing of its warders, the somber black of their serge garments accentuating the fluttering white of hands and face; and in the inhabitants of those cells, squatting on straw in one corner, haunches enclosing the head from either side, eyes bulging from between the twin-jut of bony knees, chained to one spot by no more substantial restraint than the imagined eyes staring from the hooded slit in the door, or, in the more violent wards, iron knots holding their victims in a most subtle web (collar for neck, cuffs for the four extreme appendages, and an iron belt for the narrow abdomen, one slender series of links descending from the navel to enclose the shrinking genital in its grip). Some of these creatures were afflicted with a kind of glossolalia, a frenzy that caused them to foam at the mouth with strange utterances, monstrous thickets of sound composed almost entirely of harsh consonants and gutteral clicks, in which might be glimpsed, occasionally, the shadow of some Welsh or Arabic morpheme. Others still would lure the curious spectator near to a barred portal with soft crooning locutions, promising of mysteries to be revealed, and, when the guileless amateur psychologist would hasten over, pad and pen poised, he would swiftly revert, lift his weighted chamberpot, and cast its stinking contents into the gaping face of the graduate student of psycho-linguistics or psycho-dramatics; while, in certain unmentionable cells that offended the olfactory sense with their tremendous stench, the naked inhabitants, upon excreting a sufficient amount of ordure, would ingest it once again, with many noisome smacks and relishes, and gobbets of the brown or mottled defecation oozing out at the corners of the mouth which, upon being rescued by a swift finger, were inserted into the odorous superior anus from which they had by accident squeezed. These had turned a dark brown colour, like those insects who make their home in the faeces of various animals and, after several generations of assiduous burrowing, take on the delicate tint of their environment. I still can remember gazing in one or another of these reeking cells, holding my nose as I did so and, thinking their darkened recesses empty, be prepared to move on, and suddenly glimpsing, in one corner of my vision or the room, an even darker shape moving about in search of some blacker obscurity or filth in which to bury itself.

One phenomenon, though, struck me with particular force, and that was the sudden appearance and disappearance of a slight figure in a parti-coloured garment who would hasten up to our group, make a deep obeisance, and, still holding our redundant fingers, puff himself up to an immense size, the orbs of his eyes bulging out tremendously and his lips skinned back over his teeth like strips of dead epidermis being stretched out to dry. We were not to fear this harmless creature, we were informed by our ever-present Guide, for here was a tailor run mad from pride, the only one in the establishment allowed the liberty of the ante-chamber, who had taken to strange utterances regarding the future: that man would take to the air in huge floating sausages, that we would be able to talk clairvoyantly over great distances, and other such-like wonders; as well as hissing denunciations of the present ruling house, the prediction of its speedy downfall, and the approach of a longed-for Armageddon, the day when this very asylum, with its walls, its chains, its many-eyed cells and almost impalpable hum of intercommunication, would prove a model or gnomon for the entire civilized globe. His head would loll on one side as he said this, eyes peering slyly from their cavernous sockets, then abruptly snapping erect, disdainfully, and with an arrogant twist to the narrow shoulders, as if to say, when that day came to pass, we would be the prisoners, and he the mere king of the chaos that had breeded in the innermost recesses of his soul.

What we did not realize at the time was that the entire establishment, although under royal charter and originally staffed by the King's household, stood united in its outlook upon an alien world; so that, in effect, there were no genuine rôles of warder and prisoner but each was freely interchanged, one with the other, as whim or convenience dictated. How this transformation took place we will never know; I myself believe that, under continual exposure to the disease which predominated there from the outset, the few untrained members of the original staff gradually succumbed, and were incarcerated with the rest. What a paradox it is to me now that I who am, it seems, virtually the last surviving sane member of our species, should have been almost the first to witness the initial growth of the virus which was to spread, by a kind of ontological osmosis, throughout our isle and then the rest of the globe; but stranger yet is the fact that I did not then realize what was transpiring all around me, as I made that fatal last tour through a world changing with the retreating sun: that machinery had not separated from handicraft wholly for the world's good, and that the distinction of classes had, in fact, become their isolation. I have often thought, since then, that if the London merchants of our day competed together in writing lyrics they would not, like their Tudor counterparts, dance in the open street before the house of the victor; nor would the great ladies of London finish their balls on the pavement before their doors as did (for example) the great Venetian ladies, even in the eighteenth century, conscious of an all-enfolding sympathy. Doubtless because fragments broke into even smaller fragments we—the characters on that stage of the moment—saw one another in a light of bitter comedy, and in the arts, where now one technical element reigned and now another, generation hated generation, and accomplished beauty was snatched away when it had most engaged our affections. One thing I did not foresee, not having the courage of my own thought: the growing murderousness of the world.

9

It was across the River from our customary Parish that we first established ourselves in a more-or-less permanent theatrical location, in the autumn that concluded our first tour of 1898, separated, by an expanse of some seven years, from the latter excursion that has just occupied these pages. At that time, one block to the east from our new and spacious quarters, construction was beginning on what was to be the first of many "skyscrapers" (a peculiarly undescriptive word to anyone who has viewed these tall and graceful creatures coming alive at dusk, small pinpoints of radiance illuminating, against the darkening heavens, new constellations for the noctambulator to trace—humming motes like fire-flies in a gloom-infested garden, or like the floating haze of static, due to the ageing of the film, on the screen of a perennially twilit cinema). This massive and yet willow-like tapering building, named after one of the signers of the Australian Declaration of Independence, was to grow to such heights that its upper portions were in danger of being lopped off by a too circumscribed field of vision (one, say, as limited as the eye of a projector in an old theatre dedicated to re-runs, complete with drifting smoke and dozing alcoholics). At the time of our installation into the new premises, however, construction had barely gotten under way, and the mammoth base, on the outside of which supporting beams of steel were crossed on each of four sides, was just being "topped out" when we began staging our first productions of the season. Well do I recall, on early winter mornings—the brownstones plumed with fine white vapour and the pigeons cooing and moaning in the jewel-clear, jewel-bare parks, scrabbling for bread and seed—days all sapphire and gold, with glints of burnished combed light bleeding from now one wave of glass, now another, as the dazed day-wanderer would drift through the naked trees and buildings, his eye expanded to include almost the entire shivering hemisphere and gleaning, in its revolutions, perspectives and distances only hinted at before—from behind the bare blowing lacery of twigs and branches, almost black with the cold, the rocklike eminence of that edifice containing, in its immense side, the entire solar radiance half the heavens had to offer; or, from the eastern side, as the afternoon advanced, its huge soft luminous shadow, a little blurred at the sensuous imperceptibly advancing edge, falling soundlessly through the trees toward where some frozen blades of grass trembled in the dry receding light. Day by day I would visit that adjacent park to find, in my absence, the shadow extended a little further into the narrow remaining strip the sun found and held to. Sometimes, due to double and triple refractions among neighboring buildings, a spider or skeleton of light could be found in the almost blue-black gloom that column cast, a shivering, almost disembodied vertebrae of silvery synapses holding onto its brief incarnation with insubstantial tenacity. As the maned sun dipped in its inevitable path toward the horizon (an uneven affair of roofs and gables) its fine thread-like radiating halo, multiplied by the surrounding legion of glass, from a pure yellow turned an orelike gold, then orange burning fitfully, then gules bleeding outward in thin wavering lines that caught in the overhanging twigs and stained the winter bark of the dividing and redividing branches a deep arterial crimson. At the time I am speaking of, the early winter of 1898 (as far as I can tell: there seems to have developed a fine ashy rain of microscopic motes over this field of my recollection), construction had proceeded so far as to leave, beyond the huge column of shadow, the narrowest strip of sunlit lawn and bush (shaking, with its few red berries, in the slightest breath of air); a squirrel or a large finch (it is so hard to tell at this distance!) might be seen foraging in the skimpy underbrush. There—a better focus: grey plume erect, the agile rodent scurries off and out of one's field of vision, holding an acorn or a burr-nut firmly in his champed jaws.

That season, our first complete theatrical one in the City, was marked with extreme cold; the River, almost always clear due to the salinity of the proximate Ocean, froze over as I discovered one frosty morning, looking out my window (decorated with icy script during the night) to see a clear white expanse over which tiny skaters flashed and curved and dipped, specks of blue and red and forest green in the early light. Clouds of thick white vapour poured from the rooftop chimneys around my loftily-situated apartment, testimony to the tremendous amount of fuel needed to heat their chill interiors; indeed, as I lay with the quilt up to my throat, I could feel the entire building on which my room was perched creak from the intense bitterness of the cold, as if chilled to its very bones. My breath feathered out above my head like one of those wavy balloons used to denote thought in the cartoons of the era (with the patch of colour behind bleeding into its hollow cranium). Below me and to my right and left the City spread its glittering wings, rheumed with frost; from the Cathedral's spire clear ringing notes drifted downward, breaking softly against cornice and fluted gable. Its cross burned bronze under the curve of its Byzantine roof.

On such a morning I would occupy myself in chill solitary composition, huddling before the gas heater and attempting to hollow out, in the numbing atmosphere, a warm space in which to rest my living thought. The body I was labouring over at that time was composed, Chimera-fashion, of three Ovidian myths; and as I worked over its slight form, burnished and golden in the half-light, I thought that something of my warm breathing was translated to the mute inert shape so perfect under my moulding fingers—a flush, a rosy dawn of realization, a life of its own that I could, having made independent, make mine. That that dawn proved false was, I assert, through no fault of my own, but only due to the fragility of the materials I was constrained to work with.

A translation or, more correctly, transformation, had been made of Ovid's glittering *oeuvre* some years back—I was a mewling thing of three when it was published—by a workhorse named Golding, who later was to attain a dingy fame as a composer of modern-day moralities, the most notorious of these, ever-popular with the young and illiterate, being the island-fable which has as its chief character the decapitated head of a pig; several individual tales had been anonymously done into doggerel since then; thus the myths I refashioned now were no strangers to the reading public. There were other inducements, however. I do not know how it came about, but our recent emergence into prominence in theatrical affairs generally, and within the London area particularly, brought the actors of our Company in increasing contact with leading figures of fashion in Court and the *beau monde*; chief among these were Essex and his group, a glittering array of powder and perukes, ruffs and ornamental rapiers, which included in its shifting constellation a certain devoted pederast-playwright who shall go unmentioned here—another expatriate Irishman, by the way—with large vegetable eyes who was, needless to say, a devotee of the Greek arts. He it was (I am trying to keep him down, trying to thrust him out of this account, but he is coming to life, surging up under my pen) who, long dividing the theatre of London with Shaw, was to drop abruptly from the picture in the wake of a famous scandal trial which was not to leave unsmirched the golden Attic head of his young arrogant pet of a nobleman—resurfacing, so to speak, in a tiny provincial village in Normandy, all the caustic wit that had made his comedies things to be feared as well as admired mellowed and mutated into a kind of sickly saintliness. I had the misfortune to visit him shortly before his early death (long overdue in the eyes of many); his room, as I discovered subsequently, was an almost exact model of the one he had been confined to during his two years at Reading Gaol: an affair of bare walls covered with a coarse-textured grey sacking, undecorated save, at one end, against the whitewashed plaster, a monochrome print of the Belvidere Apollo (all dimples and nipples). There was only one window in the place, a small aperture positioned so high that only with the greatest difficulty could the world outside—the dreaming Norman landscape, mottled and muted—be glimpsed and woven together; often one would prefer simply to remain in bed, gazing out at the ethereal behaviour of the heavens, and draw imaginary windows in the walls wherewith to invent a better, more symmetrical world. Daily, he would appear in the rustic village, in which he acted as something of a cross between local idiot and rare zoological curiosity; and it was indeed strange, no doubt, to see that tall, somewhat overweight, uncertain, prison-blanched figure issue from its cavernous recess and poke its way down the shady side of a lane, at whose halting progress foraging fowl, startled as by a ghost, would lift briefly into the chill and misty air. By the time I saw him, a mere three months before his demise, he had been terribly transformed indeed; the cynical mock that was wont to adorn the finely-chiselled curve of his lip had melted into a suffering smirk; the eye that had brightly impaled bogus profundities had dulled to a kind of curdled café-au-lait; he was seen often in attitudes of obvious and ostentatious prayer—in one thing he had not changed: his love of dramatic poses—and had taken to using a *nom d'angoisse* in his retirement that, in his prime, he would have laughed explosively at: "Sebastian Melmoth" (at the melancholy utterance of which we are supposed to evoke images of the picture-book martyr bristling with arrows and devoted eyes walking arm in arm, a kind of androgynous coupling, with the "gloomy vagabond," as Pushkin's greatest translator phrases it, of Charles Robert Maturin, a comfortable unbyronic Irish clergyman who composed with a wafer pasted on his forehead, which was to signal to any of his family that entered that they must not speak to him). The year was 1909—three years after her last blinding disappearance, seven years before her final re-entry into the visible world. I was *en route* to the New World, having just made a stormy Channel crossing; my trans-Atlantic steamer, the *Sir Walter Ralegh* (named after the minor poet and major Colonial visionary) being delayed by spring storms and the reports of Spanish privateers, I took the coast express from Calais to the secluded village where he was reported sequestered. The train, a spur off the more heavily travelled *Sud Express* (which thrust deep into Provençe and the Riviera) had no diner and no sleeping car attached, and the trip was, in consequence, a halting and miserable one, with delays at every settlement of more than three houses, and long shuddering stops in the middle of young fragrant alfalfa fields for interminable flocks of sheep; but I consoled myself with such landscapes as could be gleaned between jolts and halts, nothing to compare with the fields of my youth or age—those luxuriantly burdened slopes of rural England and California—but enough to fill the space between, say, one heartbeat and the next (that duration, that swooning valley, in which the entire universe might be compressed). He met me at his door, whence the tiny dog-cart deposited me: a white oval face surmounted by fashionably long chestnut waves and two fluttering white doves for hands. A young attendant prepared an English tea (complete with scones and blackberry jam). The gloom was only partially dispelled by the flickering spirit-lamp which hung from the ceiling by slender, almost invisible links. Its delicate nutation caused an army of regularly recurring shadows to march across the ceiling and down the roughly-textured expanse of the walls, disappearing where we sat in a charmed circle of light.

The features of our conversation have eroded themselves with the years, but I will never forget the facts he revealed to me about the part his circle came to play in our dramatic productions until, finally, our performances for Court were almost to outweigh our popular productions. This would not have been so bad were it not for a more insidious influence that glittering group exerted. As I have said, the webs that I spun had, as their function, the task of snaring and localizing their chief inhabitant (so that one could tell, by the faint, regular tremblings along the strands and supports, whether the invisible dweller was housed or absent); as we began to attend these court performances, a subtle, sinister effect could be noted: behind the symmetrical gleaming structures I erected there came to be glimpsed shadow houses, identical in every respect to their resplendent originals, except that they formed the negative sign, the blind cancellation of all that was so exquisitely visible; and it was this pattern, not the one I so painstakingly constructed, that she came to inhabit, albeit I was all unaware at the time. If the part I had evolved called, say, for a nymph by a sedgy bank (as painted by Corbière or even one of the French caricaturists), that nymph would appear, true; but behind her and to the rear, barely visible, almost off-stage, a gross satyr would lurk, his crotch obscenely bulging under a hairy loincloth; and it seemed at such moments that I could hear, in the deeper background, a thin, cruel chuckle reverberating. Or, at the wedding feast that would crown some lighter comedy, suddenly, at the last minute, replacing the young stalwart blessed with mock marriage to my fair, a barely human ape, a biped in a smelly pelt stuffed into a moth-eaten tuxedo, would be made to materialize; and although there came the expected gasp of astonishment from a greater portion of our audience, from one continaully shifting area of interior blackness flowed only a knowing silence. While the words themselves—those irreplaceable links—remained intact, their impact shifted wholly into another dimension, one filled with hollow heartless laughter, a glass that gave back its figure twisted strangely into bitter and alien shapes, disproportionate in some indefinable yet familiar way, like a child that has gone to sleep and reawakened under the spell of a malady that has as yet no name: his eyes glazed over, his skin tender and papery-feeling, he gazes about his tiny room as if now seeing it for the first time in his brief span of years. So here: as I looked at the scenes I had so carefully prepared, I saw, as if with new eyes, how susceptible they were of more than one interpretation; what had seemed but the purest fairy tales of man's infancy and early childhood proved, in those elegant, almost totally visual settings, to have a depth, a cavity, I had entirely unsuspected. Thus, in my Ovidian original, I would have placed, in the centre of the larger oval the stage formed—that focus for so many eyes—a large oval of brass-ringed water, so clear that one could see right to the bottom, glittering with pebbles of quartz, the edges of which were further ringed with fresh turf and grass that was always green. There, amid a clump of newly planted rushes, in a light that filtered in verdurous ripples from a quartet of stained glasses in the balcony behind which clustered waxen tapers (a precursor of the modern-day "spotlight"), I would have the nymph appear, bathing her limbs and combing out her hair with a boxwood comb, and gazing into the water whence her picture floated. In the background, surrounding this scene, an orchard whereon painted fruit blushed like the earliest intimations of dawn rose into the upper darkness. There the boy Hermaphroditus would glimmeringly materialize, succumb briefly to her importunate embraces, blush, like those hollow globes of fruit, but more like the moon than the sun when, in eclipse, she shows a reddish hue beneath her brightness. There, spurned, she would forsake her sacred springs, hiding in a thick clump of lilac bush nearby, to watch the young perfectly-formed youth shed his clothes and reveal an amazing dazzling whiteness underneath, the pallor of all things untried and newly radiant with life. At the sight the nymph Salmacis, nearest us in her fragrant hiding place, was on fire to possess his naked beauty, and her very eyes flamed with a brilliance like that of the blinding sun, when his bright disc is reflected in a mirror. Having divested himself, the youth balanced himself on the balls of his feet and, clapping his hollow palms against his body, dived flatly and with scarcely a ripple into the glassy surface of the water, that bent the light to one side as it dropped from above. As in his swift stroke he raised first one arm and then the other, his body gleamed in the clear liquid, as if someone had encased an ivory statue or white lilies in transparent glass. "I have won! He is mine!" the nymph cried, and flinging aside her garments, plunged into the heart of the pool. The boy fought against her, now on this side, now on that, like ivy encircling tall tree trunks, clinging to him, her whole body pressed against his; the shadowy chorus in the dim background echoing her unspoken prayer: "May the gods grant me this, may no time to come ever separate him from me, or me from him!'' Her prayer found favour with the gods; the chorus sighed, subsided; a sudden wind sprang up within the shadowy interstices of the trees, rustling their dry leaves together as with a single drawn-out breath, for, as they lay together in unreflecting fluid, their bodies were united, and from being two persons, they became one. As when a gardener grafts a branch to a tree, and sees the two unite as they grow, and come to maturity together, so when their limbs met in that clinging embrace the nymph and the boy were no longer two, but a single form, possessed of a dual nature, which could not be called male or female, but seemed to be at once both and neither.

Imagine my shock, then, upon seeing this pellucid picture —this unruffled surface abloom with man's earliest innocence, when, not lusting as we do with our divided natures, we gazed with single vision at the single world—broken brutally by an alien presence protruding itself upon my hermetically sealed world: that chorus materializing to a band of "sacred homosexuals"—men dressed in the religious robes of priestesses— who, hair tied firmly back, sleeves rolled up, descended upon my composite creature, my faunlet and nymphet, all roses within, lilies without, with falsetto shrieks and eyes brighter than the blades they wielded! I gasped for breath, but the surrounding ironic cackles of laughter emptied my lungs of any oxygen that might have been left by the impact of that scene. And that, fair reader, was held in the spacious halls of the Lord Chamberlain himself!

But at the time of their occurrence these incidents had no more meaning or resonance than the scraps of paper upon which they were penned; their source remained a dark ugly knot that only the erosions and entropy of time were to untie, as they do all knots, including the very mortal one that shelters, with futile twists, our flickering spark of life. Had I not, indeed, sat in that distant black room, through which tiny fish of light floated, and listened to the insistent insect voice of the one beside me, droning in the dark, underscoring my bright memoried pictures with an acid brush, I might have continued to dwell in a house of illusion, upon the bare tediously blank walls of which floated pleasant images of what did not exist.

But better, as I thought and think, better mad with much heart, than idiot with none. Those bitter fanciful injections of outside reality into my symmetrical, indeed classical, dreams, were, I discovered, a result—as the miragelike productions themselves were—of our but recently-formed alliance with members of the educated aristocracy: not royalty, mind you, but idle members of Court who had had expensive classical educations and did not know what to do with them. Sitting there in that little room with him, it seemed as though all the world I had known then, which was quintessentialized in the dramas we produced, was evoked and wrought in his voice—which, the lamp flickering lower as its small store of fluid was exhausted, seemed to disembody itself, and become purely auditory. Perhaps it was because, in his extended incarceration, he had grown used to making a narrow enclosure a model for the world, or perhaps it was simply that he had never really lost his power to weave a genuine world (albeit, in former times, that world, glittering and mordant, had all too often been confined to a drawing room); but whatever the cause, his words, as he spoke, retained all their old magic of association, and I saw anew those scenes —as if a photograph had been taken through the eyeballs of a parrot at the precise instant of death, freezing, for that one split-moment, the imprisonment of a life-time: a fretwork of golden wires on which the world is blocked and printed.

The second of those myths that occupied us during our first theatrical season in London was that of Narcissus and Echo; and due to the exquisite acoustics in the hall where it was staged it was, if anything, even more favourably received than the other. In my memory the tale is triply echoed: the voice of the youth reverberates that of the nymph, who in turn is contained and re-echoed in the voice of my narrator who has managed, for the nonce, to replace me at the unruffled pool of Mnemosyne, pure silver as mercury and as bitter. (Not for nothing does Yeats, in his memoirs, describe the work of this London wit and dandy as "too much spoiled with the verbal decoration of his epoch.") And that triple echo I imagine as reflected once again in the, I trust, elegantly appointed chamber of my reader's mind—who just may be, if I am not careful, no one other than myself. Sweet Narcissus was, of course, aided and amplified by the superb curvature of my Lord's chambers; as he called, now loud, now low, the answering verbs and reverbs rippled back to mingle and merge with the concluding portion of his cry, as well as the beginning of the next, till the effect was that of an entire chorus of honey-tongued birds in some sensuously darkened grove. There, our new director of lighting, Will Sly, worked his arcane brand of magic upon the bit of water below (his special talents were revealed by the celerity with which he could make things seem to appear and disappear, with all the instantaneousness of an eyeblink): he so concentrated those long wavering shafts of light upon the pool that it seemed transformed into a blinding oval mirror, a silvery glass before which the now silent youth, tawny with leaf-shadow and speckle, knelt; and, seeking to quench his thirst, another thirst grew in him, and as he drank, fell snare to the reflection he glimpsed within, mistaking a mere shadow for a real body, motionless, like a statue carved from some antique marble, admiring all the features for which he was himself admired. At once seeking and sought, himself kindling the flame with which he burned, how often did he vainly kiss the treacherous pool, how often plunge his arms deep in the water, attempting to grasp what could not be grasped! But he could not lay hold upon himself. Without knowing what he was looking at, he was fired by the sight, and excited by the very illusion that deceived his eyes. Why vainly grasp, one would murmur (one or another of a series of retreating echoes)—why vainly grasp at the fleeting image that eludes you, since it does not exist, and in itself is nothing? But by his own eyes he was undone; to separate himself from his body, he tore away the upper portion of his tunic and beat his bared breast which flushed rosily where he struck it, just as apples often shine red in part, while part gleams whitely, or as grapes, ripening in variegated clusters, are tinged with purple; and, like the nymph that worshipped him, wasted slowly away before our eyes (the light fading from rosy creamy skin, the tender outlines merging into dim twilight), till all that was left in the empty interior—all the gold wealth of yolk withered into oblivion—was the speaking nothing of that voice. Oh, they were charmed, were those educated dandies; it was, as the

Americans say, "right up their alley"—even to the embroidered bit of flowers running around the edge of the glade; and if it were not for the darker theme that that other voice wove into the texture of the stylized tableau I could remain, as I was then, innocently enchanted with it.

I, the weaver of the brighter thread (as that other was of the darker), was not the only one caught in its substantial-seeming web, in which the gauzy insect fluttered vainly, showing now this, now that facet of its dual design; a group of St. Paul's booksellers chanced to attend one dark and early November, arm in arm, clutching the exquisite napes of mother-of-pearl opera glasses, at the centre of which buzzing cluster, a kind of queen bee to the whole, the bookdealer Ralph Barnes floated on a continuous billow of expostulation and reply. At the time, he was considered the most "avant-garde" of the newer breed of publishers; his small but wildly successful list included such arcane titles as *Hecotompathia*, *The 120 Days of Sodom*, *Fig for Momus*, and *The Ginger Man*, as well as a whole series of translations from the Greek, Latin and Italian; and to him also were ascribed those notorious magazines of the period, one of which bestowed its adjective upon the last decade of the century, *The Yellow Book*, *The Savoy*, *Eros*, *The Chameleon*. I can yet see him from the vantage-point of all these darkened years: a slight, almost effeminate figure clad in velvet and lace, at the frothy centre of which—surmounting waves of snow-white starch—his swan's neck and fragile ponderous bird's skull lifted delicately and imperiously, glancing upon whatever object of delight or disdain chanced to move it (a notorious and profligate wit, a young filly, so to speak, in his stable of versatile writers, described him as "my cynical publisher with the diabolical monocle.") And yet, how many paltry, foolish, painted things would lie forgotten, did he not preserve them in his poetaster's hands; and that beauty, too, which was to become the burden of my song, which pervaded brave translunary things that the first Poets had, all air and fire. He looked; he was enchanted; he fell—oh, nothing so obvious as the innocence of those first scenes, but something almost sterile in its glittering unfeminine beauty. One of our Company transformed my simple Ovidian hexameters into a more elaborate metre and stanza; a typeface was chosen (designed, I think, by William Morris), a store of rich rubbed vellum was accumulated, one of the Rossettis contracted to illustrate the borders and titles with birds, creepers, and the intricate, largely non-existent fruit with which that Brotherhood was wont to surfeit itself; and an unsuspecting world was greeted, one clear, cold December morning, with stacks of small duodecimo volumes "bound in the vermilion hides of slaughtered calves" as the advertisement affectedly proclaimed, in the open bookstalls surrounding St. Paul's, presided over by rosy-cheeked lads specially recruited for the occasion. The Venus of those verses was, I remember, conspicuously absent on that date—as if she had withdrawn at the cold inexorable advance of the shadow of the now mammoth Hancock Building, whose initial stories were then in the process of being "topped out." To what remote caves or grottos she had removed herself I had, at that time, no inkling; although, as the season advanced, and then merged, with increasing rapidity, into those that followed (with all the breathtaking blurring effect of a reel of film being run too fast), I was to receive, widely spaced at first, but later more and more closely conjoined, hints and intimations as to the scenes—how I ground my teeth when I learned that I had my hand in their composition!—with which she gradually surrounded herself.

London had, at that time, nurtured within the recesses of its heterogenous body a tiny yet influential sub-community, typified, in its pre-eminence within the literary and social cosmos, by the group constellating around Oscar Wilde and Lord Alfred Douglas. These had appropriated a number of taverns and private clubs along Bishopsgate Street, north of the theatrical district, in what was to become known as "Old Town" (named, I believe, by the original settlers from the Netherlands). Nourished by the overflow from the theatres, and encouraged in their excesses by the extreme fashions of those that habitually thronged there, these darkly luminous recesses in the winding serpentine involution that was the length of Bishopsgate Street (at one point in its unfolding it ran parallel to Rushlight) soon, from being sparsely and infrequently populated, became crowded with their peculiar denizens, a gaily dressed species of whom, it soon grew apparent, it was impossible to tell male from female. These fantastic creatures were dressed in gauzy blouses that puffed out in pink and violet billows from their slender ambiguous torsos, and wide sweeping "flares" or "bell-bottoms" slashed from the knee, their arms often entirely covered with a Byzantine stack of jangling brass bracelets, and ears (usually the left) pierced through a tiny aperture by silver rims of luminence. Never will I forget the first time I entered one of these strange retreats (which have the effect, so removed their life seems, of an almost marine existence). It was shortly after she had begun a series of brief but enigmatic disappearances, often during the length of a single dramatic performance, more frequently after the last show, overnight, with no word to any of her fellow-actors and, needless to say, nothing to I who had contrived her part. During such times, which became more and more common as the season advanced and then merged with those which followed, I had taken to sitting in the windows of certain taverns that looked out on Rushlight or one of its several cross-streets, on the slim chance that I might glimpse her going from one hidden point to another, as one of those dreamers, confined to themselves, who must make all out of the privacy of their thought, calling up perpetual images of desire, so I looked out onto the naked, wet and lifeless street, agleam with the passing carbuncles of omnibuses and hansom cabs, filled with every form but the one I fruitlessly sought. A glass of wine, its ruby condensed and darkened by the surrounding gloom, would stand untasted at my elbow. Above the mahogany bar to my left the omnipresent "Bass's Ale" pyramid shimmered palely. The glass through which I gazed was streaked and beaded with cold droplets in a continuously shifting design—red, yellow, bleeding orange, as the lights flickered, failed, re-flickered in the scene beyond. Above the door to my right a fanlight glowed in a peacock's tail of amber and melancholy gold. A few couples danced disconsolately on the sawdust-strewn floor to the rear; the others sat around in coterie-like groups of three or five, their heads pressed together in an inaudible hum of communication.

It was after one such session, the eyeballs literally straining out of their sockets from the effort of glancing now here, now there, at any faintly moving object, any pale streak against the purple-blooming blackness (like watching a tennis match in which you cannot view either of the vigorous invisibly darting players who seem, as your vision blurs and blunders, to have become septi- and octo-dextrous), that I chanced upon one of the afore-mentioned lounges; its interior was draped with unreflecting sable, and the first of those strange inventions, the so-called "black light," emanated its rays from within and changed every white garment and, indeed, every bit of fluff, lint, or dandruff on one's lapel, into an eerie shimmering super-albesque substance that left residual images clinging in the retina long after one's eyes had turned away. It was a curiously stark and unrelieved interior that I entered, my eyes blinking to accustom themselves to the more intense and concentrated darkness compacted within. A group of fantastic heads, I gradually became aware, had turned toward my ingress. I stupidly blundered against one. An arm fell lightly against my shoulder, then down. Breath wafted in my ear, an almost sickeningly sweet odour of crushed narcissus enveloped me. Then long, dry, scarcely human hair rasped dryly across my exposed neck, with the effect of innumerable razor blades drawing thin red lines over tender epidermis. "Honey," a husky voice breathed, "you're out of place, you're in outer space!"—and I felt, not for the last time, myself enclosed as if in a cage of bones, the prickle of a rudimentary moustache (but silky withal), the quick hard thrust of tongue as surprisingly muscular arms gripped my head and held it close. And what was maddening, insanely maddening, was that I glimpsed, or thought I glimpsed, in one corner of my severly circumscribed vision, that ray, that embodiment of lucence and translucence, which the imprint of absence in my absurdly labouring heart sought to be filled by; glimpsed, hinted, but not seized, restrained in an embrace I abhorred, a dry cocoon of hair and nails and desert breath, that held me back, on a rack of unseeing, as when, viewing some great masterpiece of the cinema which may, for all we know, provide the transforming yeast to the dull dough of our lives, approaching in its unwinding river of light a key scene, a key image, which may form in its serrated softly clinging but sharply articulated edges the template to bind with the peculiar, the unique crevice, hollow of one's lack; and, as that form begins its slow irresistable ignition on the screen, which has now taken on the quality of anyone's field of vision, a dark bulky blocker begins its equally inevitable upsurge in the row or two beyond yours, a black and hateful excrescence, a nothing which you imprecate with every atom of your being, or would, except that that would only worsen the situation, as the boor with his soggy popcorn and balanced black cherry fizz would be certain to obliterate that beckoning image not only visually but audibly if you were to say anything; and so you sit impotently in unseeing blackness, as if that brutal eraser had, in the same stroke, obliterated you as well—as here, in that sable-shrouded recess, I groaned and grated my teeth, in a palsy, a paralysis, sure that just on the other side of my blind spot shimmered the key to the cage which imprisoned me. This cage then detached itself into recognizable limbs and figures, and I picked out, among the white faces floating around me and mocking me, a bookseller, a playwright, a scribbler of pamphlets and unactable Senecan comedies (which were, nevertheless, to form the subject of an equally unreadable cycle of essays by the banker-poet T. S. Eliot). But that image had gone from my vision's screen—left it desolate and white and empty of all save the monochrome shadings that surrounded me. Black velvet rustled dryly as if in the breath of a large and sleeping lizard. Was it any wonder, then, that to fill the space left by beauty's absence I sought to fill it with sterile images, images beautiful as the self-enclosed ideas that were their source, as bottomless, and as bereft of fertility?

10

Modern literature," as we know it today, was, during that year, going through its uncomfortable gestation and untidy birth; and I was surprised to note how many notables were gathered into the confines of the society at whose outer edges I now began to move uncertainly. The chief star of that constellation I never managed to encounter (although, as I have mentioned, I met him once shortly after his release from prison, and not too long before his admission into the more commodious gaol of death); but lesser luminaries were readily apparent as I moved from one salon to another, each vying with the other in opulence, brilliance, and banality. The school of the "New Criticism," nurtured by the so-called "classical comedies" of manners and humours then being shaped on musty old Senecan models, was just emerging, in a kind of spontaneous generation, into its present unwieldy bulk; "Parisian Impressionism" was coming into vogue with the first published verses of Arthur Symons and Ezra Pound (that monumental fake who had, during the late conflict, taken to airing broadcasts against his native America—and then justifying the triteness of those fascist outpourings with the creaky and obsolete machinery of his hamstrung, halting, cancrizantal *Cantos*). This was the school of versification which would substitute for genuine poetic achievement a London fog, the blurred tawny lamplight, the red omnibus, the dreary rain, the depressing mud, the glaring gin shop, the slatternly shivering women, three dexterous stanzas telling you that and nothing more; and it was from the awkward marriage of these two—the monstrous, almost Hegelian rhetoric of the one (a perfect "objective correlative" of the factories of learning in which they were spawned) and the amorphous vague outlines of the other, a kind of dirty blurring poetic gas, that was to bestow upon the coming century its ineradicable stamp, in the plays and verse dramas of Eliot and Webster. Composed as they were in chambers bereft of woman's enduring presence, in a kind of sterile onanism or intellectual frottage, it is no wonder that these verses, plays, and fat parasitic tomes were to inform, by second and third degree, the major institutions of modern life, and to reach, in a kind of logical reductio, that most voracious and emotionless digester of man's experience, the electronic computer.

At the same time that these tendencies were beginning to formulate themselves, of course, the mainstream of poesy continued its rich arterial life—much as the River, burdened with the sewage of indifferent multitudes, yet renews its clear sweet-flowing life in the pulse of its current. The famous anthologies of the period were beginning to unfold their rich, cream- and honey-clotted blooms, fertilized by pollen-bearing insects from France and Italy; within the space of a mere three years (a golden triumverate!)—1897 to 1900—appeared such varied, riches-stuffed treasure chests as *A Garden of Pleasant Delights* (a few of whose lyrics had been issued originally in 1884), *England's Parnassus*, *England's Helicon*, *The Phoenix Nest* (that gathering of courtiers and scholars), as well as the more prosaic *Tottel's Miscellanies*, which had begun their innumerable issues in the earlier part of the century (they had, amid countless jogging fourteeners and nimble Skeltonics, published the early Wyatt, then returned from his Italian travels with the burning burden of the "new culture" he had found there). Beauty was the burden of those songs, beauty and its celebration, in golden stanzas to aery thinness beat; and, as the season slowly solidified into its jewel-clear bareness and iciness, all the trees aflower with articulations of branch and twig, and the shadows strewn luminously soft upon the iron-hard ground, it seemed to me as if the hitherto bald unlovely streets and aggregates of buildings, warted and wizened in the shivering air, took on a gracefulness, a definite, almost iambic rhythm and pulse, that till then had been denied to the most devoted of the Muse's suitors among us; and the River itself, as if purified by the tremendous cold which pressed against it and inundated it, flowed in an almost unearthly blue current past the warehouses and boatyards that lined its banks. These lyrics, many of them the product of our intercourse at the meetings of the Rhymers' Club, appear strangely to me now in the darkened tunnel of time; for despite their fertile synthesis, the result, I believe, of the Muse's commanding presence which was rarely absent from our little room, it seems to me now that we scarcely knew anything of each other, nothing at all but the poems we read and criticized; perhaps time has eroded details or added others, but of this I am certain, we shared nothing but the artistic life. Each of us, in our separate rooms, enacted our common life; and when I visualize the time we had together in the City where we shared our existence, I see, not the rooms where we talked and argued, nor even the theatres where our life was concentrated and polished to an incredible unbearable brilliance, but the hivelike quarters of an immense and scattered edifice through whose transparent membrane-panes we, the shadows within, laboured and laboured, chiselling the stubborn element, to become, through our isolated passion, conjoint to our buried selves, till we grew to be phantoms in our own eyes, and part of that phantom whose ghostly existence we shared. The invisible links were what was real to us, the rhythm of the arterial blood in the symmetrical body we shared, not the brute fact of the walls and ceilings which separated us; and so, it seemed to us, the City received a fertilizing impulse, that made of its streets, its hurrying throngs, not merely what they were in themselves, but what they served in the impulse of our common passion; these birds, these beasts, these naked parks, these moving men and women, became but symbols and metaphors for the mind's dark well, no surface, but depth only. And when I consider the surface life into which I was gradually drawn—those elegant salons filled with scarcely-human highpitched voices, those endless charades and dinners wherein one wondered not who the vulgar chef was, but who the abominable and cruel author that arranged the scene—I think that what I missed most in that mocking design was not even her literal presence, but the interior and resonance that her presence bestowed.

There seemed, in the brilliant baroque orchestra which was then tuning up in History's wings, to be a peculiar chord or string missing, that would give the whole meaning, response, and the fertile depth which is the product of the interaction between what is male and what is female. As I circulated my alien searching presence through these so-called "gay bars" (dark and somber jewels indeed!), they seemed to me, despite their feverish and glittering life, but dead and cold satellites whirling out of reach of the Sun's quickening rays. Some of them specialized in poetry readings, others in Platonic dialogues, with an old lecher of a sophist taking the part of Socrates and divers others, golden-haired Greeks for the nonce, the parts of his sweet-limbed interrogators at the mock Symposium being staged. The spectators would sit around in languid attitudes, the postures of those used to being serviced for their pleasures; the arm of one, draped over the chair of the sophisticate to his left, might dangle free, shedding, in the close obscurity of the narrow room, a long wavering line of fire from the polished mirror of a signet ring. That ring, now that I notice, was inscribed with a flowery "S." A foot shod in muted kidskin rode up and down, left and right, in a kind of mesmerized figure-8.

These pellucid tableaux, the progenitors, by several declensions, of the recent live "sex-shows" with which we have been afflicted, were the result, oddly enough, of a theological and philosophical dispute then raging in the cloistered halls of Oxford, Cambridge, and—at a more immediate level—the pulpits of our cathedrals and chapels. This controversy, originating with Henry More and the Cambridge Platonists, transpired when that group, whose members had translated Ficino, Plotinus, and other ethereal authors, challenged the supremacy of the Oxford Aristotelians in a series of supposedly scholarly and unworldly lectures which had, nevertheless, a huge attendant crowd. Less public, however, than those debates, which often verged on scurrility, was the original meeting of this group of distinguished dons, in long flowing purple robes ornamented only with a silver braid running around the hem (meant to emblemize the river Cam), at the country seat of the indefatigable translator Chapman (who was to collaborate with Marlowe a number of years later in the composition of the immortal epyllion *Hero and Leander*), late in the fall of 1884. I had been invited there, then a lad barely out of his teens, in the capacity of secretary to the gathering, through the offices of a figure in the British Museum where I had recently begun my scholarly labours on Aristotle, Longinus, and other theoreticians of poetic method, who was in charge of cataloging recent acquisitions of Hellenic antiquity, chief among them, of course, the plundered frieze from the pediment of the Parthenon, but other priceless items as well, the Venus of Mykonos, for example, a headless, armless torso of incredible suppleness and smoothness, whose long sinuous undulation upward from the shadowy chalice of navel, the slight swell of the lower abdomen, and the fragile delicately strong articulation of the rib-cage which flowed into the firm pendulous fruit of noble breasts and ending in the stately column of a gracefully curved neck that one imagined filled not with stone but with momentarily held breath, reminded me of nothing I had ever seen before, certainly no mere mortal of a woman, rather a distinct and dangerous species which one should steer clear of, and content (if that is possible) to gaze and worship from a distance. She it was, indeed, who was indirectly responsible for my presence at that historic gathering, which was to influence profoundly, with its classical, hermetic, and idealistic stamp, the course of modern twentieth century literature, and was, in fact, to produce, by a kind of Hegelian antithesis, its opposite, in the realistic literature of the day; for in the early summer of that year, shortly after my admission to membership in that venerable institution, I found myself standing before the newly unwrapped statue who had just emerged from the cumbersome cocoon of a packing case. As I gazed, my vision, as by an inexhaustible sea-sponge, absorbed by the outlines and interior that formed themselves within, I became aware of a figure in silver and black standing behind me and to my left, that looked, not upon the lodestone which drew my eyes irresistably, but at I who was so captured. "You too," it whispered softly, "you too are a slave of beauty"—and after what seemed a suspended eternity, an infinite space between the releasing and the drawing of a breath, I reluctantly unfastened my eyes and faced the narrator of this section.

As I said, he was dressed in silver and black, a long flowing garment of midnight serge decorated with chaste moons and distant stars, and as he stood there, it seemed as though his entire being was concentrated into that compelling somber gaze. One arm rose slowly, and in between me and that stony image a dark veil shimmered through which, nevertheless, a white glimpse, an outline was strained and transmuted. His face was almost unbearably—and I am choosing this adjective after some thought—*transparent*, and one felt, in looking upon it, that one was not gazing upon the usual marble bust which belongs to the majority of men, but upon the very cranium, the seat of the thought-process itself, humming in encephalographic waves. With imperious gestures he outlined the graces of that beauty; and what was strangely incongruous in my illuminated memory of that scene was the contrast between his stark almost statuary angularity and the pliability which it described (albeit formed of unyielding stone). It was by degrees that he led me from that single isolated figure, which remains to this day in the darkened room of my recollection as a tiny pregnant figure, yet at the same time immense, and capable of receiving, with the rapidity of a blinking eye, a protean variety of shapes, along a muted echoing corridor (in the newly-constructed "East Wing" of the Museum), speaking as he did so what then were new and shocking ideas, but what I since have come to recognize, under their garment of mellifluous and gaudy plumage, as possessing all the cold pudeur of a slaughtered and dessicated barnyard fowl hung in an icehouse for some unmentionable feast. Those stony impassive divine images pass through my mind's eye as they did then, smiling faintly, as at some interior vision, the eyes blank, and bodies concentrated into gestures at once scornful and contemplative. Our passage seemed as if on wings—an effortless illusion of floating. His voice sang in my ear like an inspired insect. And despite the fact that there was no contact between us, I can feel to this day an invisible network of wires, as it were capillaries, or the dendrites of some sub-atomic nerve-system, and through which flowed pulses of secret sympathy and messages too detailed, too fantastically subtle in their linkage and structure to reproduce easily to my reader, but at the same time with all the simplicity of the units of the alphabet or those of chromosomes; and although after the initial all-penetrating stare he bestowed he looked at me no more, I was aware that my slightest movement, my minutest quiver or change of facial expression at the continual flow of his words, and indeed my entire insect-slow progress through the shadowy interior of that vast edifice, was immediately perceived and stored up in his interior eye where I was helplessly, as by a magnet or a giant sea-sponge, absorbed. It gave me, and gives me even now, a curiously dislocated and wrenching sense of a split—of moving in two places at once, both in the hollow corridor and in the more spacious, more populated, and even emptier theatre of his mind.

At length we reached a small door, absurdly low for the size of the building, coloured the rich, lifeless green of bronze that has, with the passing of damp time, oxidized into reptilian verdure. He produced a key of the same underground tint. "Here," he pronounced, "is the treasure I hold closest to my heart," and with the noiseless whirr of well-oiled tumblers that portal swung inward and, his arm for the first time interlacing mine lightly yet firmly, we entered.

11

or a considerable time that room resisted visual penetration, for my eyes had not adjusted immediately to its dimmer interior. As it swam gradually into focus I saw that it had the general shape of an egg (although the floor was perfectly level), and was lit, albeit indistinctly, by a single lamp hanging from a silver chain at a point equidistant from the gently curving walls and ceiling. The walls themselves were perfectly white and blank, but against their smooth regular surfaces was projected a train of constantly moving shadows. "Your eyes," my guide whispered, "must become used to this peculiar light in order to perceive distinctly," and I found it was as he said, for as the irises dilated to admit more illumination I was able to see the source of the shadow-play that flickered insubstantially over the interior of the room.

In a wrought-iron frame, shaped in a parallel fashion to the curvature of the walls and ceiling, were positioned, in variable interstices, small perfectly formed statues, exact, though miniature, replicas of those I had just viewed. As the lamp within revolved slowly, by an invisible mechanism, the silhouettes of these figures, gods, demons, beasts, and the numerous progeny of composite deities, were flickeringly cast on the curvature of the blank walls, populating densely what was, of itself, empty. I had, until then, remained unexposed to such phenomena of light and shade, and it was with difficulty that I managed to stabilize the swimming field of perception that surrounded me. It was as if the habitual nocturnalist, walking under his half-bowl of stellar fire-works, were to have it suddenly projected around the other 180 degrees, for I soon saw, due to the ingenious angle of frame and light, that the very floor I stood on crawled with myriad subterranean shapes. My guide gestured widely, indicating his rôle of shadow king; and his gesture was magnified hugely as its negative was caught and then cast onto the shell-like screen. I soon was able to trace other personages in the ghostly assembly, some historical, others fanciful, all with an identical indistinctness of outline, an identical core of luminously shifting shadow, that made substance out of nothingness: dukes, explorers, princes, poets, famous artists of all degrees, aye, the very apex of royalty itself in queenly shadow sat upon her unearthly throne, dispensing aery graces, and as I gazed upon that well-known figure (its silhouette, I mean; the statue itself could not be seen because of the luminence flowing around it), I saw at once what could not directly be seen—that what I looked upon was, in a sense, an emanation from my own unknowable depth. Just as the light itself did not produce vision, so we, in this shadow-world, saw directly not what was there, but indirectly what was not, and further, all which I flowed toward—all that articulation of outline so peculiarly shaped to my lack—was but a reversed curve (its symmetry twisted in its generation) proceeding outward from the black nucleic sun within. All this I saw, but confusedly; it was only later that true illumination was to come. What I was not aware of then was that my guide into this elliptically spherical world intended to place me, as he had so many others, into his ghostly pantheon; educe my form from its cringing matter by some mysterious process and place it in his world of shades; and, for all I know, so subtle was his philosophy, he may have accomplished his design and transformed me, all unaware, into some other version of that illusion we call the self.

Whatever the case, it was through his introduction that I became an early member of the Society which sometimes called itself—it had a different name among its members—"The Hermetic Students," and it was in my new capacity of a Secretary to that little-known group that I attended its initial meeting—there had been only desultory and isolated discussions hitherto—in the fall of 1884. My new-found mentor preceded me by a few days so that I rode out from London, as I had ridden in, alone, north along the winding road which paralleled the River, called in the City Michigan Avenue, then curving to merge with Bishopsgate Street, which transformed itself, as it approached the limits of the City, into Broadway and then narrowing into the tree-shaded intricate bosky involution, that sometimes almost doubled back on itself, known as Sheridan Road. The conveyance held easily my few belongings and two other passengers, a somewhat stout Frenchman or German in his early thirties and his young charge, an adolescent girl perhaps nine summers younger than myself. They spoke French volubly but it was a dialect I could not readily comprehend; it seemed to have gutteral Nordic undertones which, now that I think of it, was strangely prophetic of the political and linguistic developments that were to make of English a mere dialect of German. Her hair was a dark tawny honey colour streaked with strands of reddish gold; her ankles, exposed daringly from under a white cotton gown woven with red, suggested slender yet shapely columns of legs; her bust was scarcely developed, yet shadowed most distinctly behind the taut billow of the material. Her face was veiled, as was the fashion then, but behind it I could glimpse its faint whitened oval and its penetrating inquisitive eyes that peered out at the changing world outside the window. The veil swelled outward and inward to her breath, her words. Her companion seemed a commercial traveller or real-estate agent of one sort or another; as he spoke and gesticulated he kept a black attaché case firmly clamped between his legs. He was somewhat porcine but pleasant-looking enough; pink cheeks, flaxen hair, and stone blue eyes in which nothing of his emotion of the moment showed, contributed to a distinct impression of both efficiency and a kind of willful childishness. His hat was wide-brimmed enough so that, as he spoke and bobbed his head, it obscured now this, now that portion of his visage, so that I had to assemble it in fragments. Being at a most receptive age, I was easily shaped and isolated by what the world chooses to call "surface phenomena," and thus it was not strange that this trivial encounter (trivial because there were no words available to describe what was going on; the images were, in effect, deeper than their surface description) should remain etched, in such acid tones (yet headily light withal) in the soft susceptible tissue of my memory. Outside, the ever-shifting pageant of Sheridan Road offered vignettes remarkable for their perspectives of distance and proximity; stately boles of chestnut trees, elms, and ghostly birches, fluttered past the broad expanse of the River to our right, on which floated green-mossed barges and the tiny white triangular sails of innumerable pleasure craft. At the other end of the City, to the south, tall dark frigates were slowly being assembled, the nucleus of the fleet that was, a scant four years later, to scatter the combined might of the Spanish Armada; but here, where so many local streams and brooks were confluent with the mighty mother, swelling her boundaries to that of a small lake, that was used for the peaceful purposes of commerce and pleasure, and on whose shaded banks might be seen, reclining on the pregnant swell of the sward, lovers disported in amorous attitudes, poets withdrawn in bowery groves to celebrate that solemn progression without, all was filled with a sense of autumnal peace, as of things brought to their ripeness; fall flowers, glowing deeply in their rust and orange hues, climbed rampant under thickets of yew and bay, and on the heights above, to the left of our leisurely pace, the summer villas and casinos of the nobility nestled against the wooded slopes. Looking at the scene unfolding before my eyes, it seemed as though I was gazing at a page out of some rural fairy tale, some illumination out of the chapters of England's earliest history, and that Time itself had been made to roll back upon its own inexorable track. If Chaucer's personages (I asked myself, though not at the time) had disengaged themselves from Chaucer's crowd, forgot their common goal and shrine, and after sundry magnifications became each in turn the centre of some 16th Century play, and had after split into their elements and so given birth to romantic poetry, must I reverse the cinematograph? I though then that the general movement of literature must be such a reversal, such a return to the spring-source of its being, as, without, the varied scenes of buildings and rural landscape rolled past as on an immense reel: if, as it seemed, that inevitable progression was one-way, irreversible, to end in a single cylinder of unrevolving blackness—all those images of life and movement rushing into a flap, a hiss, and then less than a hiss—was it not my duty, however doomed to failure such an endeavor must be, to attempt to stop that mad flight toward annihilation, in which this globe, this galaxy, all the constellations glittering and wheeling overhead, seemed involved; nay, not merely to stop, but actually reverse the brutal progress toward that nothingness for which, as it appeared, all our molecules strained? It seemed to me to be so; although at the time, of course, I had no inkling as to how this might even be attempted, much less accomplished. Our approach had taken us into the suburbs north of our then rude and burgeoning metropolis, that had names like Glen-wood and Glen-lake and Glen-view, after the deep ravines and hollows of the region, and over which dusk was now beginning to spread his soft garment studded, in its gradual clinging descent, by the flickerings of earthbound lights coming alive in the wake of our passage. As the evening filled the creak and sway of our conveyance, my travelling-companions grew more and more silent, with only occasional bursts of their bright and incomprehensible tongue filling the sudden void the night-fall formed within; as we approached the terminus of our journey, a small settlement in the Ouilmette Valley called Stratford, from whence I would be brought by dog-cart to my host's manor, the silence grew almost total, broken only by an isolated singing word or two, an interrogation by the man, a response from the girl. Her veil was now completely filled with shadow; it would stir briefly with the breath of an expletive, then fall unstirring and vertical as the air of her utterance was exhausted. In the sparse illumination of the post-house they soon became but outlines that were, as they moved away, heads gracefully inclined toward each other (though I could not catch a single word: the wind, that had sprung up with the dusk, bore them all away), eroded into the body of yet another blackness. That ceaseless wind shook the withered and peeling sign overhead as a leaf clinging to its parent tree. A spiral of leaves and scrap-paper danced against a crumbling brick wall. The iron rims of an antique cart rang hollowly in the distance. Within the locked station I could hear the measured throbbing of a decrepit time-piece. The autumn stars shivered in the sky; the wind sought and found me like a cat, then as soon deserted me to stalk warily through a field of dead grass next to the station. The light blowing fitfully under the sign abruptly went out—leaving, however, that upright cursive burning on the night air long after it had vanished.

12

On the dressing table were: a blue-veined pebble of white quartz worked over by a century or so of waves and beaches (a liquid series never to be repeated), two empty Florentine wine bottles, green waves with crystal bubbles frozen into their undulations, that gathered and verdurized the light which seeped from the leaded windows yonder, a cold white emanation with crepuscules of withered rose around the edges, a bowl depicting a hunting scene in milky blue (Diana on her rampant steed, the fleeing stag), a few odd wooden pieces from an interrupted game of Scrabble—Domus, Dominus, Dominate, Dome—and an ebony crucifix on which an albino Christ was painted. He seemed irritated, not so much at the fact of His crucifixion as at being relegated to two, rather than three, dimensions. Perhaps He saw it as a kind of backhand affront to His trinitization—a sort of artistic Arianism.

My room faced west, and looked out through an orchard of wizened crabapple to a series of sunsets that reddened its bare gnarled limbs and filled, with watery vermilion, the deep bramble-choked ravine which sank beyond; but it was to the east that I was fetched each day, an east which looked over a broad expressionless expanse of River now grown to the extent of an inland lake, and one which gathered, as if it were an immense flat magnet, the entire illumination of the morning to its silver unresounding surface. Below, in the hollows, the mist would have spread its cold tendrils, and whitened each clump of dark vegetation, till one could not distinguish between the solid-seeming gas and the River that floated beyond.

Our (or rather their) discussion generally opened with a review of the previous day's activities, as morning tea unclogged their various passages, and a uniform light whitened the panes at the far end of the room where we sat (the heavy velvet curtains having been drawn aside), and from thence we ascended, as the light without did, into increasingly refined regions of the spectrum. At that time this tiny Society—the nucleus of many that were to follow, and many that were far less ethereal!—had as its founding principles several arcane, yet highly classical, tenets. These were founded upon an ancient conception of the Word—which combined, in one thrust, both the Greek and Hebrew theolatries. It seemed to these august investigators that, imprisoned in each individual articulation of a phrase, a sentence, a word, was an identical reality—the Word, so to speak, made into countless individual breaths. Fragmented as it was by these various masks, these indirect reflections of a single blinding sun, nevertheless (if my memory has been imprinted correctly) there *was* a way back, a way to educe the unity of that resplendent body from all the myriad host of its burning pieces; and this was to be accomplished (or so they claimed) by a fusion of two theories, one of prosody and one of theology—or, to have it strictly, scriptural exegesis. This concept was one founded on articulation, on the actual act of uttering a word or sentence. In its purest formulation, it stated that the sum total of an identical word or phrase uttered simultaneously by more than one person always equalled more than the sum of its individual morphemes as spoken by one person only. (Thus a notorious Argentine writer, called, once, "a forger of the script of the past", stating that he who says a line of Prosper *is* Prosper—so that if we are murmuring a phrase with a venerable history of usage and misusage, we end up with quite a cluttered stage indeed). This, by the way, was their basis for retaining features of the Roman liturgy, specifically those which dealt with communal response of the congregation.

As extended by this group of secret schismatics, however, this doctrine soon took on an eerie and apocalyptic tinge. A preoccupation with "the Word," of course, was one shared by both Puritans and those few scattered devotees of Greek culture who were the product of the English Renaissance; this preoccupation reached an odd synthesis in this tiny assembly, who held that if the entire body of "the Elect" were to utter in unison the secret names of God the world would come to an end and the day of the Last Judgment would be attained—since (and here the unmentioned and unmentionable heresy entered) the total number of the Elect would, by uttering His name, educe Him in all His reality; all those minuscule contributions, so to speak, adding up, in heavenly arithmetic, to the grand product of all that frantic multiplication: Him than whom none greater can be named (and we have named Him). The number of those Elect was, of course, severely limited, at first to the members of a very High-Church Anglicanism from which they originally were derived, then, as their doctrine contracted and rarified itself, to the large and influential school of Cambridge Platonists, which for a while included the penetrating intellect of John Henry Newman, and finally, as they dissociated themselves more and more from the intellectual currents of the time, content, within the closeted recesses of their common soul, to imagine the world that floated unknown without, the few members of that group which I have named "The Hermetic Students," and who sat, with me as their impressionable witness, on a series of clear cold November mornings, that strung themselves onto the necklace of my recollection like so many icy white stones. They spoke in whispers, I remember—a rare example of a true "conspiracy," a "breathing together"—and very cautiously, as if aware of the tremendous power hanging on their breath, as one imagines a live or sensate conductor of electricity, say in the immense floating cerebellum we call the globe, aware of the billions of crackling volts waiting to be released at its connecting touch.

They spoke, as I say, singly; and prayer consisted of joint responses from several (but not all) members of the congregation, to a catchword, which had something of the effect of a litany, except that the matter usually consisted of selections from the Greek Anthology, or perhaps some Silver Age poet of declining Rome. As dusk withered the rosepetal skies behind the bare lacery of twig and branch, and mist began to creep through the brambly hollows of the surrounding countryside, bringing with it the smell of damp wood burning, the strong overpowering stench of skunk cabbage decaying, the steady *thunk-thunk* of a solitary wood-cutter, and, in the orchards, the sweet-sour smell of apples rotting mustily away in autumn darkness, we would walk, in pairs and fours, with rosaries clicking woodenly, telling off the decades of little-known mysteries; and it is difficult for me to communicate the peculiar thrill, the thrum of some abysmally deep connection, as, in the chill gloom in which we were enveloped, striding regularly, barely visible but penetratingly audible, after the different pairs had counterpointed mystery against mystery, in a kind of antiphonal fugue, to begin, as we approached the house once more on the circular walk, the initial mystery, but this time in unison, the voices striking the same deep note of response, with only the leader—an invisible presence far ahead—hitting the key tone with his clear unearthly bass. It was then that I began to doubt the reality of all those other voices, and see that these, perhaps, were "correct"—that is "in tune"—although not until much later was I able to perceive the far-ranging constellations of resonances that they were, collectively, to strike: a peculiar sense of being at once connected with, and yet sealed off from, the hurrying worlds that revolved outside one's ken, that found its way into the slightest of the affairs and productions of the time, making them ghosts in their own and another's eyes, until, it seemed to me (or would), the very world that these pages so briefly describe, its cloud-capped towers, its gorgeous monuments, its hills, brooks, standing lakes and groves, and she whose imprint informed all, the most minute and immutable of genetic codes, would dissolve, turn ghostly and unreal, and like an insubstantial pageant faded, leave not a rack behind. Thus did I look out at everything I saw and make it a part of my own dreaming world. Back in the great house after the walk, we would sit before the crumbling collapsing flames of a huge orange-flowered fire and listen to some divine discourse on one aspect of our many-limbed doctrine, and as he spoke, it seemed as though the tongues of fire behind him irradiated his body and made of it but an echoing chamber for its inhuman element to plumb and sound. Beside me would sit one or another mentor—they soon grew indistinguishable in my eyes since they invariably had the same phrases on their lips. I had turned twenty as of last April (Old Style) and already I felt like a globe walled in glass, on whose perimeter innumerable eyes pressed. The glass was, I already perceived, smoky, opaque.

13

hen young, I had always dreamed of finding some secret spot in the interior where I could hide, safe from inspection, and imagine, free from the clinging doubts of perception, what went on without—perhaps drawn to this by an early episode of childhood when, striken with a severe bout of whooping-cough, I was laid up for a long period of time in a steam tent, and to this day, well-nigh three quarters of a century later, I can see, enveloping me on my solitary bed like the white translucent wings of some immense nocturnal moth, the moist breathing sheet, uplifted by billows of steam from the gently bubbling kettle set on a gas ring, its liquid heart exhaling a feathery plume in a regular susurration. Since then, it has always seemed to me that one issued out of such softly respirating hollows at one's peril: out there was the death of cruel air, all the atmosphere of an alien planet, the stuff breathed by species hostile to one's own; but here, one was nourished as by the breath and lymph of one's own being, no foreign meter, but one that read the rhythm, the rising and falling, of our own unique line or strand, as intimately as if the author stood helpfully by your elbow, assisting at the difficult or doubtful places.

Something of that feeling, no doubt, impelled me during the weeks I spent at this curiously removed, stately country manor, which combined in its architecture, now that I look more closely, Oriental influences as well as the more traditional English ones: its four turrets, for example, were red-tiled miniature pagodas, and the four curved roofs at the sides, descending from a level plateau, curled out at the eaves in a most un-Occidental manner. I soon discovered several remarkably well-suited retreats, during the long afternoons I had to myself, which were virtually invisible to the common eye, and from which, nevertheless, I exerted a superior vantage of perspective, and that sensation common to all creatures who get behind another—even if it be behind that mirrored substance called the self—to watch that other watch. One, found on the very afternoon of my first full day of residence, was on the roof of one of those pagodas—one that, for some unknown reason, was somewhat taller than the others, and the only one of the four which possessed winding circular steps, arranged around a massive central pole, to connect with the lofty regions overhead. Each of these steps was anchored on a moveable pin, so that they could all be placed perpendicularly to each other and thus disguise the impression of any staircase at all. It was, in fact, purely by chance that I happened to discover the identity of these stairs, while poking about on that afternoon in the vague outskirts of this large and rambling building, finding odd corners and cubbyholes to creep into, only to be routed out by a janitor or gardener making his periodic rounds. At the end of a long oddly narrow corridor on the top floor, which was lined on one side by milky ovals of glass and on the other by portraits of eminent divines (Hooker, Swift), was a small door painted a dull metallic colour; this I automatically tried and found, to my surprise (it had looked virtually immovable), that it swung easily inward. A musty stench not unpleasantly floated outward; a portrait peered kindly in my direction, and, with a quick glance round to see that this was the only sentinel posted, I slipped in, closing the door quietly behind me. The light reminiscent mustiness, like the smell of old apples gathering mellowness and fragrance to themselves as they aged, or that of old dolls releasing the odour of their stuffing, a tickly alfalfa or wispy hay, or feathery seed-clotted ticking, grew stronger, more overpowering. A few crates lay unopened on their sides; picture frames divested of their inner riches were stacked in varnished heaps near the door. A mop stood on one foot, grey curls spirocheting in all directions. It wore a wig of fine white dust. From the ceiling were suspended long loops of rope, varying circumferentially, and forming, over the width of the room, a loose cradle of sorts. Stacks of ancient volumes on theology in Greek and Latin were building against one wall. A portrait of a very old missionary was propped on the top of one of these, a Father Paulus, Frenchman, d. Canton 1859. There was a single window high in one wall, a vertical slit impalpably grimed, through which the pallid afternoon light trickled.

In the far corner to my right a massive cast-iron pillar connected floor and ceiling, and I could see, by peering behind it, those strange spadelike appendages attached to each of its segments. For a long time I stood before it, less in an attempt to determine its function, than in fascination at the curiously intricate pattern of rust and erosion that had eaten its way into the metal, producing, with its stylus of damp and air, a scrolled map of the years. As I was turning to leave, my shoulder brushed against one of the lower of these attachments, and, with a peculiarly plaintive squeak, it moved. I stared—oh, for a minute or so, no more; then, cautiously, I tried another, then another, then a whole series, moving them back and forth to the treble sounds of an orchestra of violins tuning themselves. On the ceiling to the left of the pillar, I now noticed, was a thin black line in the shape of an ellipse, and in a flash of comprehension, slow coming but none the less intense for that, I made the connection, and realized what function that pillar had. It was no more than the work of a few moments to arrange it into an ascending spiral of creaky steps up which I now arose, positioning a stair at a time as I did so.

The perimeter of the roof's tiny square was enclosed with a wall of thin red brick perhaps a foot and a half in height, thus effectively screening me from view below, and I found that by raising myself on one elbow I could view, with appropriate motions of my head, the entire expanse of the grounds extending below from my superior point of perspective. All that wild and wandering wood, confused with scrub and tangled underbrush, in the midst of which surfaced meadows and untilled fields, patches of yellow and vermilion clay, and waterlogged bogs haired with swamp grass, acquired a design as I gazed slowly and deeply at each large variegated segment below, assembling them, with slight sutures of sense between the parts, into a homogenous whole. To the west, now illuminated silverly by the ghost of a declining sun, stretched a region of deep ravines and hollows, choked with bramble, hawthorne, and half-grown aspen divested of their trembling foliage, and touched up now by the thin almost white metallic lacquer that the sun provided in its descent—a quite pleasing, if somewhat chilling, baroque bas-relief of slender twig branching and rebranching gracefully against a darker background, set off by the more serpentine Italianate cursive of creeper and withered vine. These ravines were crossed infrequently by swaying bridges made of logs and ropes. In the depths of one or another of them I could catch faint glimpses of the leaden thread of a creek picking its way through fallen leaves and branches; the wind occasionally wafted to me the faint sad musical tinkle of its passage. To the south a series of fields and meadows, separated by stands of swaying Lombardy poplar (a tree currently much in vogue due to the interest in things Mediterranean), stretched out from the border formed by the looping circular brick walk that ended and began at the manor, with a low shed or two marking its solitary passage. These were variously and somberly coloured, and indeed that stretch of land, with its strange admixture of hues—due to the introduction of different composts at different periods—had been named "The Coloured Lands," after a bizarre volume of surreal pieces by

G. K. Chesterton. Pale yellow, mottled red, and dark streaked green, varied with archipelagos of black glistening loam that looked almost blue in its shimmering refractions, they extended in orderly disarray to the relatively close horizon, a series of low foothills undulating bluely, smokily, against a slowly darkening sky. A single toiler grubbed in one field, surrounded by dark trees, for potatoes or cabbages. To the east and north swam the enclosing embrace of the River, a great and solemn expanse of inflected and wrinkled silver, almost twice as wide here as in the metropolis some twenty miles south. Islands, fishlike ellipses of grey outcropping and furze, were scattered sparsely in its strong unvarying current toward London and the Ocean. The slanting light, striking these with its cold beams, caught and rubbed to fire veins of mica hidden in their recesses. A boat worked its way upstream, its sails reefed to the wind now pouring from the west. Its hull was painted an unreflecting black. Below, following the River in its wide curve, perhaps thirty yards from its high banks, were cultivated hollows planted with orchards, predominantly apple, and in the sloping sides of which were buried dank chill fruit cellars. Mist would writhe long almost solid tendrils in between their dripping boles in early morning; now, however, they were clearly and pellucidly outlined against the darker compost of wet clotted leaves.

Within the long loop of enclosing walk to the south a carefully-plotted intricate garden unfolded, with Japanese tea-trees, well-trimmed hedges, ginkgos, and miniature shaded paths and tiny waterfalls; here human activity was more concentrated, gardeners digging beds of slumbering bulbs, pruning a tree of its dead fingers, long-robed members reading in secluded gazebos shrouded with climbing clematis ("Virgin's Bower"), one hand shading a pensive brow, or walking in pairs deep in meditative conversation, not looking at one another but straight ahead at their unknown subject of discussion. Here, on a small scale, lay, all unknown to me, the infinitely richer, more varied and voluptuous Oriental garden I was to find many years later along the misty and sun-drenched coast of northern California, on the outskirts of San Francisco, Golden Gate Park, the invention of an incredibly wealthy Japanese architect who, late in life, designed for the citizens of his adopted country an elaborated quintessence of his native one: flowering yellow-leaved trees, shrubbery stained a deep imperial purple, rock gardens dripping with silver and golden moss, flowers with long thick soft flesh-coloured tongues, all labelled with graceful masculine calligraphy in English, Latin, and Japanese. Standing pools, fed by the deep threaded flow of rock springs, reflected in their unmoving mirrors the yellowing hair of drooping willows; water ducks would glide occasionally by, signing the liquid silver with limpid V's of molten crystal. It was October, the year was 1916. The entire world was at war, but as yet America held out, and the gracious shaded enclosure of the park was an apt figure for the island of peace that this country had become. Without, war raged on two continents, made more horrendous by the introduction of such typically modern inventions as the Gatling gun and the newly launched dirigibles, which would surround defensive cities with long weighted wires dangling from their bellies, or, on the attack, dump incendiaries and explosives from their navels onto the shrinking earth below; but here, all was filled with mellow ripened peace; the sky was of an utter cerulean hue, with a shimmering mist about the edges, the effect of the moist earth exhaling in its flowery labour; goldfish speckled the deep waterways with flecks of reddish yellow, lily pads sucked deeply at the liquid hearts of their pellucid ponds, and on the soft banks, thickly textured with grass, clumps of giant sunflowers swayed to the musical breeze, hovered over by furry golden-dusted bees gorging themselves on their hidden sweets. These bees, their shadows blurred and luminous at the edges, moved under the shadow of a cypress tree, attracted by something yellow and vibrant reclining there. A shadow of hair floated to my right, a lighter shade within a shade. The bees danced and hovered, hovered and danced, as if to an ancient music, not landing but maddening themselves with excitement at the scent and vision of so much sweetness and passion. About the cypress, a grove of fruit trees spread their laden arms, interspersed with those of fragrant-scented myrrh and eucalyptus, and, varied as they were, they seemed to compact all seasons there, for from their branches fruits hung, some ripening, ready some to fall, some blossomed, some to bloom. In the distance, above the heads of the nearest trees, a range of mountains to the east lifted their silhouettes, blue with remoteness; and on their snowy crags the light leaped like a goat. Time, in that brief moment, seemed suspended here, Time whose golden thigh upholds the flowery body of the earth in sacred harmony.

After a journey of some days west I had come through those high baleful mountains, the Sierra Nevadas, which wall in, with their overpowering bulk, almost the entire sky, shrouded, now, with early autumn snow and mist, to this valley in the sun by the sounding Pacific, in the bay of which was erected the bridge-girt city of gold and mist, of hills and perspectives, San Francisco, a former mission expanded, after the fabulous Gold Rush of 1849, to a vigorous metropolis. North of the City extended Napa Valley, famous for its vineyards, which, due to its cool sea-misty air, mellow sun, and dry grainy loam, rivalled those of France for memorable vintages; and north of that, the forests of giant redwood trees, parks of fabulously deep and rich shade, the droppings, from a tremendous height, of the largest living things on the globe. South of the City began the legendary El Camino Real, later U. S. Highway 1, which passed along the coast, winding its intricate way through mist and sun-spangled mountains, with the Pacific always visible or audible, over far-arching bridges, the greening side of a mountain leaping upward into drifting white, or, in fields carved out of the living sides of these hills, the golden orange of pumpkins glowing in the mellow October sunlight. The top of the car was down and I could see, out of the corner of one eye, flashes of sun-tawny skin, the impression of a full young throat laid bare to the radiance of the mellowing autumn sun, growing warmer as we drove south. To the right, the Pacific lifted tall white plumes of vapour above the craggy coast; gulls and cormorants flew in wide looping circles, screaking and mewing; occasionally, herds of sea-lions might be seen basking on some wet black rocks. I lifted my head back and drank from the proffered bottle; young sun-warmed red wine flowed into my mouth in thick tingling spurts. We parked by a roadside rest-stop, a small half-circle of sandy turf overlooking the ocean, booming some five hundred feet below. A mountain rose dizzyingly, in a green gasp, at our backs. I turned then, my mouth still winey and wet, my eyes dazzled by the sun exploding in the sea. I put my arms around—

14

The spacious mansion where I spent several weeks of my lingering youth, late in the fall of 1884, dated back before Tudor times and even that series of minor skirmishes which came to be known as the Wars of the Roses, and there was, in its venerable, vine-covered, respectable exterior, little that hinted at the complexity which was hived within. It now, of course, has been restored by act of Parliament and made into a National Monument (long lines of children fidgeting, chewing gum and sticking it under tables of ebony inlaid with mother-of-pearl, old ladies from Kensington blinking at the wrong bust because they are on page 37, Bards, instead of 73, Buffoons, of the Guidebook to Local Curiosities), but even then it stood in excellent repair, and there is, somewhere in the cavernous recesses of my memory, an aerial photograph which showed—it was impossible to get it any other way—the design of the whole. It remarkably resembled a sleeping child (it is true that this was taken on a day of mist and drift which allowed the outlines to merge into a beautiful distinctness). One wing, relatively new, dating from the reign of Henry Bolingbroke, bent a chubby brick red knee all the way to the stout torso, complete with glimmering navel (a candle burning in the diamond of a small port window); the head was the humble servants' quarters, shrouded in vines, with windows that blinked to the raising or lowering of blinds, now shuttered in sleep. A weather vane atop the peak swung erratically to all four corners of the globe. One arm was tucked in close to the body (a porch for the viewing of aquatic phenomena); the other was flung wide in the abandon of unconsciousness, complete to the details of a balled fist and a bent elbow (an addition on an addition). Oh, and there were other details, too intimate for the eye to catch at first, but revealed to the memory in reviewing her illuminated pictures: folds of creamy skin, pink nails with miniature half-moons glowing behind, the strawberry clock, a kind of tiny spiral nebula, of a birth mark; and more . . . But perhaps, you will think, I am being too fanciful. Certainly none of this was revealed to me at that fog-dogged time; the interior of that large and unwieldy structure was as mysterious and unyielding of symmetry as, say, the circulatory system was before Harvey mapped its intricacies in 1916. It was, now that I re-examine those blurred impressions, remarkably like exploring the fluid structure of a one-celled organism from the point of view of, say, a sub-microscopic investigator, or that of a blastula being invaded by a curious virus: a sense of rooms, corridors, galleries being nothing more than the wandering interior of a large and amorphous amoeba, specks of nucleiotidic matter, crystal encysted spheres cloudy with nitrogen or luminous with phosphorus, floating past one as one drifted deeper into the interior. It seemed to me, although I did not realize it clearly at the time, that I was searching for one tiny room in particular, from whence all the others radiated to form the vast and shadowy edifice around me; a nucleus, as it were, wherein would be contained, fantastically reduced, the code for the whole. An event had taken place there, I knew, that had been responsible for, indeed had shaped, everything I was aware of. To find it, I gradually realized, became an increasingly impossible task, for those chambers soon came uncannily to resemble each other, even down to the hanging of portraits and the pattern in the thick carpeting which extended from the centre. Windows there were on the elusive perimeter, slender slits of light or large mellow ovals or banks of leaded greenish-tinted waves, but as one penetrated into the interior these abruptly disappeared, being replaced by musty moving velvet, or intricate tapestries from the Gobelin mills, or, in many cases, deceiving mock windows either mirrored (their silver suggesting similar rooms on the other side) or masterpieces of virtually photographic painting wherein landscapes were magically made to seem to appear, exactly as they would had there been no intervening wall to block the view: a dreaming segment of River, its current reproduced in darker streaks against its silver, with tiny islets precisely positioned, the colour and shape of their vegetation changed faithfully to reflect the passage of the seasons, empty, however, of all navigation (that would reveal the motionless quality of the scene), or the woods, autumnal now, appearing to bend under the weight of a chill breeze, the bark reproduced with such silvery exactness that the tiny holes of burrowing insects might, upon close examination, be viewed, or the lines of stress caused by their skins contracting at the approaching cold. My search, however, took me away from even such plaintive deceptions as these chambers had to offer. I wanted, I recall, nothing to distract me from the warm and shifting interior. Some of these rooms, abysmally tiny, were purportedly guest rooms, but had grown musty from disuse, and in these I often spent entire afternoons, lit only by a single kerosene lamp, gazing on the dingy high white ceiling or on the walls where the negative imprint of absent portraits lingered (here the sun has not rested, the young body of a beach-bronzed lover tells her beloved). Footsteps would hesitate outside and echo long after they had left. The smell of dust, a not unpleasant aromatic tickling in the nostrils, would rise around me. Sometimes I slept—a sleep in which the tiny oblong room usually figured, taking on the character of a large whispery cocoon or that of the stomach or colon of an immense unknown animal. In the early dusk of five o'clock I would slip out unseen and join, after feeling my way through interminable corridors, the other guests in the spacious and well-lit refectory, with its stained glass windows behind which tapers were lit, depicting various Oriental or Indian or Egyptian scenes in shades of green and silver and more sombre browns, a crowded gathering of storks, ibexes, sacred cows, many-breasted deities, phallic fencing, and other even more indecent encounters dignified with the name of divinity. At the head of the long rectangular room, rowed with two series of polished pillars, was an elevated dais, whereon our hosts were seated for the evening meal. A lectern to its left contained a tall figure which read to us during much of the repast, usually Cicero, Marcus Aurelius, or the aphorisms of Epictetus. Silent figures in black, an order of lay brothers, waited on our needs, which became, I noticed, sparser and sparser as the weeks passed. It was as if all our appetite, our need for outside sustenance, were concentrated in that reed-like voice, winding its way among limpid austerities. Soon dusk would be replaced by total night, and as though in response to our entrance into Pluto's kingdom the tapers dimmed, the tables, cleared of implements, bore only the imprint of our shadows, and the voice, as if it were a pearl concentrated into its own milky essence, became tinier, more polished, penetrating. Under the solider dome of the heavens (solid because of the emptiness compacted and condensed into unswaying blackness by the firing of those shivering pinpoints) the recurrent script of the evening was being drawn on its more imperishable slate as, in evanescent fashion, we reduplicated that calligraphy within.

On other days, I abandoned these more formal elements of my master design—these rooms which had, after all, regular appointments, the obvious stamp of an interior decorator—for crevices, cubbyholes whose main distinguishing detail was the brute fact of their being enclosures; low closets that one had to stoop to get into, for example, almost unnoticeable at the rear of some withdrawn little sitting room, folding doors meant to merge with screens and tapestries, now removed, and revealing their outlines in a thin susceptible black line. These had to be pushed gently in certain hidden spots—and in the right order too—before they creaked unwillingly inward, releasing a warm dark odorous flow as they did so, as of viviparous mammals that have hibernated for incalculable winters, a not unpleasant smell, that of things withdrawn into their essence, contracted into a knot which, upon being unwoven, releases its distillation of years to the outer air. Many of these were hiding places for unreformed Catholics during the purges of the last Henry, and as I moved into one or another of these shadowy cocoons, drawing after me a flap of concealment, arranging around me its inner darkness like a protective membrane—many of these retreats were no larger than the figure of a crouching refugee—I found myself as one with the Jesuit trembling behind the protective mimicry of wood or plaster, breathing with him over the respiration of decades in a night we both shared, and wondering, as that darkness branched into the brachial grape-clusters of my lungs, what martyrdom my unknown confrère had suffered, what lances had pierced his side, what fire turned to unbearably burning gold the red of his webbed arteries and capillaries, as if it were not he but I who had to undergo such an ordeal. Sometimes, in the back of one of these life-giving pockets, I would discover yet another valve of egress into yet another chamber, making it a kind of bivalve heart connected with a tenuous aorta; and, beyond such a series, a long intricately winding passage-way often began, seldom more than waist-high, moving into the interior recesses of the vast body in which I was confined, with many branchings-off into one or another limb or organ; and often, too, I would find myself, after some hours of wide circuitous wandering, back in the same chamber whence I issued, dusty, bedewed with the sweat of my passage, but with the sense of having encompassed, in some subterranean fashion, the corpus in which I was, embryo-like, secreted. In these slow cyclic revolutions I would pass more familiar sections of the manor, manifested to me by the sounds that welled from without; and I cannot tell you how strange it was, in traversing a long loop of dusty tunnel, to hear, through the thin panelling to one side, a butler or janitor hurrying on a well-known task, humming the tune he always did at such a time and such a place, or, on the other side, a veritable waterfall through the dancing pipes as, strictly on schedule, a lecturer in Pythagorean theorems released his fragrant burdens into the commodious bowels of the house. I heard—transformed, as it were, by their passage through sleeping forests of oak or walnut—discourses on topics as varied as Aristotle's lost tract on comedy to the best positions for enacting sodomy, but from such a dreaming distance, it was as though I were drifting by on a different planet entirely and overhearing the speech of an alien genus or phylum (some trunked or tailed inhabitant of a so-called "SF" narrative, really no different, despite the Halloween masks and mutations, from any of the numerous stock two-dimensional cut-outs that were outdated when Trollope tucked them into his tidy novels). Soon, however, even these tenuous links with an outside world released their ghostly tendrils, one by one, uncurling at the tip-end of their sound; and the utter depth of silence was broken only by the internal ruminations of the edifice into whose heart I was descending, liquid gurglings of elbowed or improperly muffled pipes, the steady sustained hushed rush of vast heating ducts trembling with their mighty breathings. At length, after days of assiduous mole-like burrowing, during which I had managed, almost entirely with the tactile sense, to map the anatomy of this unique species of building (there were corners and walls I would carry around with me always), I felt myself approaching, as along the filaments of an immense web, the pulsing centre of that design, that gave out lymph and breath to the whole; and as, in the dewy deadly yet living structure of an arachnid's bowels the patient noiseless spider may, by resting at the precise centre of his gauzy labyrinth, feel any tremor, any sign of alien life, along the sensitive filaments extending in all directions, so I, as I approached that invisibly receding point, felt a peculiar pressure increase on all sides, but one that acted from within, sensitizing all surfaces to the detailed transpirations above, as a child, wasted by fever to but the essence of himself, feels his dry papery skin so incredibly tender that the slightest change in temperature or even atmospheric pressure is recorded instantly on his shrinking epidermis, or the motions of his nurse in the next room preparing medicines, or the muslin of the sheet shrouding his tiny naked form, or as, in the long respiration of an involuted serpentine yet perfectly balanced sentence, one approaches the energizing and all-transforming verb that gives meaning and connection to the whole, and from its soft clinging tactile interior touches and caresses and controls the minutest and most remote morpheme, so did I, in my slow and inevitable descent, feel connections crowding on all sides as I drew near the chamber which awaited me. That tight terminus surrounds me yet, a long virtually imperceptible loop part oval, part figure-8, its dust laid by the beads of moisture condensing on the walls and ceiling, with the faintest luminosity provided by tiny piles of phosphorescent wood gently mouldering away into lightlessness. The palms of my hands and knees were clammy with the distance I had crept. The air was close but not unpleasant; it seemed to be fed from some deeper subterranean artery that passed, at levels unguessed at, over cold clay and wet layers of shale. I believe I had reached the sub-basement at this point, a low-ceilinged many-pillared space in which an even moderately tall man would have to bend his head to stand erect. This was excavated at some depth, as I realized upon poking my head out of the small sliding door; the clay walls were beaded thickly with silver globules, and an overpowering odour of earth assailed my nostrils as I drew my first deep breath. Across the thickly textured phosphorescent gloom that extended into dimness, at the far end of this hollow at the house's foundations, a low door, almost indistinguishable from the surrounding wall, manifested itself by a steady pulsing light under its lower edge. I floated toward it as a moth toward the flame that is to illuminate and consume it. Within, I could perceive a regular unvarying throbbing suggestive of great power held in reserve, and something else behind it—a liquid murmur, but not as of open water gurgling, but of fluid passing through innumerable convolutions of pipes and conduits. Already I stood before its flesh-coloured softly textured flap, that with the rhythm behind it seemed to heave and subside. With a gasp of recognition—or, rather, the sigh that our molecules must give when they settle into the pattern which is to be theirs for the term of their mortal existence—I pushed at that loose skin-like covering and stood revealed before the throbbing heart of light. A vast system of tubes and arteries ran in and out of its muscular contours, a crystalline network alive with rivers of moving luminence, molten gold and clinging globules of silver, tiny encysted specks of fire which coded, in their regular dance, the movement and meaning of the whole. My face, I knew, grew rosy with the effort of contemplation. A massive hum arose from within that ordered tangle, as from the imagined centre of an immense hive humming with sweetness and regulated life, the cell, its opaque yet translucent walls trembling in the surrounding rhythm, containing the invisible presence of its Queen. As in the story by Wells, I bowed before the Lord of the Dynamos; and if it were not for some invisible skin of separation, I believe that I could willingly have been absorbed into that hidden nucleus of flame, and merged my own tinier flicker with the rush of its solid hollowness. The entire house seemed to tremble in unison with the beating of its mighty heart. A network of stairs surrounded, at some slight distance, its glowing carapace; and it was through these, as if I were a tiny speck of seeing matter in a branching bloodstream, that I circulated for the next several uncounted hours, hovering in a regulated dance around its luminously shifting surface. Above, I could sense the myriad life of the structure transpiring; the breathing, the entering, the withdrawing; the merging of images and their splitting; whispers and faint furtive communications made mouth to mouth. A robe rustled and parted in a distant room. Two smiles became one withering long drawn-out sigh. A starling cast its floating shadow on a section of red-tiled roof and then slowly, as if being drawn in on an invisible inexorable string, sank down to meet it. An elm was stripped of its dry burning hair; its skeleton rubbed against a weathered cornice, then reached upward tenuously to tap against one echoing square of glass (the same it had beleaguered now for these past forty years). A mouth shaped itself around an unknown word or mouth. In one corner of a remote laundry room a faucet released a surprisingly pellucid series of bright polished droplets (these pearls that were your eyes). Two rats sniffed suspiciously at a crumbling chunk of poisonous green cheese. In the bell-tower a brazen womb prepared its silver offspring of notes; in my moistly respiring interior I felt a hollow slowly expanded to receive their fertile seed. I placed my hand against the warm glowing side of the furnace. Upon its illuminated field it made a black negative imprint.

15

Oh how often have I, since then, longed to touch my own heart, as I did at that moment! And since that time it has seemed to me that my life has been but a continual circling around that hidden point of contact, a detour away not merely from what I most desired (then as yet unincarnated), but from that without which I would remain unfinished and incomplete, a statue as yet not annealed to its single form, a poem without the breath of its life-giving utterance. How many miles of walls, corridors, unreflecting glass were to secret their skins, husks, carapaces, between my paced retreat and that enigmatic contact; and how many times since then have I, in dream or in that second dream we call waking life, sought to penetrate to the radiant nucleus of the hive called consciousness, only to be stopped short by some anomalous mass of black wax against which my fingers pressed in vain! Oh, the treehouses of my summer youth when, in a cradle of greeny branches, I would rest all the long day, lulled by the crooning wind's limpidity and those high fleeces of cirrus! Then, I felt convinced, I was not as I would be: a creature with all the capacity in the world for viewing himself, but powerless to touch the organ which perceived. And in looking on these coloured memoried slides, that flicker and coalesce with many a rubescent sigh and violaceous quiver, I am made aware all too painfully of the tediously blank wall which lies under their heartlessly thin skins (the etiolation of things that in themselves are nothing); the whitewashed shell of the prison which surrounds one. I am reminded in this connection, now that I ruminate on it, of an obscurely famous uncle of mine, for many years curator of a great museum in the Middle West of the United States, but at the time of my protracted youth, recuperating from a long nagging heart ailment, he was employed as a commercial artist by a large internationally-based publishing firm. To escape the boredom of work, which he never turned to but under the pressure of necessity and usually late at night, with the publisher's messenger in the hall, he had half-filled his studio with mechanical toys of his own invention, and perpetually increased their number. A model railway train at intervals puffed its way along the walls, passing several stations and signal boxes; and on the floor lay a camp with attacking and defending soldiers and a fortification that blew up when the attackers fired a pea through a certain window; while a large model of a Thames barge hung from the ceiling, to be joined later by other even more intricate mockups, the Tower of London, a Spanish galleon with tiny slaves bent over the oars, St. Paul's, complete with worshippers in musty finery and the Dean in the midst of an elegantly-wrought sermon. In Windsor Castle, through the fan of a French window, a royal couple might be dimly glimpsed, the King looking out into an aery park, the Queen before her dusky mirror, preening, spreading the trembling corolla of her ruff, shadowing the white tenuosity of her face with one graceful hand. When he entered, the room, which had hitherto appeared desolated and unpopulated—dry husks of marionettes rustling in a little breeze, their strings loose and slack—suddenly turned all related and alive; the houses hummed with activity, the soldiers stood at attention, and all those little figures, till then limp and inert, were transformed into the dynamic inhabitants of a busy microcosm. He had the knack, I have mentioned this before, of changing any white emptily staring wall into a field rich with the shadowy creatures of his imagination; and it is this that he effected with the cramped interior of his attic studio which was, all in all, but a dingy little mouse-hole in itself. Its single rather high window looked out, I could see, with a little firm assistance from behind, onto the brick wall of the building across a narrow alley. The light issuing thence was uniformly pallid but, due to the subtle blue shading he had indued to its pane, metamorphosed the interior into a kind of luminous subaqueous shadow, a little terrestrial Atlantis anchored in the air. Such, I often liked to imagine, were those islands in the stream of the Thames, that from the perspective of the City looked so remote and blue, scattered like sapphires in the twisted almost ornamental current, and, from the vantage-point of a barge or pleasure craft, loomed like the immense bulks of sulphurbottom whales, come upstream to mate, spouting in clumsy graceful fashion (indeed, some of them substantiated this fancy with their occasional geysers of hot water and steam that plumed out of the rocks of their highlands). And because of the unique manner in which the River enclosed the City's bulk in its blue embrace (that transformed, as it were into air, the earth and concrete of its corpus), it made of that essentially earthbound phenomenon, a metropolis, the aery floating mirage of an isle, that appeared, as one floated in from the more massive billow of Ocean, as one of those dream-cities of the Cibola, a fabulous moulding of gold and mist, that manifested itself out of the heart of one's direst need, at the moment of abandonment when, the throat parched and saline, it is incapable of uttering what it desires. A dream city indeed! I knew only too well the bricks and mortar of unliving cells that went to make up its sprawling extent (not for nothing do the inhabitants of a certain strategic insane asylum call it, according to their fantasy, "Chicago," an uncouth Indian name which means, insofar as I am able to guess, waste matter—literally, offal, faeces, excrement). But such is the working quality of imagination that it is able to superimpose upon inert matter its own reality, make what is solid a shimmering insubstantial edifice, capped with clouds and emblazoned with the labels of its genus. And that is how I am able to think of it—not the city of wartime industry, bombed and desolate, nor that of a booming peacetime economy, humming with commerce, that "city of shopkeepers" which the foreign philosophe so glibly clichéd, but an almost mythological structure that one might evolve out of the depth of a solitary dream, ornate and stately, with all the passion and pageant of those creatures of chance that one endows with the greatness of life they themselves lack. In the spring of 1900, our second year as a Company in London, the river-girt City, it seemed to me, grew polished to an almost unbearable brilliance, its many facets, like those of some great complex jewel, seemingly capable of absorbing and refracting an almost immeasurable quantity of light. As one would drift down the River in some rented pleasure craft, the light aery bridges arching overhead, their supports rising green and dripping from the regular arterial inflection of current, then pale yellow, the colour of sticky new leaves, as they merged with the spidery catwalk, the spires and towers would rise into one's field of vision with all the regular crepitation of a recurrent fantasy, burnished with a solar radiance which seemed to issue from within; and the very warehouses on the western extreme of the River's curve, squat and dolorous, seemed to coagulate into mixtures of sunlight and dusty gold, a substance beaten out of some rare metal by an alchemy now lost or forgotten. To the left and right of one's dreamy progress, moving between buildings and crumbling loading docks, issued the tiny channels of sub-arterial tributaries, many barely deep and wide enough for the barges they were dug to accommodate. Several of these buildings had fallen into beauteous decay, and it was not uncommon to view, between broken pillars and crumpled paving stones, amid fields of shattered fiery glass, tall clumps of untended sunflowers nodding gently in the soft spring breeze. Further north in one's looping progress—leaning on the oars in pleasurable exhaustion, face shiny and tingly with sweat—loomed, on the westward bank, the huge edifice of the Main Post Office, the largest, at that time, in the world, which, despite its considerable bulk, managed to produce the effect of a stately aery grace, due to the light yellow shale-like stone used in its construction. Bending forward, then rhythmically back, one would shoot, with oiled celerity, into its soft clinging shadow, exactly two city blocks long, capped at either end by two taller shadows of towers, used by various governmental agencies. The sun would strike across the broad back of this large protective creature, stroking to life, with its flooding fields of radiance, details of deterioration and renewal, weeds flowering with a shy springtime temerity amid the glint and glitter of cans and abandoned carriage wheels slowly being resolved into the ore of their genesis, clusters of wire trembling slightly in the westward flowing air, reminiscent, proleptically, of the huge almost house-sized clumps of sagebrush that would blow endlessly across the interminable plains and deserts of western America, in my fragmented trip across that continent some fifteen years later. Rows of windows, set deeply in the ruddy retiring faces of decrepit buildings on the eastern bank, released long almost liquid tears of pale pollenated gold from the mysterious depths of their irises, and in the broken sockets of some of them could be perceived, silvery radiant against the sensuous gloom within, webs spun out of the bowels of invisible spiders in which tiny jeweled insects glinted. As the prow glided from shade to light I could glimpse, in the north end of the monolithic Post Office, a small room set to the rear (so far, indeed, that only the most fugitive of reflected beams—those wandering searching needles of illumination—could find its retreating core of shadow); and in its bare contours, its gaunt radiators and cracked smoky ceiling, I recognized, or would, the unadorned interior where much of the present account is being composed. Some six blocks further the River curved to the right to connect, nine blocks eastward, with the broader artery where it originated.

It was at this confluence that the royal progress began in the spring and early summer of 1900, celebrating the Queen's Golden Jubilee following fifty radiant years on the throne, to culminate, on August 7th, with the various floats and flower-hung barges that had decorated its waters in months past joined together in one single unbroken moving circle of praise. It was, indeed, a solemn moment when, the shores packed with an enthusiastic variegated populace, the sky, of a blue which suggested not so much the infinite nausea of space beyond (a vacuum into which all matter tended in a sickening rush) but the solid band of colour caused by the mixture and ignition between air and fire, and, in the gently swelling waters, the loops and coils of foam caused by the numberless hulls and keels splitting the amorous liquid (so many, in fact, that the water level rose several feet at the height of their passage), to see, at the head of that procession, the royal barge connect, by means of a flowery chain, with the vessel ahead: so solemn and so moving that it seemed as if the very energy of the four elements, till then split into countless impotent fragments, were united and released in the crucible of some cosmic alembic, turning the grosser constituents into aether and flame. And the barge itself that she sat in, like a burnished throne, burned on the water; the poop was beaten gold, purple the sails, and so perfumed that the winds were lovesick with them; the oars were silver, which to the time of flutes kept stroke, and made the water which they beat to follow faster, as amorous of their strokes. As for the person of the Queen herself, it beggared all description; she lay in her pavilion, cloth-of-gold of tissue, as if the flowing River had aureated itself and, from the foam, condensed this Venus. On either side of her stood pretty dimpled boys, like smiling Cupids, with divers-coloured fans, whose wind (even I could see at a distance) glowed the delicate cheeks which they cooled, and what they undid did. At the helm a seeming mermaid steered, and the silken tackle swelled with the touches of those flower-soft hands; and from the barge, in its billowing rising and falling progress, a strange invisible perfume hit the sense of the adjacent wharfs. From the liquid flotilla a music floated to me on the water that contained, in its dance, all the thousand moving mirrors of the channel, each with its sparkle of sun, each with its fragment of indigo heaven, composed in honour of the occasion by another lover of intricate waterways, the Venetian Antonio Vivaldi; while, as I pressed through the crowd to keep that central barge in focus, I came to that section of the waterfront adjoining the Gold Coast, a limpid curve of silver-sanded shore where, most intimately, the print of my fair idea lay, and whom, now, its milk-white swans adored, in the gradual advance of the royal presence, gliding upon the blessed brook refined by her eyes. The populace grew larger and more adulant with that slow majestic progress; the City, that year, was full to bursting with foreign visitors and innumerable streams of rustics from the provinces; not a vacant room was to be had—and even such of those as were already let were often divided and sub-divided by flimsy screens and curtains; and the public houses were nightly packed with an enthusiastic celebrating mix-mash, from Barons in velvet train to stable-lads still perfumed with the ointment of their trade. All these, it seemed, and indeed all intelligible peoples, that might be willingly gathered into a net of meaning, were gathered here, radiating outward from that central liquid crown with all the geometric prolusion of a hive held in humming consonance to its queen bee. Past the immense steel-bound leap of the Hancock Building, now approaching completion, and the sensuous undulation of the older skyline of brownstones and weathered yellow-brick apartment complexes and condominiums, the Queen's flotilla tended, burdened with the weight of flowers flung from the banks, most of which dimpled and ruddied the gentle eddies and parted lips of the stream (those nymphs with roses in their mouths). And as the mighty flood intersected with smaller tributaries, those swirling confluences were, it appeared, crowded with tiny witnessing craft, shallops and scows and tugboats, and long graceful scullers from nearby universities, their dripping oars at rest, the shapely perspiring arms crooked at the elbow in a half-embrace, glistening with viscous gold, tufted at the pit with burnished copper. The sun balanced at noon and stripped each mast of shadows as, at that precise moment, the hived shores set up a tremendous shout that seemed to echo and re-echo between the azured vault overhead and the earth whence it issued, giving, in the utterance, an incalculable impact of depth, of burgeoning sound-seeds. And still that procession dipped and floated, floated and dipped, drawn on as by magnetic rapport with the queenly vessel which glowed on the shimmering mirage of water: so rippling and so unreal that it appeared as if it were suspended on nothing but inexhaustibly proceeding waves of light. At the section where the River bends westward, curving around the central City, a group of itinerant musicians gathered, and set up a counterpoint to the floating music of the waters. One of them, a young woman just approaching her fertile prime, with long waves of tawny hair in which strands of reddish gold glinted (and where the condensed vermilion of a carnation glowed), held a curved bow in her prehensile tapering fingers, and with it struck, to measure, her tall shapely *viola d'amore* on its taut mouth. Her lips were parted a little and very wet; her eyes were almost closed and showed only two white slits of their inward-looking balls. Nothing of that music was audible, however, only its effect, as it were, upon the rhythmic inflection of wind and water, rippled fire and the regular saying breath of the populace. The sun, at its zenith, had reached the tallest of these floats, and crowned its flowery head with liquid gold.

The spring and summer of that year retain, in my memory, a green and growing space, from the tiny kernel of its germination—hard buds glazed in a spring squall, mists condensing in the parks pale jewels that trembled in the lightest breathing, as if the inanimate were quivering toward the determinateness of a life-form—to the sudden astonishing flowering of its promise, the trees laden with the rich sticky burden of their foliage, a yellow-green deepening verdure, the swollen shrubbery along the boulevards dusted with tenuous ochre, the lilac just verging on the stained purple of its many mouths, and the forward violet, once peeping in isolation from under protective beds of moss, now lifted in thick clusters the pale moth-like markings of its central corolla against the darkening flush of its petals. Often during that season—when, it seemed, the delicate pastel hues of the City were being subtly drawn out as by a master artist—I would loiter through the water-glazed lanes, enamelled with shimmers by a suddenly unveiled sun, its windows splitting into dazzling fragments the arrested celestial radiance, its signposts limned in wiggles of nervous light, the foliage of the overarching trees like the downward-burning flame of her rich hair, and the gleaming cobblestones, buffed to flowing brilliance by the alchemy of water and fire, standing out in my dazed perception like the fluid, mingling, splitting letters of some dream-alphabet, feeling at my side the playful vernal wind, all warm and amorous, nuzzling against my ankles and neck, and breathing softly, with long respirating sighs, into my ear, and, as the morning would slide imperceptibly into afternoon, the advancing shadows of trees weaving themselves into shifting meshes wherein the sun wrote his gleaming script, casting upon the flushed brick faces of the larger buildings traces and laces of their branching nerve systems. Oh, those streets, those lanes of my fertile passion! What difference did it make to me that, even then, its elusive object was withdrawing (indeed, had been withdrawing ever since I had become aware of it)—all objects are curled up into themselves—since, in any event, she had become so generalized, so transmuted into the very aether and the luminence which, like radiant plasm, filled it, that in effect I could no more be without her than I could cleave to her?—since that signature found its way into the minutest and most trivial of the details that continually bloomed around me, the liquid brilliance of rooftops staining, in their copiousness, the worn brown fronts of their warming gently expanding walls, the flutter of shadow wings over the swelling sponge of the park's turf (with the invisible rush of their passage audible overhead), the folded leaves, on the fingers of slow-sapped trees, being woo'd from out their buds by the teasing influence of quickening air and amorous sun; and, as the mist and snow of a seemingly endless winter dissolved into a clinging vapour about the shrouded heads of buildings, and the City, held fast in the embrace of a reviving countryside, flowered with the madrigals of strolling musicians in the parks, and the people emerged from their recesses like shy shoots from under their autumn bed of damp and decaying leaves, showing prison-whitened faces to the warm sympathetic influences without, it seemed as though an immense and symmetrical body were rousing from sleep, stirring its large shapely limbs under the breath of the season formed by the earth's imperceptible tilt on her axis in her long elliptical journey around her star, combing its hair out in sighing restless breezes, lifting its blank and beautiful face to the sun's ruddy pencil to be drawn into life, to be described.

That year saw the opening of sidewalk cafés along Rushlight and other intersecting streets, and the mornings and early afternoons would invariably find one or another of us under a gaily painted umbrella, imbibing, along with our *café-au-lait* and croissants, the fragrant growth of a new day. The most popular of these among our group was the bright and bustling Café Royale, where, slightly less than seven years ago, Max Beerbohm had originated his incomparable sketch of "Enoch Soames" with a minimum of incisive corrosive lines—which produce, nevertheless, a more forceful effect of "reality" than these more weighty overdrawn creatures did who daily crowded this piazza with their exaggerated presences, like parodies that haven't the good taste to stop before the shrill extreme. This was located at the nexus of the "T" formed by the intersection of Cedar and Rushlight Streets, in view of the steadily growing Hancock Building to the south and east, and was sunniest in the morning and early post-meridian hours, when the broad radiance struck without obstruction onto the tiles and tables, glowing and humming with vivacious human intercourse. A series of aspen trees, filagreed with wrought iron, shaded that portion of the terrace closest the sidewalk, and the shadows of their young leaves would flutter in mute converse on the milk-white enamelled tables as we more audibly vociferated below. To the right, partially separating us from the neighboring bookstore, a hedge of flowering lilac arched, a deeper indigo against the lighter purer cerulean. And in the low wall enclosing this square were sunk pots wherein daffodils bloomed, shaken in the soft breeze, their petals gathering the honey luminence of the air. The shadows they cast on the table trembled in the spring animus and clustered, with little yellow suns between, on the long shapely arms to my right busying themselves with a flute of effervescence (that had beaded bubbles winking at the brim), brushing away the bees attracted by the fragrance and pollen, combing back a loose strand of hair drawing a fiery line in the shy day's breath. The sun tilted at noon and began its curving descent down the opposite side of the heavenly concave, and as it poised itself between the building behind us and that brief row of flowers, it deflected one shaft through the cone of amber fluid that left me dazzled. Oh, I realize that the pronoun "I" is being overworked here (is indeed probably the most faithful well-worn cog in the vast mirror-machine known as language), but let it rest, let it stay. I am so tired, I am so rarely allowed to hover in one space, in one closing gradually vanishing place (those valleys of the heart eliminated in its contractions). There is so much to be noticed and remembered before the light fades, cut off by the building to our rear and then the more massive curve of the earth itself; for instance, to the left, across from the fuzzy presence to my right, I could pick up, through the stinging images of flame and fluid, a figure etched in black and white, his face invisible under the wide brim of an elegantly curled sombrero, slender hands tapered around a goblet of crystal and silver (one of the fingers encircled by a broad signet ring blank as his face), crossed legs encased with creased French piping, the object of his intent regard impossible to fathom. I would have leaned over, despite the restraining hand on my arm, but just then an ample German waitress rolled her bulk between (a stomach like a punching bag, breasts like a heavyweight's fists), and my vision cleared just in time to note that under the blonde lurked a brunette (the bleached hair revealing its melanic root). Mist obscured the upper regions of the Hancock Building (down which the first of four workers had plummeted a scant month ago), but the sky overhead was miraculously clear, with only the faintest and most fragile of cloud-wisps drifting in its empyrean depths.

This season, so brief in duration, so lasting in its feathery effects, saw the appearance of the first of her many pseudonyms (only the last of which has been given), a name soon to burn in ruby and garnet from the marquées of the long ellipse that formed the theatrical district proper, the immortal Florence Farr, the original of which, I believe, was a restauranteur's only daughter who spent her days as a waitress and her nights in dissipation in the cheap bars and wineshops around Soho; taken up and transformed it became something rarer and stranger than that hinted at in its base genesis, an alchemy of flowers and distance that soon was to generalize itself into the very atmosphere, as if I were perceiving the City not geographically but botanically, through the cross-section of a petal, say, viewed microscopically, the light seeping through the stained filters of innumerable proliferating cells. At the time she took this epithet to herself she had attained a dramatic brilliance that was well-nigh unparalleled, in the two performances of her prime, the masterpiece of a River and that of an Ocean (the one actual, the other imaginary, but both elevated to the same transcendent plane of reality), where she played in one the daughter of a magician and in the other the momentary Queen of an imperilled tropical kingdom of the mind—I can yet see the tenuousness and aeriness of the one, the ornamented amber and beaten gold of the other, weaving empires with her words; and, at the same time, *horribile dictu*, in a series of low music-halls and baudy burlesque houses, that melodrama of war and lechery based loosely on Homer's slapdash affair (wherein one is asked to imagine discarnate spirits and armored humans copulating to an inane measure), the first, despite its obvious claims to being an "entertainment," of those black "dramas of the absurd" which purport to present to an essentially indifferent audience the banal "anti-hero" (stripping off the masks of bloodshed and bloodlust only to clamp them the more firmly on the proffered visages of a complaisant public). What I chiefly remember of those sombre scenes—their glades dripping with incense-like moss, the sinister encroachment of huge hunchbacked shadows—is not the dreamlike encounter of hostile soldiers in the eerie twilight, antlike and carapaced, silent and deadly, with even the furor of their blows muffled and sickening in the impact, but those other even more noiseless and enigmatic encounters, in lighted tents that revealed only the moving shadows of those within, or windows partially shaded containing, in glimpses and glances, scenes of betrayal that stung me to the root of my vision. These scenes, I have no doubt, with their elements of the peepshow, endeared them to the lower classes which filled these houses nightly, coupled with, of course, the realistic views of swordplay and a new set of almost cinematic devices which gave, through the interplay of light and shade, a nauseatingly believable impression of a man being eviscerated and emptied onto the steaming battleground—and, placed as they were in conjunction with the laid-bare core of lechery that formed their pululating heart, it made for a concoction (equal portions of gore and cheap perfume) which the critical and popular gourmands of London were not lax in devouring, with many noisome smacks and relishes, and sharings with their neighbors at the trough. Such, at any rate, it seemed to me: those honey-bodies, honey-words, clung together, humming and sticky with globules of syrup, hearts, my own not excepted, beating thicker than a feverous pulse, wallowing now in lily beds, now on the crimson started by that voluptuous pressure, as the shadowy shaft wounded and then tickled the rosy sore, love's arrow, those bodies, as clearly as if carved out of solid light, entwined in a tangled conjunction of limbs, a generation of still-breeding vipers. All this, I swear, I saw—the treachery, the traducery, the betrayal, with backward-looking glances and gasps, that seemed to be and yet was not the thing it was; for in all this fair-seeming show, as in all of Cupid's pageant, there was presented no monster: and yet, if this beast with two glistening dorsal surfaces was not truly monstrous, what could be called thus, as it moaned and made love to itself? Those open mouths spoke and yet did not, pressed as they were together, soft cave against soft cave, sucking and tasting the nectar at the root, saliva and chewed syllables dribbling out one corner in wet ropes; and as the light dimmed and those bodies merged, what I became aware of was not the luminous corrosive picture of what was in essence artistic betrayal (fastening herself to another's design), nor even the literal faithlessness unfolding its serpentine evolution before my eyes, but the heavy breathing that filled the air around me, a dry drawn-out hiss, as of wind being sucked in through many apertures, or the laboured gasps of an animal being suffocated. If it were not for my realization that this was a play—that these parts were not, in effect, those who played them—I could have, I believe, joined that scene for a brief moment, as an actor not called for in the script, and torn those bodies apart with an instrument that did not regard the fabric of their juncture. Mesmerized as I was with the lighted tableau-like quality of the moving picture I could not, myself, move, but only gaze with clarity and hopelessness at what swam outside my grasp. That darkness, I suddenly am able to notice, was becoming increasingly like the one that now caps my head in its black helmet: a miniature projection room at the impossibly distant end of which floats a bright image of what cannot be attained. The monstrosity of love, I saw, is precisely this, that the will is infinite and the execution confined; that the desire is boundless and the act a slave to limit.

The picture changes, as in Byron's poem, by an alchemy of rippling light akin to the mutations of montage. A wide table is visible through the doorway of a tent (the flaps pinned back like large ears). Tiny figures can be seen on it, and the intersecting grid-marks of a design that one cannot make out due to the low angle of vision. It is suddenly apparent that bulky shadows are hunched around this table, some in armour, other brawny and half-dressed. One huge forearm, covered thickly with coarse black hair, pushes pieces around on the surface. A gutteral murmur, as of immense gears made of bone and gristle straining together, rises almost palpably above the table. A harsh laugh is heard. A thick hand scatters the pieces.

Again the picture changes. It is night; a storm-lantern casts a flickering uncertain pool of radiance on random walls. A sound of singing from within. A huge warrior stumbles in, unstraps his armour, scratches, flops back on the divan, cries without. Another figure, of slighter stature, enters mincingly, his war-gear draped in feminine garments. He curtsies; the tip of his ornamental rapier protrudes like a mock phallus. Hollow laughter resounds; an arm, mailed at the wrist, sweeps forward; a grunt; the lamp is dashed out. Struggling sounds subside into a rhythmic squeaking. An appreciative murmur from the audience, interspersed with hearty lip-smacks. The light returns wanly. It is dawn. The Queen is alone on the battlements. She looks onto the field of battle, so soon to be reddened with sunlight and blood. A smile blooms on the utter whiteness of her face. She loosens her gown; it ripples to her feet. The figure is so white, so deadly, so drained of colour, that despite the exceeding voluptuousness of its contours one is forced to look away. At that moment the sun lifts its bloody visage. It is a fiery head helmeted in glowing iron. A drum begins thudding within. The Queen veils herself, withdraws. The furrows bear their dreadful harvest; armed men spring out of their crevices and begin to strike one another. Soon blood flows through these as through the irrigation ditches of an immense plantation. The light withdraws, returns. The statue of a hooved animal accretes its outlines as if being drawn by some stage assistant. Suddenly it rolls forward, revealed in all its golden bulk. A great shout; the belly swings shockingly open, a ladder is produced, and up its rungs a seemingly endless file of tiny deadly insect-mailed warriors clambers and is inserted into the caesarean aperture above. The monster creaks and sways with the additional weight. Anticipatory breathing from the audience, as if in the grip of an approaching communal climax. Once more the picture transforms itself. The silent animal, pregnant with death, is surrounded with old counselors and young women. Some of them have infants in their arms. A buzz of inquisition rises above their heads. Great battlements dwarf the statue's bulk. Through a window high in one tower a woman is either dressing or undressing; she is visible only in the mirror where her beauty is bared. A sword on one wall seems to hang above her head. In the last scene we have entered this room. Cries can be heard from without, high-pitched shrieks and the animal grunts of intense gratification. At one point which I would prefer to forget infants may be seen through the open window being tossed high and then impaled, in their unmelodious descent, upon the waiting tips of pikes and bayonets. The Queen, naked to the waist, watches impassively. A rosebud nestles between her breasts. One hand is dangled free and reveals perspiration lines of excitement. The lips are parted slightly, wet and glistening. She seems to be listening to music. The door behind opens suddenly and, without stirring, she motions for some other to enter. A bulk obscures our narrow view (the slit or cranny we are peering through). Those watchful outlines, alert and soft, are covered as by a sheet of gross corporeality, circled with rings of leather and brass. An orange arc-lamp suffuses the scene with its lurid stain; this is counterpointed by the flames darting up from below the window. The picture dissolves in a liquid ripple, as if we were viewing it in a sheet of water suddenly disturbed by an interior discharge, or as if a milky fluid had spilled over its surface, causing it to sigh in waves of downward-running light (the effect of a veil abruptly twitched by sensitive stage hands). Arms push themselves out of the thick neck, as though out of the skin itself; they twitch and tremble, then grasp the gigantic shoulder blades as if they were the twin spurs of a massive overhanging precipice. Flames consume the fabric of this vision and leave us, at their last expiration, in crumbling glowing blackness. Something brushes my cheek—a current of air or a filament of floating faery hair. There is, was, the general sense of dawn after an orgy (the clammy stickiness, the befuddled attempt to recognize strange faces, to sort walls and windows into the makeshift of an edifice), except that this dawn brought no illumination, only the sense of a communal darkness. I was not surprised to see, once I made my way out of the building's depths, that night had fallen along the entire length of the unlighted street, and that the City itself, begemmed with slowly kindling luminaries, was shrouded in its accustomary colossal blackness. A building across the Park (which would come to be known as "Bughouse Square,'' after the Puritans, Communists, Fascists, and other crackpots who filled its arboreal recesses with their rantings) signed the night with fiery initials—one limpidly curving branch acting as a kind of parenthesis. Then its trunk bent forward as we made our way and played the predictable part of an eraser—a broad sickeningly empty and black stroke that, with an almost audible *whoosh*, eliminated the bright pulsing signals yonder (strange, that I never have been able to locate that mammoth tree during daytime walks—the park is almost entirely filled with tall shrubbery and, at best, a slender birch or two).

16

Adjoining one broad side of that park, to the north and catty-corner from an ancient Scottish Rite Cathedral, was a monumental edifice constructed of huge black slabs of granite, and with closely-knit iron grilles covering the infrequent lower windows. As one would sit on a newly-painted bench across the street, the ascending sun to the right would strike through the interlacing branches of elm and birch that lined both sides of this meditatively shaded thoroughfare, the Walton Street that transforms itself, after passing through the streams of several major arteries, into the narrow remote aristocratic length that is East Wilton Street. The early radiance would pass, I say, through that intricate living mesh, causing rhombs and corymbs and coronas to momentarily flower on the gravelled walk at one's feet, and, simultaneously, would attain the easternmost of those barred portals, that, upon being blindingly reflected, appeared as if caged in a black negative mesh. Couples, many homosexual, would stroll through the shaded paths, sometimes seeking a denser bush to conduct their private business; and, after dark, the local beggars and tosspots (several of whom would act as unconscious models for a series of historical plays, more properly historical comedies, some years later) congregated in the shadows for their evening journey into laughter and unconsciousness. Now, however, the fair face of the day revealed itself in all its milky curdled freshness (with the blue of the bowl luminous behind the liquid); it rested its soft cheek against the stippled shadow of the turf, hollowing and rising in its puffed breaths; it closed its eyes with the almost palpable dance of a pliable vigorous young leaf, then winked dazzlingly open as it formed a crevice in the living roof for its warm overflow. On the walk extending to the right and left flocks of pigeons would waddle, foraging for the crumbs and corn of various lower-caste philanthropists, and often I noticed, after they had passed, one lone stray struggling to keep up with the others, a scrawny dark bird that, I suddenly saw, had only one leg. It would pause to gather its meager store of strength, and then, in a frantic series of hops, rush after its fatter sleeker Cadillac-like brethren, and at length, exhausted, stand in the middle of the walk on its single thin leg like an imperfectly formed blot among the other shadows. One day, from early morning till early afternoon, it stood unmoving on one isolated stretch of path (the occasional pedestrian almost stepping on its flat little outline, only swerving at the last moment), and when I returned toward nightfall found it in exactly the same position I had left it, a chill evening breeze ruffling the feathers (the only part about him that was moving at all). He stood in the park accumulating shadows to himself, a darker patch of gloom among the night-flowering densities that shifted and sighed and subsided, found a deeper shade to merge with, merged; and next morning, when I hurried to the spot, my eyes still moist from nocturnal excitement (a continual train of bright coloured images), there was nothing there, nothing at all. It was as if, during the long night, some immense eraser had taken the trouble to pass over that bit of pebbled path, leaving nothing for the light to reflect (though undoubtedly that eraser was somewhat more tangible than I make it out—a predatory tomcat, a group of playful adolescents with a can of kerosene and a box of matches out for an evening's entertainment). The sun that morning, I remember uncomfortably, seemed almost bland, as if it knew something and wasn't telling.

The building with which this segment opens was known officially as the Newberry Library and, actually as well as officially, it housed a magnificent collection of rare books, manuscripts, and incunabula (with rich concentrations in the late 16th and 19th centuries); it was a well-known but unmentioned fact, however, that it also housed, deep in its bowels, beneath even the immense inlaid pillars of the central corridor with their intricate richly glinting mosaics of mythological scenes (Grecian air aureated into a shimmering thin-beaten skin, an antler rubied suddenly in one's downward-moving perception as if dipped in a maiden's ivory abdomen) a revolutionary clinic for the study and cure of language disorders, a class of ailments that, among the literate population, was becoming increasingly common. At the time I became acquainted with this building's formidable interior (the late summer and early autumn of 1900) I was ransacking those recesses, lit up from without by broad mellow washes of sunlight filtered through sealed crystal, for newer and even more ethereal material to keep my imagination's stage occupied (as if a temple, never mind how weatherbeaten and ordinary, were polishing the hollow of its interior to constrain its fickle deity to remain); and as I daily pushed my way through the thick glass door of the entrance, decorated at each of its four corners with golden masks of Apollo, it seemed to me as though I were penetrating not merely an accretion of stone and concrete but the polished cap of a huge brain, muted and golden in the radiance of early afternoon; for as I began to move within that spacious resonating interior, columned with pillars of sunlight in which an occasional insect glinted, its various interconnecting rooms and alcoves filled solidly with the red and gold backs of rubbed and oiled tomes, the stairwells and balusters glowing secretively in the almost scholarly dimness that flowed from deeper inside where more recondite collections were stored, it grew upon me that the billions of hived words, letters, marks of punctuation, were not merely the inert inked characters of a language now (alas) unfortunately as close to dissolution as I am as I write this, but the animate humming cells crackling with innumerable interconnections of the brain of some unfathomable creature; not the isolated prisoners of sealed morphemes, but the joyous verbs of an unending undulating sentence that formed the meant world in microcosm. In the large oval centrally-located reading room, ringed with mosaics of quotations from the ancients and moderns against a background of gold leaf, whereon, arching to the centre of the reduced celestial vault, the branching and rebranching body of a tree was intricately traced, meant to represent that of knowledge (here philosophy flowered, there botany bloomed), the concentric rings of reading tables would burnish and burn in the full afternoon luminence seeping from the windows clustered around half the hemisphere; and, gathering like bees around the corolla of some golden flower, the busy humming heads of readers would flutter and hover, sucking the pollen of knowledge out of the opened petals, their hair dusted with powdered gold by the all-seeking radiance penetrating from without. Against the glass of display cases, slanted to reveal their inner riches, this light would gather and spring, leaving the eye momentarily dazed as it feasted upon some limpidly curved wave of illuminated manuscript, burnished by the light sifting down, or the vegetal layers of a woodcut illustrating an early morality or interlude (the Devil in a tophat, Death in courtier's ruff and brocade, with the ribs poking through). Further within, I soon learned, were stored the rare collections centering around early myths and histories; and it was to these that I made my dulceotropic way, as though I were penetrating to the core of the layered cerebellum, the governing seat of knowledge and desire and will, the dusty golden haze floating around the perimeter remaining, in retrospective perception, as a kind of pre-dawn glow to the combustion igniting within.

That way led, I recall, up a spiral staircase, off which floated, to the left and right, spirocheting intersecting tendrils, that reached, at ascending angles, still further upward. These were pierced with clusters of small hexagonal windows, milkily opaque, but of such a density and clarity as to admit a dazzlingly incandescent, yet perfectly even, flow of mature luminosity. The parquetry on the gently rising staircases and curving corridors was waxed to a soft brilliance; the walls and ceiling, curved like those of a tunnel or artery, with many waves in their undulating surface, scaled over with hexagonal gold leaf. The collection I unvaryingly found myself secluded with was located in an early version of the now-famous "geodesic dome," formed, in this case, of hexagonal slices of amber crystal annealed into the contours of an immense light-absorbing and refracting beehive which appeared, viewed from without (from, say, the imposing Salvation Army Headquarters situated just across the Park), struck to vibrant colour by the sun coagulated in its depths, as it were filled to overflowing with an abundance of honey; and, from within, as if the gathered syrup of wideranging fields were pressed against its cellular surface, and seeping, with the radiance that bled through, in long clinging amber strands of light into the hollow being thus filled. Such it appeared to me as I ransacked those hidden recesses of their stored riches, stacking dripping combs, as it were, on one sweetly burdened table, to suck, one by one, their essence out, the sun warm on my neck, my shoes removed and one hand poised, at the proper phrase, to dip into the honey-pot and write. Many tales and legends of those I then uncovered I might recount, except for fear of repeating what is too commonly known; but two in particular my humming thoughts revolved and hovered around, bright with the fire issuing from their hidden hearts. The first of these was that of the young hunter—one version places him in the most remote regions of the Hartz Mountains, another in the higher more inaccessible reaches of the Black Forest—who, wandering far outside his usual territory, finds himself toward late afternoon, as the light angles, with many reflections, through the queerly twisted black branches of an unknown species of tree, in a glade filled with the high detached atonal angry whine of a strange breed of wild bees (another version transplants them from Africa, still another from northern India); and, being hungry after his exhausting and fruitless search for the elusive snowy mountain goat or the high scornful blackantlered chamois, he traces that wavering pitch to its source and eats of the dripping dark comb, falls immediately into a trance (an early fragment, the "Hippolytus B" in the Bodleian numbering, calls his food a "faery honey"), and when he wakes, or thinks he wakes, finds himself transported to an earlier time, the "Golden Age" of the classical poets of old; and of his former condition, remembers only such fleeting and fading memories as serve to accentuate the lush and fertile landscape where he has been removed (we must remember that this myth received the form through which we know it in the classical age when Rome was beginning its slow autumnal decline—an age not unsimilar to our own in its unsteady position on a ridge of time that looks back to an Edenic existence, and ahead to one that our novelists have stamped with the dreary telling phrase: "anti-utopian"). He cannot, however, entirely rid himself of that former life; and so, as he wanders through now this enchanted grove, vibrant with the lyres of legendary poets, or that fertile orchard, heavy with perpetually ripening fruit, he glimpses, as it were out of the corner of one eye, odd pockets of neglect and decay, patches of ruin and artifacts alien to the life he senses all around. In the literal sense of the word he "sees double"—or, rather, weaves two versions of the world into a single, if spottily ragged, fabric: a shimmering, intricate, bewilderingly shifting weave wherein figures appear, vanish, and insect-like metamorphose, bright threads interwoven with duller and more delirious ones, that change as the light changes its angle or intensity. Another, much later version, composed some time toward the end of the Middle Ages, and ascribed by some to the second author of *Le Roman de la Rose*, reverses the telechronation; that is, has our displaced wanderer originally in some forest of the Golden Age, and, after his trance and awakening, places him in the midst of a preindustrial village, loud with drays and hawkers, with piles of rotten fruit in the gutters, or in the slaughter-house of some prosperous butcher, washed with rivers of blood, confused with loops of intestines draped over the stained and smoking rafters. Both versions have their virtues; I, for reasons that I hope are obvious, prefer the former, if only because it leaves the basic fabric of the vision, its fruits and flowers, untouched, albeit qualified by the dingy haze of that later time (thus may a visitor to the land of dream speak of the insubstantial mistiness of his waking life—the one, however, into which this much more transcendently, luminously real world will be, upon the return of that inferior mode of consciousness brought in with the dawn of awakening, dissolved); the same haze, I liked to think, that with the tilting of the earth on its axis presaged the ripening of all things toward their fullness and their grave; not even so much as a fog as yet, but rather the merest smokiness attendant upon a glass that has stood out in the sun too long, and in the ardour of its rays lost its first crystal intensity, or like the larger lens of the atmosphere itself that, with the pilings and burnings of the season's husks, grows more opaque, diffusive of light, making the bright inhabitants of an imagined world but their wavering fading reflections; the same subtle virtually imperceptible metamorphosis that occurs, for example, in the smoky interior of a drinking house, filled with the loud vociferations of tipplers and the shrill cries of barmaids calling their orders in. At first glance all seems permeated with a boisterous community of friendliness and good-will; there is much crashing-together of tankards, drinking songs, and that irreplaceable staple of the English pub, the delicate contest of darts. A group of regular patrons is clustered in one corner; by gazing assiduously, through smarting eyes, one may make out the well-known faces of several prominent writers and playwrights, among them that of an avowed atheist and advocate of loose living, who provided the topic of many a rising young Puritan's ranting sermon—and yet who, with the honey of his sonorous blank verse, had revolutionized the English drama as we knew it till then. The others, a collection of pamphleteers, prose-mongers, ballad-composers, are appropriately vague. One spot remains persistently blank—the locus from which one stares with watery eyes. A drawn-out argument is in progress; voices are high, hands smite the table, drinks jump as if surprised, eyes glitter through drifting smoke. The figure across the table shakes his golden head, laughs; his mouth moves but the words cannot be distinguished. To the left, on the table, a muscular arm rests, naked to the elbow, dusted lightly with tawny hair. It twitches nervously as if it wanted to grasp something. The voices rise to an impossible crescendo. Suddenly, in one of those unplanned lulls that are all the more shocking for being unexpected, the arm, with preternatural quickness, blurs down and then up. It holds something long and cold and hard. There is a flicker of white light. A shriek rents the smoke and buzz of the interior. A blinding flash explodes. When vision returns—a long black interval between as if the eyes were bandaged—the world is at once greyer, smokier (the gold tarnished into a baser metal), but against this monochrome field an unmoving figure is stretched, half its torso across the table, its arms flung out, face half-exposed to the lantern swinging deliriously overhead. It is totally drained and white. A strand of gleaming hair falls over the open mouth but does not move. From behind one closed eye—the right, that looks out, or the left, that looks in—a black thread trickles. There is a sound of many feet approaching, and abruptly, in the hushed sickened silence, the unmistakable noise of numerous doors being closed and locked.

17

The second of the legends that I garnered and polished during those long slanting afternoons of early autumn was that of the warrior who, in old age, turns beekeeper, and makes a hive of his notched and battered helmet (this legend is immortalized in two lines of the poet-journalist Peele)—perhaps drawn to this simple and powerful image (the instrument of war muted and mellowed and metamorphosed) by one of my seemingly endless childhood, humming and remote, that I spent, during a series of linked and dangling summers (a necklace I yet keep and treasure), on my grandparents' country estate in County Sligo, Ireland, in the midst of low rolling green hills, on the shore of a tiny sapphire of a lake that glittered in the beams of a sun that seemed (so powerfully does recollection work) suspended in its solid azured vault. There, I would row out in a tiny shallop and anchor myself in its spring-fed depth, a dazzling blue that sank to peacock green and then violaceous ice-cold layers of ink, watching tiny chains of silver bubbles dance waveringly upward to explode against the surface; and, hooking a berry on a thread, dangled it enticingly over the edge, and lay luxuriously on the hollow bottom, listening to the somnolent gurgle and whisper of water underneath (like overhearing a conversation but not being able to make out the words), dazing and easing my sleepy vision with sun-spangles and sparkles, a green watery reflection moving against the sides of the boat. The sun would paint my partially closed eyelids with a warm mixture of red and blood (dipping into my capillaries for the other ingredient of his alchemy), and my sense was even then, as now, one of winding endless streams of bright and changing images on reels that were stored in interior darkness. On other days, overflowing with sun, I would withdraw to the tiny outhouse that was situated by a musical creek disemboguing from the westernmost shore of the lake, amid whose lighter voice I might hear the deeper plashings of bullfrogs, snapping turtles, and carp, and there, the partly-opened door admitting an elongated parallelogram of yellow, the various chinks wandering tenuous honey-threads of trickling luminence (as if an old shell or hat had been left out in all kinds of weather and developed a pattern of random yet beautifully symmetrical holes in its worn surface creating, as the aery syrupy radiance without gathered thicker and more condensed, constellations for any inhabitant within to note and marvel over), there I would bare my nether parts in the sun-shot shadow and watch the bright world revolving without, loud with the thrum of cicadas in the high deliriously green trees, begemmed with drifting dragonflies and horseflies and those elusive hazy companions of my childhood wanderings, the bluetailed flies, no relation of the common or housefly, but more akin to the larger more varied dragonfly, that would hover with deceptive lassitude above the reeds and oozy marshes surrounding our lake, their long torsos and transparently-webbed wings a dreamy extremely light almost atmospheric yet concentrated bottle blue—the colour of glass that has been licked and rubbed and wetly nuzzled by a playful river for some dozens of years. As I sat there, secreted in my shady cocoon (the metamorphosis from unseeing sunlight to seeing dark only begun), these evanescent creatures would hover above the stream yonder, twitching to one side lazily and effortlessly to avoid some real or imagined peril, with such unbelievable rapidity that the eye could not follow the movement, or see, even by means of the faintest blur, how it got from one place to another—so elusive of place, in fact, that I never managed to capture one, despite long hours of virtually motionless stalking. On the placid regular inflection of the creek I could see, in between marsh-grass and the hollow whisper of reeds, its glassy surface inscribed by water-spiders and water-skates, delicate long-legged creatures suspended by means of surface tension and their own slender jointed legs beaded with tiny air bubbles. The trees which cooled one side of the outhouse were a species of Colorado Blue Spruce, and I could see, through a cranny to my left, loosened needles dangled on a strand of cobweb dryly and bluely luminous against a soft moving background of gloom. Soon my odours gathered and mixed pungently with the ones of fir, ripe spring-fed grass, and the lime used to break down the ordure heaped below, and I breathed it in deeply as though it were a rare and exotic perfume prepared for me alone. I had, even then, the sense of being invisibly in relation with all the layered world without, for it seemed to me as if the shifting tendrils of radiance that filtered the blackness I was wrapped in extended outward as well, weaving tenuous filaments into the air and light that drew the world into description—as though I were touching, with millions of sensitive nerve-ends, the contours of the beloved face which remained as yet unknown. I cannot begin to describe the luxuriant sense of place or positioning—the exquisite tingle that permeates every atom of our being when we fit exactly into a space hollowed for us alone; and, at the same time, an infinitely heightened awareness, as of a flexible string capable of endless modulation, tightening or loosening, in its reception of strokes, of vibrations, as I rested on the polished green enamel of the smaller hole (there was a larger, higher one for a larger species) engaged in long meditative excretion; and often, surfeited with impressions, as if my humming thoughts had been so many far-ranging bees of a common hive sent out to absorb the varied essences of field and dale, I would fall asleep, crawling with coloured images that were burdened with pollenated sweetness, moving from cell to cell of my brain, filling each chamber with what it had found (a leaf with its lip curled like a nose, the flutter in a frog's jade back, a sunwarmed cow-patty burrowed with insects). Outside, night would have fallen from the dusky tops of trees, but already the constellations had rubbed themselves to fire, and below, in the gloomier groves, over the fields of dark and stirring grass, the wavering yellow of lightning bugs, as of lamps shining through shades of old parchment, began to signal across the growing void. Later, as the evening deepened its sensuous hold on the slumbrous earth, I would wander out, equipped with the hollow shells of blown eggs, to capture these airborne flecks of luminosity and imprison them in translucent white; their pulsings were visible through the thin wall as moving aureoles of faint moonglow lighting the empty interior.

Such a metamorphosis I underwent, it seemed, in the lighted dome where I was immersed in my labours, for as the afternoon imperceptibly shaded itself into dusk, the luminence that guided my imagination gradually withdrew and concentrated itself into a single vibrant yellow pool on the table where I sat. From below me, too, the evening spread its insinuating fingers, up the sparsely lighted stairwells, along the darkened corridors. I could hear the creak of mops approaching and retreating and, somewhere in the gloom overhead, a large moth beating its wings against the glass. It suddenly occurred to me that I was the sole occupant of the room and that now, as never before, I was visible to anyone standing without that glass bell. To extinguish the lamp, whose shade was powerfully reminiscent of the one that accompanied my nocturnal solitude on those dark summer nights in Ireland—its yellowed parchment, like a leaf aged into veined and amber translucence, was bordered with a deep vermilion—was but the work of a moment, and, eyes aswarm with residual midges of brightness, I slipped into the darksome stream flowing noiselessly into the regions below.

18

f we view the evolution of the seeing faculty from, say, that of the higher insects to that of our own species, the one compelling fact to which our fascinated attention is drawn is that the impulse is a unifying one: the monochrome fragments with which the faceted eye of dirty diptera or industrious orthoptera, or the more ornate odonata, flatly perceives the world, are gradually annealed together, with only dry wisps of sutures between, as the organ grows more complex and receptive to light; and, at the same time, that world (the one created in the act of perception) gains fabulous shadings and mouldings and counterpoint of detail, far beyond the need of any poor organism to survive. Again, if we consider the evolution of linguistic ability, that secondary sense for forging the world into a whole, what we mean, or should mean, by sophistication, is not, of course, elegant phrasing, or dulcifluous periods, or any of the 200-odd devices of rhetoric catalogued by Wilson in 1853, but the power to unify what is disparate: to bring into humming consonance all the variety that is capable of being perceived. The words, that is, are not to be viewed as the ugly discrete little fragments or figments that they appear to the eye at first sight (the hieroglyphics of some obscene strutting bird), but as innumerable transparent panes allowing the inhabitant thus magnificently incarcerated out into a newly unified, luminous world—a world, in fact, fresh from the creator's stamp. Such an Adam, let out into this Eden, wandering dazedly through halls of vaulted green, suddenly aware of depths where before he had known only surface, must not forget, however, the tenuous nature of his vision, for it is ready, at the slightest shake from within or without, to be resolved into its components and dissolve, helplessly and hilariously, into nonsense—the last stage being, of course, the banal surrealistic poem entitled "Death," wherein all our phonemes and morphemes, so carefully gathered and arranged throughout a lifetime, are ruthlessly blown and scattered by some punning mouth (the mouth, I always liked to think, that practices by swallowing us blackly each day).

Some such dynamism operated, I believe, in the extensive and exclusive asylum situated under the Newberry Library in the London of that time (just under the collection on Early Americana, which included a famous treatise on whaling as well as some manuscript poems by J. F. Shade, a lesser known member of the "Tribe of Ben"). Those regions, rarely penetrated by the common citizenry, became a fascination to me as, in the early autumn of 1900, I carried on my more illuminated labours above; for the form of insanity which they dealt with had to do with the communicative faculty—with the way in which the world is linguistically perceived (a tendency that I myself, to be perfectly honest, have not been unaffected by, as even the most remote and polar seas, imprisoned for untold aeons in frozen crystal, yet feel the tug and pull of lunar gravitation when the earth fatally tilts). These disorders, almost exclusively confined to members of the educated aristocracy, grouped themselves into two main categories, which took their names from the rhetoric of the time—those of "Paronomasia" and those of "Syncope," the first a disorder of excess, the second one of deficiency. Well do I recall being admitted into the thickly padded cells that housed those afflicted with the former malady! As I approached the first of these, accompanied by a silent warder (indeed, now that I mention it, those entrusted with the immediate custody of these unfortunates were all, or nearly all, deaf-mutes), my impression was that the tiny room was inhabited by a multitude, for from the barred oval in the thick studded door issued an unending stream of expostulation, reply, query, peroration, declamation, soliloquy, cross-examination—indeed, a most complete compendium of rhetorical devices, all in an astounding range of pitch and timbre, from basso profundo to squeaky castrato, so that, were it not for my present orientation, I would have believed myself in a theatre given over simultaneously to several companies for dress rehearsal. My astonishment at viewing the tiny crouched figure in one shadowy corner of the room cannot be exaggerated. At our abrupt entrance the flabbergasting sounds that issued from his distended mouth did not slacken in the least, indeed seemed to heighten to an impossible rate; but his eyes, a clear, utterly mad blue, gazed at us imploringly, in absolute terror, and his hands, till then limp at his side, flew up to grasp desperately his working jaw—which, however, continued champing up and down of its own accord, as if driven by an immensely powerful steam engine. The effect of his speech was minimized, as I have noted, by the thick padding with which the room was furnished; for if it were bare I do not see how a person could have survived in it sanely (unless he were, as these warders all seemed to be, deaf). By some unexplainable trick of respiration he managed to gasp for air and talk at the same time, and this had contorted his features to such an extent that they were stained a throttled purple and wondrously transformed, so that he appeared hardly human, but rather some simian breed, or even the speaking rump of a baboon, splotched with riotous colour. Indeed, so powerful and multitudinous were the words that were wrenched out of his gaping gullet that I half expected the organ at the other end of the long sinuous undulation of intestine to join in the choric threnody (devoid of palatizations, alveolars and fricatives, but full of a rich range of the bubble-bursting noises linguists call "labials"), but, of course, such rectal rhetoric would have been muffled by the ample hospital gown with which all these creatures were swathed, a fine flowing linen fabric of the most dazzling white, with a wavy border of gold running around the hems of skirt and sleeve. It was as if that unwilling actor, in one person, played many people, a bursting stageful compacted into his tortured lungs, for now the noble periods of royalty flowed out, and now the obscene buffoonery of some Fool, naked of all but his poor wit. Indeed, anyone who has felt the world pressing in daily, with innumerable plucking fingers, heaping protean shapes upon the trembling imagination whose nature it is to take the shape of other things, can empathize, as I did, with this unfortunate, through whose fragile skin the world, misshapen and monstrous, threatened to burst, as though a clown were inflating a circus balloon with long meaningless gusts of laughter. Mock windows were here, as elsewhere, painted on the walls (had they been genuine they would have offered a view of yellow-green clay intermixed with layers of rough gravel, together with what fossils the centuries had accumulated); the scene they purportedly opened upon was that of a dreaming English countryside, with brook and heather and hedgerow, after the manner of Constable or Rackham. Other inmates, afflicted with the same strain of dementia, were constrained by some inexorable inner mechanism to speak only in rhyme, usually in a mixture of dactylic and anapestic hexameter, which sounded much like W. S. Gilbert doggerels speeded up; although one or two of this type, melancholy and dignified, uttered classically rhymed heroic couplets in varying degrees of nasal twang. The section devoted to this queer species had the audial effect of an aviary: countless notes chiming and discordant, rising to break against the ear with a hollow tintinnabulation. One such creature had been on his poetic machine for years, and was well-nigh out of fuel; he had exhausted, in his mad tour, the richly varied vowel sounds of the English tongue, and now was moving on to more gutteral Teutonic locutions, that sounded, in his metronomic voice, like a large scavenger devouring his piece of offal. Yet another was under the illusion that he was John Clare and, when forced, would come forth in remarkably pure Northamptonshire dialect. All his simple, effective rhymes, with many pellucidly clear detailed descriptions of the landscape his mad mentor had lived in (the horse-blob swelling its golden ball, and the fine focus held on the oak's slow-opening leaf, of deepening hue) were directed, he said, to her whose image he carried over his heart—and here he would close his eyes and, for once, fall silent.

Disorders of a somewhat different nature were lodged in the north wing, among them several senile specimens, linguistic wrecks of a once fertile capacity, one of which, a former director of this and other even more famous sanatoriums, was the well-known philosopher, psychologist and poly-linguist (chiefly English, French, and Russian), Dr. Ivan Veen, who occupied a luxurious cell where, in his vigorous intellectual and sexual prime he had interviewed, examined, investigated many of his best-known cases (as well as those more anonymous ones involving at the terminus of treatment a discreet intra-muscular injection), and who had taken, in his somewhat gongoristic decay, to odd local remedies for whatever arcane ailments gnawed him, such as the fairly revolting "plaisir anglais" (as he termed it) wherein the patient allows his bladder to fill until a certain degree of discomfort is attained and then, in a tubful of steaming hot water (or, alternately, and even more nauseatingly, of a temperature the same as his body), voids himself long and lassitudinously into the warm viscosity—whereupon the gratified tubber has the unique pleasure of bathing in his own urine. Akin to those with defects of speeded-up speech, etc., were those whose organs of articulation were not atrophied in any way, and yet were never known to utter a word. Their disorder, it was quietly explained, was that of a radically heightened hearing that could perceive conversations at the other end of the building, the fall of leaves in autumn upon the roof, the rustle of pages in the reading room overhead—the most thoroughly deranged of these being the one who could not shut out the sound of his own blood circulating, or, during the stillest depths of the night, the very sound of the earth revolving on its axis and engaged in its long bottomless fall around the sun. His ears, I was able to notice, were of a normal size, but so thin and shell-like as to be almost entirely transparent. Sometimes, to demolish and cacophonize these intolerable sounds, he would plug and unplug his aural passages rapidly, producing a soothing meaningless stutter—much as, during a long night of sleepless illness, a nurse or mother might croon to a child wasted by fever or waking dreams: the air flowing through the open window, billowing the white linen drape ghost-like inward, the creak of the rafters overhead under the weight of a nocturnal animal or the more solid restless body of the night itself, the glowing trembling circle of the tiny bedside lamp, all the artifacts of his intolerable agonizingly sharp consciousness, are resolved and soothed by the flow of that unvarying somnolent voice. So should we sleep, so should we wake. In the east wing were the cells devoted to the more disturbing diseases of syncope—that malady which blots and blurs the world into disjointed fragments by leaving out key pieces that describe it. At the soft centre of a word, a phrase, a sentence, something weakens and collapses, leaving the remaining fragments in bright and meaningless conjunction. Examples of this occur in common speech (fo'c'sle, bo'sun), but in the psychosis of this development the abridgement happens in conjunction with no known model of comparison: walking along the outskirts of a perfectly normal sentence, the hapless wayfarer will suddenly, inexplicably totter, stagger drunkenly, and drop from sight—reappearing, if at all, on a totally different stretch of road, his hip-boots tarnished and muddy as if from a tremendously long journey. Let us say, for example, that such a one—a salesman or mechanic in real life—wishes to utter something like, "I love you, darling—isn't it queer how many times I keep saying this?"—which might come out, "I love you queer how many times," a phrase that has, one must concede, little of the sentiment of the admittedly prosaic original. Or (jotting something down in his appointment book) "If I don't see you Monday at 8 I'll see you Wednesday at 2"—but what his puzzled prospect hears is "If I don't you ate I'll see you Wednesday too" (as if dinners were being mixed up with deliriums). Such sentences, it should be emphasized, sound perfectly normal to the speaker, although in the early stages of the illness, if the patient is at all linguistically aware, he may, some moments after uttering such an anomaly, catch it (as it were) in mid-air and turn it over and from side to side in puzzled surprise, as any parent might do upon seeing for the first time a queerly deformed offspring, wondering how he ever could have generated such a creature. In its terminal development, however, there is rarely such awareness, and the patient is, in effect, speaking a language known only to himself, and, as the cancer blooms luxuriantly, with profuse offshoots and creepers, in its final assimilation of the organism that has acted as its host, an unending stream of babble froths and bubbles from his mouth, the fractured kernels of sense, unreducible atoms of language, vowels, consonants, dipthongs randomly jumbled together until all that can be heard echoing from the bare walls of his cell is a ceaseless unbroken scream of absolute terror. When that has been reached—and only then—the patient, in a simple virtually painless operation, has his voice-chords removed; but that this expedient is but a local palliative there can be no doubt, for, although cut off from external expression, these voices continued, as I learned, on the inside; so that the effect this operation had was but to lock up the inmate with that inhuman howl in an even tinier more confined cell, which produced the inevitable result, if it had not been attained before, of driving him totally insane. The only patient known to reverse this process, the Irish-Russian poet Rosca Dildow, informed me, in simple, halting sentences, of much of the preceding account; and it was as if a space-wanderer had returned, after untold centuries, to confer with his former fellow-men, the void of his passage still with him, his eyes searching now here, now there, for familiar artifacts to guide his awkward way. The means of his limited recovery, an astounding accomplishment which had many reverberations in psychological and linguistic circles, was queerly akin to the method by which transformational grammarians generate sentences with a model grammar. Virtually speechless after his long bout with the illness, he was given a basic lexicon of perhaps fifty words and a series of simple rules whereby to generate kernel sentences. He was able, after diligent practice for long years, to combine these kernel phrases into fairly complex sentences ("She is coming", "She is here": "She is coming here"), although he never developed much beyond this stage.

What they exaggerated, of course, with their atrophy, was a tendency common to all articulating animals, that of missing, not noticing, leaving out, key details in one's field of perception (whether that field include a sentence, a landscape, a face)—as if one were gazing, not through the transparent pane of some lofty view (the light that gives birth to the consciousness surrounding one with its crystal and amber), but through the shadowy bars of a prison that one carries around with him always (the gaoler just inaccessible with his tantalizing golden key). Through that mesh, though, the landscapes float, dizzyingly and dazzlingly, and if they prove to be lacking certain elements (a tree, a shapely shadow writhing in the wind, a stretch of fertile loam swelling under its solar weight), that is all the more reason for the imagination—ever responsive to the draw of a vacuum—to supply, through the pulsater of an artery, those forms that the heart lacks. For these, though, there was no such relief; for them, even after being released from their more obvious confinement, the City must indeed have appeared to be that spectre of the mind's night, Chicago, then, as now, a rude frontier city growing on the shores of an immense inland ocean of America, destined to become, in the middle years of this century, a great livestock-slaughtering and meat-packing centre, as well as the major inland grain shipping port of the United States. At the time I am writing of, however, it had all the ills of civilized life and none of its advantages; nightly it reeked with the odours of leather tanning and brewing, and rang with the shouts of drunken brawlers and the wheedling cries of prostitutes plying their immemorial trade (now, as then, under the protection of the local constabulary), and the whole illuminated, in its muddy clangorous ways, by torches of smoking vile-smelling tallow thrust into the sides of buildings. How anybody could confuse the one with the other, even in the depth of the most abysmal fantasy, has always eluded my most searching comprehension, for they are, in essence, almost perfectly opposing complements, for the one, in its susceptibility to subtle and deep metamorphosis, and the other, in its impermeability to such processes, exist at the apex and nadir of imagination's starry vault; so that, to this queer and growing cult, whose world, originally a rich and fertile field of perception, was now a flat affair of stage scenery and sawdust, the London of that day must indeed have appeared drained of all its vital content, the mere husk of its rich pulpy core remaining to trouble them with the simple easily assimilated stage property of the modern realistic novel. It is agreed, of course, without any argument whatsoever, that the London I describe in these pages, and the Chicago of some sixty years later, coincide in many respects (that is but the marvel of, say, a brilliant-blooded insect imitating the coarse grey texture of the concrete it happens to rest upon); here a street, there a park, or here (again) a building or the massive shadow of a building may be fuzzily reproduced in that other time, that other clime; but between the two exists the skin of a shimmering rainbow bubble, formed of dual awarenesses on either side—my own and those allied with my mode of perception, and those others with their mirror-reversed city and time—much as, side by side, invisible each to the other, the dual cosmos of matter and anti-matter exist, or are said to exist by the poet-scientists of *my* world, simultaneously. Thus the starlight falling upon the roofs and gables of a sleeping springtime city, creeping in an opened lattice and reborn in the crystal of a bedside glass, thence to find a glimmering rest in the half-open unseeing eyes of some fair sleeper, may, for all we know, proceed from a sun now dead, and yet be, for all that, the more illuminating, the more heartbreaking in its searching revelation of tender inaccessible detail. Some such disparateness—the struggle of two dimensions against three, that of the shell against the life expanding within—operated here, in the colony that grew daily from the discharge of this asylum, so that, as the century accumulated years like a stalagmite growing under the calcified drip of an immemorial subterranean sore, the vision of a gratuitous world that we are offered at birth gradually blurred, wavered, and threatened to dissolve as other, secondary, flawed versions began to gather, challenging its primacy, its purity of line and outline. Often, in the years that followed, walking through the theatrical district or one of the adjoining areas, I would catch myself doubting my own perception, as the droves of aliens that increasingly populated these streets and lanes would loiter on the corners or in the parks, the buzzing of intimate incomprehensible conversation floating above their heads, drifting in directions and centres of communication and control that were impossible to fathom. It was, I think, in secret response and sympathy to this growing influence, that the course of history began to edge out of the unruffled waters it had been gliding through, to take on the turbulence and repression that have become its dominant characteristics; for it was simultaneously with the opening of this asylum at the foundations of the Newberry Library—designed, now that I think of it, by two architects who helped fashion a famous university in Hyde Park—that the first of many "Long Parliaments" was declared, brief shadows of the dark night of totalitarianism which was to follow. That night, I now can perceive, was, in the years which followed that dazzlingly luciferous season, to cast a perpetually growing twilight upon the City and its environs, so that its memory has become one of lighted pinpoints outlining rather than illuminating the structures that bulked around me, the interconnective periphery changed into a kind of terrestrial constellation, indicating sparsely and broadly the darker design of the whole.

Those years, darkened in retrospect, saw the opening of the first "singles bars" in the theatrical and night-life district—the gathering-places of the young and dissolute whose lurid lights and pulsing beat disturbed the night with a powerful tropism, as, in the insect world, multitudes of flying organisms are attracted from long distances by the radiation of "black lights," so, in the tiny cosmos of this section of the City, these centres where our animal life was packed into a nervously burning vitality exuded a strong invisible magnetism through the inspissated blackness—one I found myself almost immediately a prey to. As that season wore into those which followed—rubbing away, as it did so, like patient repetitive water over a slowly reducing stone, the City that I was erecting as a stage for my passion's enactment—I began to haunt these nocturnal jewels, set glimmeringly into the looping necklace that this district roughly described, at first from loose-floating curiosity (resembling in weightlessness and indeterminancy of association an adolescent's unformed lust), then, as the circles I drew around them became tighter, more mesmerized, the whirling of a still lava-hot asteroid around a breathing and baleful star, from an unconscious attempt to fill the hollow that was expanding within. The "new dance" that has, since then, divided and redivided into countless sub-species, was just beginning to spread like wild-fire through the greater London area (transplanted, like a rare virus, by some unknown process, only last year from the New World)—much as, in the early decades of the last century, the waltz raged like plague through the civilized nations of Europe, and was considered, as our own would be, "shocking," "daring," "scandalous." I think that the prototype was known as the "twist," although this may have become confused in the myriad variations that were to follow; but whatever it was, this new species of gyration was characterized by a curious split, one which seemed against the whole notion of the dance (the movement of opposites together into some variation of the unity the sexes are but fragments of): this was simple but admitted of countless deviations; it involved the separation of the two partners during the act itself. While these throbbing dances were in progress, that is, there was no contact whatsoever between the participants, who moved as whim or the vogue of the day directed—and not at all in response (and here the tantalizing split widened) to one's partner, who might, for all practical purposes, be on Venus or Vega, or any one of those other bobbing figures, as the one that twisted slowly before him. I cannot begin to describe the unearthly quiver my monstrously mutating soul underwent when first exposed to this phenomenon—which seemed to have been concocted for me in particular, for my own queerly flawed twist of vision, by some uncannily and devilishly inspired demiurge or semi-urge. When I look back on those years now—which seem all the more luridly lighted for being viewed through the darkened decades which were to follow—I think that my disembodied all-seeing presence must have been suspended in some unnoticed corner of these rooms, for despite their varying shapes and colours, despite the fashions of motion and sound which came and went, I am isolated, in my act of revisitation, upon that floor, which seems to extend dimly and infinitely in all directions, and is filled with shadowy figures turning like puppets on strings of ruthless melody; I am absorbed entirely into the act of seeing, absorbed so utterly that it seems nothing of myself is left, nothing at all except an invisible organ of perception, a gigantic vitreous slightly bloodshot eyeball revolving to the movements of other bodies, and that is nothing unless these bodies move and cause it to exist; for the eye, that most pure spirit of sense, I soon saw, does not behold itself, except reflected in the other's form. So did it come to seem to me, although, at the time, little enough had been revealed, only so much of an inkling as the abyss opened suddenly beneath the gazer over a stony parapet whose eyes had rested on a clear ocean of solid mist that abruptly a rip in the gleaming fabric had caused his entire perspective to totter deliriously on the very brink of balance, a glimpse into what lay, at untold depths, underneath, that sucked his vision into its sickening vortex; and yet, above, the sun beckoned yet further on those peaks of impossible longing, until one could not decide which was the more terrible, the height to be attained, or the depth to be sounded.

The earliest of these establishments—a scant half-block from Rushlight Street, separated by a wedge of triangular tree-shaded mall—was called "The Stair" (from the spiral that led up to the dance floor above the bar); it has since, of course, been replaced by a huge apartment complex, alliteratively named after an American chronicler of bullfights; indeed, all of these gathering-places, so brimming with vitality and humming human intercourse in their day, have given place to these later emptier developments, parking lots awash by day with the blue haze of gasoline exhaust and deserted by night, with only the isolated tinkle of a tin can blown by a restless wind to disturb their unpopulated reaches, or broad governmental slabs inhabited, seemingly, only by the ceaseless whirr of computers communicating with themselves. This prototype was founded at the turn of the century by a group of fashionable sportsmen (whose fields of endeavor shifted between bosk and bed), and they attained an instant popularity by attracting droves of unattached young women to their premises through the singularly inspired stroke of employing as bartenders and floormen handsome cleancut brawny athletes, who acted at once as protectors and as erotic objects. These in turn—secretaries from the central business district, nurses, coeds from nearby universities—became the magnetic focus for the one constant in an otherwise varied world, free-floating male lust, under the force of which the cash registers of this district rang merrily and madly, only to be extinguished by the same edict that was to eliminate all places of public entertainment, and indeed the conditions that these make for artistic expression. At that time, though, they were packed to the bursting-point with a tangle of sweating pumping bodies, above and around and through which an unvarying music flowed; while outside, lines might stretch as long as three city blocks, waiting to thrust their restless lengths within as the interior emptied. At the door two muscular bouncers would be checking "I.D.'s" (due to a curious local ordinance, modeled on one of the United States, restricting entry to those over 21 years of age). These years were the ones that saw the introduction of the "mini-skirt" and its near cousin the "micro-mini" (the terminology of which penetrated even the cloisters of Cambridge where a lecturer in the finer adumbrations of Thomism was wont to refer, amid an uncomprehending astonishment, to the "macro-cosm" and the "mini-cosm"—his one concession, I believe, to any event occurring after the Reformation); and for one who later was to experience the excesses of Puritanism as, earlier, those of Catholicism, it came as something of a shock (not to one's "morality," whatever that is, but to one's sense of differences, of disparates) to see, in the moth-attracting radiance of the gas-lamps, the naked shameless sunhonied flanks of these daughters of the rich and educated exposed almost to the crotch as they balanced on bar stools, rubbing their thighs together in time to the unrelenting music, or, on the floor, wiggling their rounded cruppers till the abbreviated skirt, the merest concession to modesty, would ride up and under the bouncing twin globes, surrounded with their own tantalizing numinosity of atmosphere. Once I had inserted my presence into these throbbing interiors I would work my way, surreptitiously, making the conflux of bodies aware of me as little as possible, to the whirling nucleus of the dance floor and, once there, find a vantage point from which I might most completely experience the raptures of perspective, of distance and proximity: an outline, a shape, into which I might flow, with the most exquisite of sensations, that of appropriating a form alien to our own, yet shaped exactly to the contour of our lack—the sigh of the key, not knowing its own serration, as it seeks and then finds the template from which it was made, feeling the tumblers fall into position with a quiver of at once fatality and freedom.

Moving into those darkly lighted caves was, I now recognize, like entering the flickering innards of a cinema, or the even tinier skull-like projection room of a solitary screening, alive with shadows; and as, in the revolution of seemingly endless reels of film, certain images are bound to recur, just so I began to notice a persistent variously shifting picture, or series of pictures. I forget exactly in which of these lairs it began to obtrude—whether in the Sitzmark, the Zoo, the School, the Rush-Up, or the Spirit of '76 (a bow to its transatlantic ancestor that has latterly transformed itself to "Mum's")—but standing there, amid a press of dancing shades, I was gradually made aware, after God knows how many fruitless impressions, of a recurrent pair: the girl alternately in an abbreviated mini decorated with suns or medallions, or tight pants and yellow top, hair falling shimmeringly below the shoulders, somewhat small-breasted, exquisitely narrow abdomen billowing out into the full splitting swell of hips, eyes long lashed, the rest of the face in shadow except for an aquiline outline of cheek; the man a huge Nordic specimen who variously appeared in this or that place as a bartender, a bouncer, a parking lot attendant; once in a while others, which may or may not have been produced by parthenogenesis from their original (sometimes squatter, sometimes taller, sometimes heavier, at others almost baby pink). She would usually face the surrounding crowd of watchers as though on display, shifting through ninety degrees of her invisibly woven circle so as to afford side and rear views; and although her partner invariably kept discreetly to one side, it seemed to me that, as the dance, and the delirium, proceeded to its melting climax, he always managed to obtrude his bulk upon the terminal image: a maddening practice that, position myself as I would, I could not nullify. There were other blockers as well, glossybottomed riverhorses in disguised maternity tents, knots of footballers with insignia emblazoned on the backs of their dayglo jackets (various bars sponsored different teams), businessmen, curiously anomalous in suits and ties, standing awkwardly about, beer warming in their sweaty palms; but none of these approached that one as an effective eraser, possibly because of his proximity to her image. They were playing, that fall, a sentimental favourite by a popular crooner which was constantly on the juke-box in between band sets, a quietly melancholy piece that counterpointed the emptiness outside against that lurking within; for through the window on the second floor, steamy with the heat of many bodies, I could see the blackness of the autumn of the year, the wind blowing restlessly and heartlessly through the deserted streets, the trees, still clingingly green, tossing to and fro, like patients afflicted with melancholia tossing on their long white rows of hospital beds under the ominous influence of a persistent nightmare; and though the year itself had been a very good one—its vernal essence distilled as into rows of musty old casks—yet it was as though, with the bringing of things to their fruition and harvest, we had been but hastening them to their bleak and lifeless end. Here, however, was a beginning of a different kind; and as I watched the growth of that fatal image, I was reminded, or rather would be, of nothing so much as the last decisive picture that haunts the seeing faculty as the eyes close sensuously into their voluntary darkness, the one that the devoted sleeper carries into the inner night of his stupendous palace, and that will carry him, as gently as a mother carries her child, into the dark current bearing him he knows not whither. Thus was I carried into the season deepening and withering all around me. First at one, then at another of these places I located, amid the whirl of alien bodies, the one that made the packed room empty; and it was even thus, as a mosaic is filled in gradually, the various fragments accreting separately to form a single symmetrical whole, that I began to glimpse the bitter truth concealed in those feminine, those undulating outlines. From the perspective I have now laboriously and painfully attained I am able to realize, for instance, that I could not have been viewing one character, but must have fused several into a single powerful figure (a sort of reversal of those films where a versatile actor plays a half-dozen parts during its course); for the one I began to track through the streets and winding alleys, at first desultorily, then with all the insistence of pointless lust, could not have been the same one who, for example, worked as a coat checker at the Rush-Up (I can still experience the shock of ungodly recognition as I saw, amid the rustling empty garments, the identical shape I had left but a few minutes before in the foyer of an exclusive hotel two blocks eastward). At the time, though, I can confidently state that I took such apparent bilocation entirely for granted, as if it were an astigmatism or blemish of the eyesight that one carried around continuously, and not an event in the world without that we are pleased to term "real."

On another evening, alive with flying grit and the flapping wings of torn newspapers rising in whirls and spirals around the wavering gas-lamps, I managed to track what I was beginning to regard as a recurrent fantasy to a lair on North Astor Street, a secluded lane of mansions and brownstones named after an American millionaire. The lobby, brocaded in black and red, was empty, but against its bare tiles yet lingered the tapping of retreating footsteps, and I bent, with some trepidation, over the names slotted next to the doorbells. I did not, thank God, have to look far. Outside, the wind, caught in the naked branches of an overarching oak, howled. There was no moon. It was late and I was already past due for a performance (a minor part in the burlesque comedy "Soilust And Dessicra"). I found a perch in a gnarled laurel tree to the rear of the building, three stories up. Just opposite, the window of her surprisingly tiny room was wide, and from behind the curve of a branch I peered within. A single lamp provided a withering yellow illumination. It seemed the entire room was dangled with clothes, hung from wires, knobs, overflowing from the half-opened drawers of dressers, depending from, and multiplied by, the unobtrusive crystal planes of mirrors; a rustling, breathing, sighing flutter, filled illusively with life by the chill presence entering at the vacant window, blouses puffed out and skirts swirled gracefully and emptily, a slip shaken in a sudden gust, a long length of hose rippled into an aery dance. It was as though the entire tapering building were in the act of lengthy respiration—or, rather, as if the huge painted pads of a clown's lips were invisibly pressed to the open aperture, and exhaling relentlessly into the helplessly trembling interior. For a long time I hung there, unable to move, hypnotized by the emptiness stirring so tangibly and untouchably, almost numb with the cold and the wind, tiny fragments of débris stinging my face and getting into my eyes. Then, just as my grip was loosening from the branch overhead preparatory to an ungraceful and necessary descent, I noticed what I should have been noticing, the window, closed but naked, one floor above, wherein a flash, a gasp of white lingered before being extinguished to glowing blackness. My chagrin and surprise were such that I nearly dropped to the brick piazza some thirty feet below (thus breaking my neck as well as my heart in the process); but I somehow managed to sink my claws into the bark and awkwardly, blindly, descend.

Other nights brought different fruit (those russet, bitter apples that, upon being split, either acidly blind or mellowly bathe the cultivator in washes of living light). It was exactly three years after the turn of the century, and three before her final disappearance into that other world (whence I vainly attempted to follow her—but that is reserved for another account entirely). We were then at the height of our success and popularity, and were sought everywhere by noble houses for private performances; our more general dramatic art had not yet suffered its latter neglect, and our daily matinées were invariably packed to the bursting point with a newly-created leisure class. Among that crowd might be glimpsed a conspicuously tall character dressed in French ruffs and cape, invariably in deep conversation with Burbage or one of the other actors; this was our former director of lighting Will Sly, the famous French impressionist and mime, who could so change his visage and manner that you would swear, during two successive moments of his act, that he was not one and the same person (in one routine, for example, he would play the parts of both the country squire who has caught a poacher on his grounds, and that of the coney-catcher himself; in another, a dissolute nobleman, reeking of sweat and brandy and cologne, seducing a simple Yorkshire serving-maid, and then the whitefaced wench herself, backing slowly to the bed, one hand over a heaving dimpled bosom); and it was not long thereafter that he was smilingly inserted into our group, first as versatile actor, then as assistant and finally stage manager, the director of all our shimmering veil of illusion. When I remember him it is as it were through an eyeshaped rent in some rich brocaded curtain, that allows the light of the pageant within to seep out, with all its amber accumulations of leaf and lymph, reproducing, in miniature skiagraph, the action transpiring on a larger scale at some unsuspected level of the interior; for he remains at that point of my memory's canvas which, by reason of its ocular position, arranges the rest around it by unblinkingly viewing it. At the time, though, his instrumentality lay chiefly in his drawing me into contact with an obscure inventor, Lee de Forest, whose main contribution was yet to have profound implications on my world; and it was, I think, significant, that it was simultaneous with my induction into the "singles bars" of the time that I began to frequent his sparsely furnished laboratory, a garret in some noisome corner of Cheapside that he had appointed with all the artifacts of his little-known art. He was of a diminutive stature, with a thick shock of steel-white hair falling loosely over his fragile dome, and the folds of his long sable cloak gave him an almost priestlike mien as he drew me beckoningly into the queerly resonant interior of his room. A single fanlight over the door spread its peacock's tail of colours and stained the worn carpet with a richer spectrum than it of itself possessed. A neon sign outside the one window pulsed redly and consistently, pumping a bloody light over the walls and ceiling. With one hand he fumbled for a match, with the other drew me in. The floor shook faintly to an invisible vibration, produced by the secret workings of a toy factory located in the basement of the same building. Then the gas jet caught and I saw, in its flame, innumerable blank and questioning eyes peering at me from every point of the room's perimeter. Its colourless flame ignited in each a minute flickering iris.

19

hese came to life, I discovered, upon depression of a master switch, and looked, not inward, but out, into a world far beyond the range of ordinary perception. They were the precursor, in fact, of the more recent "security systems" that have so pervasively infiltrated our institutions and buildings both here and abroad—those roving closed-circuit cameras that sleeplessly watch entrances, exits, glaringly illuminated interiors. At the time of my introduction, though—the early winter of 1903—

these portable viewers were still in an embryonic state, and monitored perhaps a dozen restaurants, public edifices, and apartment buildings throughout the City. I can still recreate a shiver of far-ranging perception as I recall the moment when my companion lit these screens that viewed so distantly and precisely—as if my sphere of awareness had extended to include the entire corpus of the metropolis itself. What a shock it was to me, then, when I discovered the object of my focus at the time, that I had followed fruitlessly till then, swimming now here, now there, into the various hidden eyes through which I peered! The orb that looked coldly into a fashionable East End Italian restaurant, with cascades of glittering Venetian crystal and murals of petrifacted Roman ruins, soon picked out a familiar shape, dressed in a gold uniform with wavy red edging around the pockets, neck and hem. The skirt was, I noticed, short, and the neckline cut deeply and narrowly down into the bodice. She moved quickly and nervously against a background of mirrors, drifting silver planes, rich leather, heavy curtains. One small oval glass reflected a rural and Virgilian scene—a herd of mythological cows grazing in a green and bowered Arcady. A bull, I was able to see, possessed a fine set of heavy swinging udders—a bow either to some obscure myth or the zoological ignorance of the painter. The owner was a corpulent man in his fifties, invariably dressed in a greasy tuxedo—his notion, I suppose, of British elegance. When he entered the picture—or at least that portion I was concerned with—his massive arm would fold around that slender golden figure and make it seem somehow tinier, duller. All this, remember, was revealed not wholly but in fragments—the various pieces corresponding to the different positions of the cameras. I often had the feeling that I was viewing these tantalizing scenes through the faceted eye of some immense insect—the cold observer of an alien world. She would arrive early in the morning—before seven—and begin her duties by filling up pots and shakers with sugar, salt, pepper. A sleepy expression would remain on her face until just before noon. In the afternoon she would serve cocktails in another room to groups of businessmen and tourists. It was harder to pick out her figure then because of the general gloom and the press of other bodies. At three or a little before she would get out and hurry down a long corridor decorated on one side with a single undulating mountain in the shape, I now recall, of a camel's back. One of the humps looked distinctly like a monk in the attitude of prayer or, perhaps, an ape dangling by one hand to an aery pinnacle. A leather door studded with brass rings would swing shut and leave an immense area of space empty. These were soon balanced with other scenes. Afternoons and evenings would be spent in gambling hells, casinos, and other low dives, among which figured the necklace of bars I myself was beginning to frequent. The most prominent of these was a huge emporium atop a manmade mountain of concrete and glass whose name formed a perfect palindrome (its original was located high in the Sierra Nevadas of the United States, on the shores of a lofty mountain lake); there she would rendezvous with her "steady" or another itinerant figure, drinking innumerable glasses of white wine as she sat before spinning wheels of red and black (upon which were painted garish visages of the goddess Fortune). Long rows of slot machines extended from east to west; these were haunted by restless shapes who inserted coins and depressed levers to make their invisible mechanism whirr impassively. Tables of green felt quivered silently under the impact of yellowed ivory dice. Croupiers with longhandled rakes, like bony and prehensile appendages, drew, as by magnetism, quantities of symbolic money into their orbit. Chandeliers, caught between planes of opposing glass, extended infinitely in each direction, from east to receding west. An ashtray rested at her elbow and slowly accumulated its ration of smouldering lip-printed cylinders. Because of the position of the camera her back was invariably toward me. Her hair fell long and straight in a goldenred cascade over her shoulders. A body intervened, then released that image. Someone bent down to the nape of her neck and seemed to drink. His shoulders were wide, his hair almost whitely yellow. The camera swung deliriously. A manufacturer's plate on the side of a machine came into focus: Nevada Mining Co.—maddening by reason of its meaninglessness. Still later another screen bloomed into flickering life. I am probably condensing several such sessions but in memory they retain a single ominous progression. Outside snow had begun to fall, and the flakes, drifting aimlessly in emptiness, were stained by the neon sign just outside the window. My silent companion seemed no more substantial than the images chasing themselves across the screen. The weather stations, I remember, were unanimous in their reports: snow was general over all the country and indeed, from east to west, covered it as with a shroud, and swept it into the dissolving ocean. It tapped against the cold pane so persistently that I thought the dead themselves were trying to enter. Then the terminal ocule (as it was technically called) swam into focus. The effect was that of peering through layered clusters of petals, or perhaps the cross-section of a vital organ, carrying on silently its inner processes. A series of veils blew ceaselessly against the camera's searching eye. A bird stood in one corner, gripping its perch with jewelled claws. Its head was shrouded in black velvet. The bulk of a young mastiff rose in another part of the room—a burly brindled animal shackled firmly into place by a stout chain and a thick studded collar. The window was open and seemed to be paned with a solid square of blackness. The flakes that bloomed therein appeared like the motes of fluff cast by the beam of an old projector, or the specks produced by the eyeball's capillaries thudding dully upon receiving an excess discharge of blood. I believe some foreign dignitary had occupied the room previously—the ostensible reason for the electronic eye, which peered out, or so I was told, from the impassive face of some Renaissance Venus—Botticelli or Giorgione (there is, of course, no way to check on this, short of entering the picture viewed). Through the window, obscured by veils of drifting snow, one could make out the glittering panoply of the City, outlined by the darker surrounding current of River. A solitary ship, probably Spanish because of its overhanging bulk, made its laborious way upstream, sails reefed to the wind now pouring from the west and straining with the effort of invisible bending rowers. Then a kindly wind or poltergeist blew a curtain aside and the room suddenly doubled in extent. A heap of clothes grew beside a sofa of indeterminate shape. The floor was of a peculiar dull parquetry, covered at odd intervals by dirty white throw rugs that resembled miniature squashed polar bears *en somnambule.* A chair to the left of the sofa had a jacket over its wide shoulders, and seemed to be watching the scene unfolding within. Methods of description, I have had cause to notice, are psychologically imprecise, precisely because what they describe are not detachable objects (if only they could be thus disembedded!) but impressions upon the impressionable subject; thus—in terms of the description only—there is no essential difference between a real and an imagined object, an event that happened and one that only might have occurred. I am here not only because of an absurd conjunction of events (the production of a mythical, if real, inventor with the flash of a conjuror's prestidigitating fingers—that inane patter going on all the while), but also because of their inexplicable absence—as the sense of poetic meter is effected not merely through the trite trochee or dull dactyl, but the valleys, the swooning hollows between, that curiously, with an uncanny imitation of living plasm, change shape and texture. Thus my description might be the result of any stray beam of light striking random incurious eyes: but that these are open, it might be you or anyone transfixed by the crossgridding of intersecting waves. Her lips were moving but, of course, no sound could be heard. A shadow bent over listening. Her face turned half away as if in fear of being struck or kissed. A series of shadows seemed to be watching. The delicate melting curve of cheek against the open window's blackness . . . Kissed? No. Better never. Better never to have kissed. Never to have kissed.

The overcoat hung on the chair moved as if animate. A black bulk before the eyes. Curse all obstructions (erasers, rags of forgetfulness). Then, with all the clarity of an anatomical drawing, she lay outstretched upon her naked bed. Everything was in order, I tell you, everything, from the white gasp of skin to the raven swoop of hair (produced by the monochrome iris through which I stared), and the eyes half open to expose their impassive whites; the curves, the curves swelled out and in with the exactitude of a compass's descriptive arc; the clear articulation of the tiny perfectly formed bones through smooth almost transparent skin; the hand held palm exposed, tenderly dewed with moisture; the hips with that peculiar incurving at the small of the back, as if to receive a fertile impulse;

the smallish breasts; the knees slightly bent. Then what was wrong? What was terribly, sickeningly wrong? Had the whole world gone mad, that I could not focus on it? A conspiracy, a collaboration to hide, to obscure, to taint, to adulterate. At the focal point, where all the lines swept together, and all the orbits ran into their dark radiating sun, something was monstrously out of place, something was monstrously mutated. My heart was almost battered out of its seat as I looked. A series of violent lurching thuds were indistinguishable from those of, say, a squadron of secret police battering down a door preparatory to a dawn raid (on "undesirable aliens"). "Isn't," a voice whispered at my side, a queerly effeminate voice, "isn't he lovely?" That ubiquitous overcoat gratefully filled the screen with its hairy bulk, that seemed, as the air filled and emptied it, to be breathing heavily. A door slammed. The lights abruptly went out. A hand found its way into my abysmal blindness and, as I did not stir, began moving downward, with all the delicate sensitivity and hesitation of a crab or some other exploring arachnid. The fluid from the warm river-current circulating outside was sucked up by the colder atmosphere and crystallized, then sifted down upon a sleeping City. A few flakes fell upon my arm but did not melt.

20

uch images make up, I discovered, one's life—or at least so much of one's life as one is aware of; and if the play of images upon the screen of one's consciousness seems random, an armful of autumn leaves, of disparate species, tossed to the winds, fluttering madly away out of sight, that is only because a connective thread or theme has not been found, that binds all the shapes into a varied whole, the fragments into one piece, the dazzling delirious colours into an unbroken spectrum arching the vault of one's imagination. And underneath? I hear a fair philosopher inquire (Truth's handmaiden, indeed, Truth's whore). Underneath, my dear, is a mess, if you inquire too deeply; in truth, I saw a woman flayed the other day for a petty or imagined offense, and you would not believe how much it altered her appearance for the worse; all those tubes and conduits, and delicate interconnective tissue, became so much rank and steaming meat; indeed, as the grisly operation drew to its conclusion, I formed the unshakable opinion that it would be far more advantageous, from the point of view of virtually any system of aesthetics, had she been filled with nothing more substantial than gas (and in fact does not the Philosopher himself term man a "speaking bladder"?) Such a gruesome process of denudation—the opposite of the effect I am attempting here, the weaving of a rich garment of associations—is strongly reminiscent, or would become so, of the series of civil disturbances which were so radically to transform the City and indeed all the surrounding country as the century wore into its third and then fourth decades. I had flown in from Los Angeles the very month that the Parliamentarians had seized control of the House of Commons, by the series of manipulations and delays which had come to characterize that Party; and as the plane touched down on a newly created field on the outskirts of London I was rudely shocked at the queer and dangerous turn History had led my erstwhile country into. The brownshirts which were then beginning to populate the cities of Central Europe were here producing their first ugly excrescences, under the influence, although we knew it not then, of the embittered Austro-Irish interloper Cromwell, who had been impelled into petty politics by a combination of the military defeat of his class and country by the Allied powers in 1919, and his utter failure, because of his utter mediocrity, in the profession of his choice, that of artist and designer. As I boarded a topheavy omnibus *en route* to the City—my sudden return was impelled by a much-needed revision of the so-called "First Folio," which had been issued, as I have mentioned, in 1923—I was struck by a phenomenon well-nigh staggering to my native-bred sensibility: the majority of that vehicle's occupants did not speak any dialect of English I had ever heard, but rather some unwieldy Teutonic crossbreed, in which Gallic and Anglican flashes occasionally gleamed, but for the most part as outlandish and cacophonous a collation of syllables as I have ever endured, reminding one not of the harmonious synthesis, the delicately powerful merging of meaning and form which language, or our language at any rate, ideally constitutes, but rather the grinding and rending and flying apart of molecules in mutual abhorrence, the chaos of some universe of anti-matter fragmented by the deadly radiance of a black and negative sun. And yet these were, or my eyes deceived me, born and bred Englishmen. A Yorkshire lass leant on her beau's arm, a ruddy soldier from the Midlands; navvies on a half-holiday jammed into one corner, their raucous conversation impossible to decipher; bankers and businessmen returning from commercial trips abroad, their lips twisted into strange shapes, their fingers counting over unknown foreign currencies (although, for all I know, they may have been reciting poetry to each other). Indeed, it was not like returning home at all, but rather like entering, for the first time, the alien confines of a different country altogether—one that, for all practical purposes, might not have been discoverable on the face of the globe itself.

As the 'bus slid into the Charing Cross depot (a newly-created icosahedron of steel and glass overlooking the River) I was shocked at the changes that had been wrought, during my protracted absence, upon the body I had once known and loved. The lanes, that had limpidly effloresced, in vegetal curves and whorls, from the main arteries and thoroughfares, had now unaccountably straightened themselves, until they resembled the limbs of a corpse stiffened in rigor mortis; and the flickering gas-lamps, that had flowered nightly along those leisurely undulations with crests of ghostly flame, had been replaced by the ghastly uniform pallor of electric arc-lights. And the trees! where were those stately collonades of elms and birches, trembling aspen and the more massive overhanging oak, that had formed rustling, sighing arches, and mosaics of leaf and light, vast windy cathedrals indeed for the lay worshipper to wander under? In their places were monolithic pillars of dense black granite festooned with interconnecting wire—the neurons, I was told, for the new system of communication that now obtained throughout the metropolis. And in the tiny flowering jewels, the meticulously tended and sculptured parks that were wont to decorate and fertilize the City's shapely anatomy, were now, in place of blooming beds of fire and amber and turquoise, the uniform slabs of concrete that have come to typify the form that London had evolved into.

But my greatest dismay was reserved for my inspection of what had been the theatrical district, bounded roughly by the intersecting branches of the Thames. On the surface, it is true, it had not changed as radically as one might suspect from the foregoing (this was, after all, the architectural showpiece of London). The usage, however, to which these venerable structures were given, with the accompanying internal transformation, determined in no small degree their effect upon one's naked perception. Thus, while the external shape of certain antique buildings might be respected (the Rookery, for example, a wrought-iron and rosestone masterpiece dating back to the end of the last century), their rich core of associations was utterly eviscerated and laid to waste, for their interiors—those living plasms of light and shade and stone filagree—were, in all cases, sucked out, to be replaced by what, for lack of a better term, I will call Newtonian space (the geometric void described by an obscure physicist of the 18th Century). The Rose Theatre, for instance—or what had been the Rose (it was now a motel or a mausoleum or a municipal hall)—had, as one penetrated its familiar ruddy exterior (those scrolls and salient curves, those deepest leaded irises, with their flickering flames behind), nothing of the inner life it had once possessed. Where once the solid space within was flooded with broad planes of amber and rosy light (thus one imagines the deeply stained light of the outer world penetrating to the heart where it is in darkness transformed), catching and stroking to a second life the woven glinted details in the warm folds of hanging brocaded curtains and tapestries, exploding against fugitive mote-shapes drifting in the luminous air, absorbed into the deeply softly polished surfaces of moulding and panelling, finding stray bits of embedded glass to ignite into miniature suns, glassy green, marine blue, or those yellow Venetian waves of haze and honey; where it had illuminated, randomly and richly, that focus for so many transient eyes, that portion of the imagination's interior where we evoked our passion's enactment, and where, on the field of so many witnessing wondering heads, it had rested, as though to bring them to fruition and harvest in one and the same act, and, on the walls and ceiling, were revealed no barriers to the mind's expansion, but rather illuminated windows opening out onto the starry mythological beasts of the heavens, now was made empty and sterile through a subtle insinuating metamorphosis: an exhibition-hall for automobiles or hardware or textiles, perhaps, the curved inscribed shell of the interior bricked in with cinder blocks or plastic or structural steel, echoing with electronic voices paging for one or another visiting "V.I.P."

The City, indeed, as I began to wander through this once-familiar district, now beginning to be streaked with the ghostly lines of hard-driven snow, had transformed itself radically since my abrupt departure some twenty-odd years earlier. It had always been a metropolis of great congregations and gatherings, and in this it had not, at least on the surface, changed; but now these great comings-together were not those of the theatre and the arts, or the progress of some noble family, visiting dignitary, or that of the ruling house itself, as it had been until but recently, but those of business or trade conventions that gathered their members from the entire inhabited globe (concentrated numerically among a peculiarly ubiquitous "Midwestern" type dressed in expensive and ill-fitting clothes and with a standard "crew" or "flat-top" haircut which revealed, beneath the stubbly surface, the pale pebbly lunar surface of scalp)—until London was to forget her noble heritage, the bequest of artists and kings, and call herself "Convention City." Without the great halls and hotels, however, all was empty and unpopulated—the result, in part, of the new edicts and curfews sent out from the sequestered conclave of the Parliamentarians (later they were to call themselves, after their originals in Germany, National Socialists and then the brutal-sounding dissyllabic "Notzi," a coinage of the Lord Protector who was fond of eviscerating words into new and grotesque shapes—not to mention other more complex organisms). I walked north from the Bus Depot along Bishopsgate Street, crossing as I did so the northern branch of the River; and as

I gazed up and down its dark swelling extent, obscured by veils of drifting snow, I was suddenly able to see, through random vents, that its liquid length was pierced by many new bridges and crossways, and as my gaze extended to the muffled horizon I saw that it was hidden completely under these bands of unvarying iron. Still, closer at hand, it was comparatively free of obstructions, and in its dark cold current were reflected the ghostly masses of overhanging warehouses and exhibition halls, the most massive of these being the immense squat bulk of the Merchandise Mart, constructed with ill-gotten war profits immediately after the First World Conflict. There was little or no traffic, and this passed me sparsely and silently, yellow headlamps lowered furtively, the inhabitants invisible in black shiny glass. The stiff angular shadows of derricks stood on the carapaces of some buildings, and on others cylindrical water-tanks, left over from the days when highpowered pumps had not been invented to supply their denizens with water. Blue lights drifted here and there on the periphery of my wandering vision, the emblem of the newly-motorized "SS" troops that now patrolled the greater portion of the City's corpus. As I walked past Ohio and Ontario Streets I noticed, beckoning with jewelled fire through white snowy swaths, a familiar marquée; it was not, though, the Swan Theatre that I had known of old (in whose gracious spacious wings I had so often lurked, waiting for a chance glimpse to bloom upon the darkness), but a building called the "Image" (at the intersection of Bishopsgate and that avenue named after an Indian tribe which I have an odd scruple against pronouncing just now). It had, after its transformation from brilliant theatre to ill-lit movie house, been used for the screening of foreign films; but this somewhat elevated usage had deteriorated into semi-pornographic sexcapades, until little of its original function could be descried in the coupling of banal images on the stained and tattered screen. The names "Marlene Dietrich" and "Emil Jannings" glowed luridly from its perimeter, two Teuton stars of doubtful repute; it was, insofar as memory serves, a murky pornocopia, with lots of gloomy German atmosphere, about the seduction and corruption of an essentially innocent if simple-minded *Profesor* by little more than the white flicker of the inverted V a pair of shapely naked gams forms: a dull bit of sordid sport, if one goes in for that sort of thing (I still recall with depression the comic mournful lust of that solemn yokel, crowing in the barnyard of his sullied, rather useless ideals, German metaphysics of the usual sort, his unspeakable desire—and the masculine, or rather masculinized feminine figure lifting one shimmering leg against the applauding blackness, encircled by a garter whereon bloomed a single banal rose). This, and other indications I found throughout the district represented, although I did not clearly realize it at the time, a tendency, slight at first but increasingly irresistable, which had grown with the century, that found its clearest expression in the accumulation of English real estate by foreign interests (this was paralleled, to take but one example, by the gradual gaining of control over the machinery of domestic government by the foreign usurper Cromwell). These were dominated through the local firm of Burbage and Rubloff, which quietly began, after the War, to accumulate scattered parcels of property; and I am reminded by this insidious process of nothing so much as the slow luxuriant unfolding of a cancerous growth in its unsuspecting host, as now one vital organ, one extremity, is gradually usurped and supplanted, until where once the organism, in its splendid symmetrical anatomy, proclaimed its varied unity in every gesture, the flow of all its life-processes, it now became but the loosely-assembled fragments of any stray aggregate of molecules. If one were to gaze at a map, as I am doing now in retrospect, one could see, as though one were inspecting the x-ray of some yet unimagined creature, the deadly clouded milky fungus spreading, from Walton Street and the easternmost extent of Cheapside, where, under one of its many dummy corporations, whole strips of ancient buildings were being razed to prepare the foundations of what was to become, after the War, "Sandhog Village" (named after a mediocre but popular poet of the American Midwest), to, on the other extreme, from Oak Street all the way south to Grand Avenue, the land-fill project which was even then reclaiming from the River's bounty additional territory to aggrandize. The Hancock Building, long since completed, loomed over the River, its summit crowned with a searching beacon whose eye was never lidded, so tall that from its height one could view four adjacent counties. Further south along Michigan Avenue the Standard Oil Building was being constructed on a corner of this land-fill; the lease was, again, held by these irrepressible entrepreneurs. Within its shadow, to the north, thrusting into the River's bosom, the peninsula of Navy Pier stretched, against whose docks were tethered the shipping of the world. And along "Theatre Row" itself, crowding out the defenseless huddled structures I had known so intimately, loomed the stone-and-steel bastions of governmental agencies and apartment complexes, gigantic garages and, although it was kept a secret then, disguised factories for the production of munitions and war *matériel.*

The City had become, I saw, virtually unrecognizable; and if I linger on this particular spool of impressions it is only because, within this mutation, another beloved body lingered, not yet entirely assimilated by its digestive processes (as, in reconstructing the evolution of a particular elusive species, the passionate scientist, or scientist of passion, may note and record traces, vestiges of earlier stages of development hidden here and there in the anatomy he is studying); indeed, its present state reminded me of nothing so much as the vast metropolis situated on the shores of a large inland lake of Northern America, a heterogeneous heap devoted now almost entirely to commerce and trade. Here, in the whirring inanimate dynamo the City had evolved into, inhabited, as it seemed, by stiff automata, pure surface phenomena with no depth to them, was stated plainly what had only been hinted at before; what I had felt growing within my own consciousness, with many monstrous mutations and foliations, coldly and clearly, like an immense crystal that gathered all illumination and colour to itself, was here externalized, made solid, something to block the rays of the sun and cast a shadow; for now I saw, with a clarity none the less blinding for being tardy, that I had prepared the way without knowing it for a great satirist and master of irony, whose print I saw apparent all around me, for master works stir vaguely in many before they grow definite in one man's mind.

The transformation from the one to the other was nowhere

more apparent than in the few isolated jewels that formed the theatrical life of the region, shortly to be closed entirely by the Edict of 1942. Most of these had been given over to the screening of pornographic films and an occasional burlesque house; the remaining theatres, set back from the main thoroughfare secretively and protectively, were devoted to satires and comedies (the forgettable flatlands of Beaumont and Fletcher, Webster and Eliot), with one or two of these, since the War, specializing in "avant-garde" spectacles and dramas of the absurd. If, before, in the early years of the century, these tendencies were barely beginning to pronounce themselves, as the elusive subject of these pages shimmered, changed in outline, and began that slow inevitable withdrawal which was only to end with her explosive exit from the world, here they had come full circle and attained their fullest expression, as the moon, in passing through her phases, attains to her darkest and brightest at opposite points of her cycle. As it chanced, my arrival in London was synchronous with the opening of Alfred Jarry's *Ubu Roi,* at what was now called the Théâtre de L'Oeuvre (it had been bought by Burbage from Will Sly upon the latter's death in 1916). Here the Word, it seemed to me, received its most total fragmentation, for the theory of language which treats its subject as discrete unrelated phenomena to be combined "aleatorically" here found its perfect expression (I will not give samples since any talentless Yahoo can toss alphabet blocks into his blockhead's hat and juggle them to his inane satisfaction). I had found simple lodgings at the Hôtel Cèdre, where I had stayed upon first arriving in the City many years ago (it was located above the now-moribund Café Royale). After a frugal meal, I issued early into the already-darkening streets; a partial black-out or "brown-out" was in effect, and this gave an even gloomier aspect to the chill wintry canyons that divided the monolithic buildings. A scant three blocks east I could hear the River groaning as ice-floes impacted, building a mighty glacier-like mountain which was eventually to encircle the entire central portion of the metropolis. The snow, that had fallen throughout the waning dimming afternoon, had visibly slackened, but still drifted here and there in long white blurring streaks, like lines or motes of static in a film that has aged imperceptibly with the years. The luminous top of the Hancock Building was shrouded in a cold white cloud of vapour; I could see its head burning ghostlike within that helmet. It had been transformed into a warlike fortress, using its elevated perspective to watch for hostile ships-of-the-line, destroyers, and the newly-introduced submarines or "U-2's"; before the decade was out there was to be installed in its upper portions the first of those probing devices that could feel through the night like a blind man's fingers, the great sonar and radar cones.

The theatre was situated off the main sweep of Rushlight Street, so secluded and withdrawn that I almost overlooked it in my blurred passage. A garnet glow attracted my attention, however, down a narrow slit between two irregularly-placed buildings (where a bar called the Backstage had been located of old), and I followed its watery reflections against the glazed walls back to a miniature marquée. There, a wildly-attired group was loosely congregated; they were dressed in a theatrical fashion, but one which transformed them into dolls, marionettes, toys, fantastic automata; mice waltzing with porcupines, ducks with dogs; skull-capped *saltimbanques* lolling against patchworked harlequins, purple-lipped *soubrettes* in wire corsettes embracing stiffly what appeared their reflections, wooden-faced figures clacking thick lips together, pliable floppy ones with dry stuffing seeping out of their joints, weeping powdery tears. Wires, almost invisible in the half-light, ascended upward into darkness. A small orchestra sawed and shrilled in the gloomy rear. On an elevated dais to the left a cameraman had erected his equipment: hooded phallic eyes that swept aimlessly in half-circles, now to the light, now to the dark. A clacking sound could be heard in the background, a noise as of a toy train revolving endlessly on its prescribed circuit, its thin yellow pencil of a headlamp piercing its minuscule portion of night, always illuminating the same sequence of images (thus the widening cone from the eye of an ancient projector: now this, now that image is caught in the flood of its flickering emotion, which exists only to outline the artifacts of its desire). A hum, too, as of innumerable miniature mechanisms in whirring activity was audible as I drew nigh the low-browed building peering out at me from under overhanging eaves.

Within, the effect was immediately one of incredible compression and condensation; the darkness seemed thick, syrup-like, a sooty substance that had bits of grit and abrasive granules floating in its viscous fluid, and this heavy concentrate was only accentuated by the pinpoints of floating luminence that hovered in random clusters here and there. As my eyes adjusted to this murky atmosphere I saw that the interior was crowded with the same stiff figures I had noticed without; here, however, they seemed more perfectly suited, the exaggerated, stiff inhabitants of a doll house or toy factory. Then the red curtain rose like a waterfall of blood in reverse. The ceiling and walls could now be seen more clearly; imps and demons, gnomes and gargoyles leered and peered from every conceivable angle, a spilled cornucopia of bulbous noses, wintry joints, livid lips in hysterical profusion, exactly the scene (I thought to myself) of a charnel house just after a miscellaneous and random butchering. The stage curtains were reproduced in various vermilion hues throughout (depending, I suppose, on the different stages of coagulation in the arterial rivers flowing from a slowly chilling corpse). Midgets in a sort of soiled yellow uniform marched up and down aisles, directing the costumed patrons to their places. The orchestra had moved to a pit just under the proscenium; their sawing and bobbing and tootling continued unabated. Feathered plumes and corsages (made not of flowers but clusters of wire) kept ragged jerking time. A confused clearing of throats could be heard in a kind of mock counterpoint. Someone snored stentoriously in the rear—or else was breathing very heavily. My own lips were parched, I remember, as by a long drawn-out desert wind that has passed over uncounted thousands of miles of arid sandy waste, a white and sterile sheet rippling monotonously to the horizon of one's perception—the very desert of one's need, I like to think, out of which one builds the fertile image of what he lacks.

Invisible cameras whirr. Film slaps. Light weaves erratically around on the stage. Slowly it is becoming occupied—but not by the usual characters; as much as I am able to pick out, objects, momentarily animate, scampered and clattered in reckless, nervous, jerky vitality about the resounding boards; mops and feather-dusters, pots and stiff stately brooms waltzed, bumped into each other, whirled madly, sadly, throwing up a cloud of dust as they did so, as if possessed of a common demon, some humorless post-Reformation poltergeist now merely running down on steam left over from a more vital, believing age (thus had the "kitchen-sink" dramas and comedies of the century's opening evolved)—or as if a housewife, gone batty from boredom, were tossing things about her cold-water flat, except in that case she must have been invisible. Then the assemblage fell silent. A word was spoken. The light dimmed. Wind blew through a mock window to the left; brown burlap billowed inward. A mop balanced precariously on one leg bowed his powdered head—not ordinarily given to becks, let alone nods. The tenuous light reached to the rear and drew a vague booth hung in dusty mahogany curtains. They rustled in and out as if they were part of a breathing organism, then parted slowly, cautiously, revealing their warm musty interior.

She was incredibly old, but had lost none of her yellowed, almost amber beauty—although perhaps this was the effect of the thick caked layers of makeup that obscured the clear face underneath; it was, indeed, almost as though she were being viewed not through the medium of our skittish three dimensions but through the faded celluloid squares she had been wont to inhabit. For a long time she sat motionless, as stiff as the stuffed owl that perched awkwardly on one corner of the booth, her face half-hidden in shadow, her lips parted but with no sign of breath whatsoever. I noted her dress: deep purple edged with glowing scarlet. Her lips compressed suddenly.

"Venus atop Mars in the first quarter. The royal houses . . . uninhabited. Temples in ruin. Apollo hollow, Ceres sere . . ."

No, she could not have said that, or indeed any other gibberish: her mouth, I remember distinctly, was closed tightly the entire time—or if it did open, the words were not synchronized with its motions, as if a director whose attention has wandered were to absentmindedly dub in any haphazard collation of noises.

"I see a great empty space . . . I see plains without end . . . I see mountains piercing the sky, cliffs of fall . . . I see snow, eternal snow . . . beyond . . . "

On she droned, in a cracked voice (or something droned through her), chain-smoking brown cigarettes all the while, cylinders of fragile ash growing in her stiff curved claw, on which burned rubies and garnets and unwinking cats' eyes. The audience seemed to have fallen into a trance, or perhaps it was only asleep.

There was, abruptly, a tremendous thunderclap. Plaster shook from the ceiling. Curtains on all sides rippled to the floor, revealing an ugly brick substructure. A huge warrior in black mail materialized in the midst of the débris onstage She stood behind him, dwarfed by his bulk, and directed him in the activities that followed. Her face had drained utterly white—or perhaps powder from the falling plaster gave it a new coat and colour. With powerful sweeps of his arms this large automaton, his bristly face carapaced in iron, gathered certain limp sagging members of the audience and stuffed them in a bulging sack. Cheers broke out from those remaining. Once his arm slipped and a neck snapped loudly, with a dry hollow popping noise, as the head of some unresisting unfortunate was wrenched backward at an unnatural angle. The applause redoubled. In the excitement the woman had, I noticed, vanished, but her robe lay in a heap on the stage. There were stains around the middle and lower portions. Mirrors maneuvered. Whips whistled. Portions of someone's anatomy—a buttock, an arm, a belly convulsed in terror—were fragmented by their canny planes. Soon they were rivuleted with blood or red ink. Sighs, hisses. I rose to leave, slipped on ooze that coated the trembling floor. Shrieks began to ring out in earnest now. I saw that brownshirts armed with long leathery saps were darting here and there, striking indiscriminately. I slipped again. I was halfway to the exit when it dissolved in a flash of absolutely white heatless brilliance.

21

he spoor grows weaker after that—this is, after all, my last attempt to resuscitate its lingering aroma, its unearthly stench—much as the flow of a once-unified film, resplendent with light and shade, and stipples of those nervous dancing motes of vitality that are the sign of a living creature, is gradually chopped and segmented by a casual butcher of an editor, until only disconnected flashes and glissades of its original symmetry can be discerned through the flicker of those horrid scissors. As this circular, or rather elliptical chain of images evolves—much as one conceives the genesis of the solar system, the lumps of molten gas flung out in excess of desire cooling imperceptibly over the untold aeons that are but moments to such stupendous organisms, then assuming random inevitable orbits around their mother sphere—I am increasingly reminded that the very language of its composition, let alone its subject matter, must remain incomprehensible to the erstwhile members of my species; that if I am talking to any hypothetical listener or reader I must, in effect, have invented him, for certainly the inhabited globe is devoid of that once populous creature. Written in a dialect unparalleled for precision, complexity, symmetry, and those beauties of vowel and veracity that are not to be found in any other known medium (and that make it, along with the Arabic and Chinese, the mother-lode of the richest poetic tradition in the world), its universality that, in a network of fine golden wires fretted this globe, has been through a quirk of history relegated to the stagnant linguistic backwaters inhabited by such curious specimens as Manx, Lower Northumbrian, and Choctaw, by the Teutonic glottals of a second wave of barbarian invaders. Well do I recall the unearthly whine of the low-flying "buzz-bombs" that, like a wave of locusts, presaged their first assault, landing under the shadow of Dover's white cliffs in the first chill of the autumn of 1939!

France had fallen only the month before and now was ruled by the puppet-government of Vichy; and this flabbergasting collapse was counterpointed, across the Channel's margin, by the traitor Chamberlain turning the reins of government over to the interloper Cromwell, who had but recently consolidated his control of Parliament through the House of Commons (that of Lords, as always the last bastion of conservatism, as yet held firm). What formed the final wedge, though, that was to split the country into warring factions was the defection of the Church's power and authority to that of the many Dissenter sects: these were united in their opposition to the union of Church and State in the person of the royal Head of both, and all the golden pomp and pageant, including that of our own theatre, that it represented; and this grievous defection was emblemized by the treacherous alliance between a number of High-Church dignitaries and powerfully-placed militant members of the trading classes who were, nominally at any rate, Dissenters all. Soon the breach in the country's fabric widened irreparably, and civil war raged throughout the City and the surrounding country; columns of Parliamentarians, Cromwell's newly-created middle class army, clad in iron grey, wound over the smoking and desolated countryside, while only sporadically, among the houses of great nobles and country squires, armed resistance was beginning to be mustered, supported by the same staunch yeomanry that had been England's strength of old. Rallied by the inspiring though somewhat ineffectual leadership of Charles, the second ruler of the House of Stuart, they had managed to overcome the grim doggedness of those iron troops (which included such techniques as "parched-earth" warfare, the burning of fields and foodstuffs before an advancing army, or around a retreating one), through a series of lightning-quick brilliant maneuvers that the Royalist forces contrived under the consummate generalship of the King's young nephew Rupert, fencing in, as it were, the leaden advance of the rebels with blinding flashes of light, when the death-stroke fell, from the most unexpected quarter of all: invasion on England's vulnerable southern coast. Simultaneously, from the fastnesses of northern Scotland, ragged legions of dour Highlanders descended through the Cheviot Hills upon the distant northern border, the hard-core remnant of rebels from conflicts nearly two centuries earlier, bearing broad claymores on their powerful knotty shoulders, kilts swirling, led by the banshee wail of bagpipes and the leadership of a curiously effeminate, almost dainty Scottish nobleman, Sir James Boswell (a remote ancestor forms the subject of a biography by the great Litchfield lexicographer and critic). Soon the country was divided as by malignant invading microbes; Dover and Ramsgate fell almost instantly under the *blitzkrieg* of armoured panzer divisions, to be followed with sickening celerity by the absorption of Portsmouth, Plymouth, Bideford and the major arteries that fed the greater London metropolis. I have before me, in the beleaguered war-room of my memory, an illuminated map of the series of rapidly shifting contours that my mother-land had become, with ash-grey, lead-grey, clay-grey for the encroaching control of the alien (and his domestic counterparts), and blood-red, fire-red, sun-red for the valiant resistance of the indigenous Royalist forces (these included the disbanded theatrical companies who exchanged their cardboard armour and wooden swords for more durable stuff). Sussex, Kent and Essex are blighted before the invader's mailed advance, one reminiscent not of the brightly decorated hammered Renaissance foliature of the opposing forces, but rather the dull massive carapace of various antediluvian Coleoptera, creatures adapted to endure through persistance and indifference to local conditions rather than any skill or sagacity of their own; as yet Berkshire, Surrey, Suffolk, and the western counties held out; and from Wales into the Midlands territory is actually gained, a rose-bright edge of flame bursting across the countryside with almost vegetal splendour.

I was employed at the time as entertainment director of the Shropshire regiment (whose prowess is celebrated in a famous volume of poems by a Cambridge classics professor), and my duties brought me into increasing contact with the various skirmishes and sorties that characterized our campaign: riding out on chill autumn evenings, the Hunter's moon high and white and baleful over the billows of the darkly cresting hills, with their foam of bitter green furze, the silver tympany of the horses' harness keeping musical notation of our progress, the muffled thud of hooves impacting against the frost-rheumed turf, warm breath vapourizing in icy plumes above our bent intent heads, bracken occasionally crackling dryly as we swept through a new arc of field, or, fording streams whose musical gurgle was muted by the skin of brilliant ice accumulated in the shallows, fragmenting the cold white stone of the subaqueous moon, that troubled the living stream, into splinters of blinding quartz; then the raid itself, the horses' hooves wrapped in burlap, our swords shrouded in thick capes, the enemy camp silent and watchful, the sentinels struck down without a sound, then the bitter explosion of conflict as we swooped down upon their slumbering tents, laying torch and steel to the left and right, the cherry-red, rose-red flames leaping out into the offended night, the screams of the butchered horses, the half-dressed footsoldiers fleeing panic-stricken into the frozen fields to be cut down in mid-flight by our relentless horsemen, falling by tree, by stone, by icy pond, darkening the smoking ground with the liquid of their expirations.

As the months of conflict lengthened into years the enemy introduced peculiarly repulsive methods of warfare, the most abhorrent to the native citizenry being the hiring of alien mercenaries who soon, because of the uniforms they affected, became known as the Blacks and Tans. These brought into our country techniques of interrogation previously unknown outside the notorious cellars of the Gestapo in the innermost recesses of Teutonia: immersion in water, exposure to extreme cold or heat, long periods of questioning during which the specimen was fastened in the intersecting grids of blinding arc-lamps, the application of electrodes to the testicles, etc.—all the banal and brutal psychology, in fact, which has been the doubtful blessing of the modern police state; and I recall with some reluctance scenes sketched with bitter corrosives into my memory, the utter stillness of a provincial midnight split with the exhaustless scream of a creature, one could not tell whether male or female, pushed to the limits of mortal existence, or, down secluded lanes that one dared not probe further, behind discreet leafy curtains which once had shrouded a more gentle activity, the moans of some creature that had been beaten into a sponge and then wrung of its few poor tortured particles of information. The hard core of resistance against such tactics came, oddly enough, from a group of expatriate Irishmen (just as the artistic exploits of the earlier part of the century had issued from equally alienated natives of that beleaguered island); and it was my fate to be an unwilling witness to the betrayal and wanton murders of the members of one "cell," including one that had composed verses in Gaelic; I put their names down here not because of any unique accomplishment of theirs (they were but pub-frequenters, middle-class club-frequenters, and as for the verses of that affectedly wild Gael, they were but the minor stuff of all provincial poetry), but because the momentous event in which they were unwittingly involved has transformed them: they are changed, changed utterly, into a terrible beauty, MacDonagh and MacBride, Connolly and Pearse, changed from the petty days that had till then been their lot. The willows were green on the banks of the stream where we found them, green as though fed by a mixture of their own life's blood, so lately spilled, and the crystal braid of its current. The trampled muddy ground, the clumps of turf torn up, the bushes violently parted by the stuttering of hysterical sten guns, an empty dress drenched with beads of condensed mist embroidered with wild nodding poppies, and a strand of golden hair running through the soil, told their tale all too plainly, the steelshanked hook hidden under its bait of white flesh, a creature out of some tale of older times vanishing through the glimmering air into the mist and magic of her begetting, leaving the grim reality unmasked underneath, piercing them with its bone and monstrous beauty.

What gave these Teutons, indeed, their inevitable victory, was not merely their superior military juggernaut (in whose unfeeling pincers the once-unmarked body of our fair isle writhed), but treachery and division from within, an internal susceptibility that allowed these insect-like, insect-mailed invaders undeserved entry, through duplicity and deliberate lowering of resistance, as though an originally vital organism were to purposefully lose its immunity to an alien and malignant strain of microbes, or some rare crossbreed of virus; a genetic deficiency; a link missing from the strand, the sentence-like inflection of chromosomes, until the parasitic swarm overwhelmed and assimilated to its myriad crawling pseudo-life its irreplaceable host, like those insects that propagate by ovulating in the eggs of other species, invariably bees, leaving their young to suck nourishment from that foreign store. So had it transpired here, in the native land of my birth, until the beloved contours of that ovule grew blurred into a different species altogether. I recall, in this connection, one scene in particular, in which the metamorphosis from the one to the other was most clearly delineated. The winter of the last year of war was drawing to a bitter close, and spring was raising, with its blighted green, a false hope throughout the torn countryside. Capitulation was expected daily among realistic strategists; the counties surrounding London were occupied by the antlike tents of the enemy, the air by the reek and smoke of fields and fodder laid to the torch. Only in the central City opposition held firm, supported mainly by bands of roving guerrillas, like the last few phagocytes fighting off a mortal infection, that made existence impossible for the hostile forces pressing in from without. All day we had fought, shaken by the bone-wrenching thuds of V-2 bombs falling all around us, striking indiscriminately cathedrals and tottering tenement buildings. The King had been captured and executed only the week before, but yet we held out, impelled less by any present hope than by an unquenchable memory of something that had been, the Queen who yet ruled in our hearts. I had been sent with a raiding party into the occupied districts across the western branch of the Thames; and as the day attained its leaden noon and wore on toward dusk, was forced to take cover with a few comrades in the gutted shell of an abandoned apartment complex. Immobilized by the heavy concentrations of enemy troops without, we gazed through the cracked cobwebbed panes of the basement with sinking hearts as endless columns of tanks, trucks and jeeps wound eastward toward the last pockets of resistance, all painted a uniform grey with the iron fylfot on turret or hood; and it was then, I believe, that the last gauzes of illusion fell from our eyes as, hour after hour, those leaden troops streamed by (dubbed after their leader the "Ironsides"), the very bones of the street and surrounding buildings trembling under their implacable impact, and, as day blurred toward dusk, a buzzing chant arose from that mighty column, a great unholy battle-hymn that affronted our ears with its harsh burden, shaking the very panes in the crevice where we cowered: a dirge as of countless insect voices raised in groaning stridulation to some carapaced divinity, for, indeed, it was as incomprehensible as if it had been produced by the tiny whistling tracheae of such an order. What threw us into breathless despair, however, and overwhelmed our last lines of inner resistance, was the vision granted us as dusk possessed the streets. We had cursorily taken notice that the building across the street had been appropriated as some kind of headquarters for the ingress of aliens; but our attention that long afternoon had been absorbed by the mammoth flow of men and munitions on the street, and beyond the fuzzy recognition of long official Mercedes limousines, flags, insignia, we took no further notice, intent upon the more manifest preparations and our own highly dangerous position. With the transformation of day to dusk, however, and the passage into obscurity of the last of that barbarian train (one of a quartet of pincers crushing inward), the windows in the commanding building came flickeringly alive and shed their heartless pictures to the watching darkness. Sentries stood by the various ornate entrances gazing impassively outward; the light seeping from the building erased their faces in the negative shadow it cast. A centimetre above the building's dark mass a single motionless cloud hid the disc of a new moon: her face was now invisible from the embattled obscurity of earth, swept with confused alarms of struggle and flight.

Two floors of windows were in full blaze, we could see, and through the indifferent hangings miniature figures darted about as if driven by clockwork. In one room a map covered an entire wall; it glowed as if with newly-let blood. A single room in the dark tower that lifted noiselessly above the squatter bulk below burned as if with fever or delirium; and my attention—magnified by a pair of powerful field glasses—was gradually attracted and absorbed by that trembling luminous square, in the interior of which I could make out the marionette-like figure of a general, in a Sam Browne belt, black undecorated uniform, and a harsh white staring face interrupted by the dark wet gash of a clipped moustache, sitting stiffly behind a large solid desk, and, stretching herself out languidly on top, crystal goblet encased with slender fingers, one knee bent to expose a soft white glimmer of thigh, her mouth partly opened and tongue distended wetly, hair falling in a gold wave that was almost white, fingernails, I could see as I brought my instrument into focus, painted with a dark flush of crimson, so that they appeared as if filled with blood, the regal reclining figure of the image that had till then reigned haughtily in our hearts. All her imperious manner had crumbled, however; but it was with a familiar scornful gesture that she flicked her cigarette in a fiery arc to one corner of the staring room as the dignitary's clawlike hand began to climb up the velvety column into darkness. She parted her legs a little wider to accommodate the arachnid. As it paused to feed upon a pocket of amber or honey she lifted her glass and drank of a dark fluid—a drink, I was able to see, currently much in vogue, named after a Catholic queen who reigned in the preceding century, called a "Bloody Mary," for when she lowered her glass her mouth was rimmed with red, as if she had been feeding on an artery. One black arm pushed her out flat on the altarlike desk and tore at her vestments. A smile bloomed on the utter whiteness of her face (now that I think on it the angle of vision would not have permitted such a perception, but let it rest, let it stay). Her eyes were partly closed and through the veils, the curtains of flesh, their whites gleamed blankly. A wind blew steadily through the empty street, blowing into dancing spirals dust and grit and the torn wings of newspapers. Some of it got into my eyes; and by the time I had wept out the burning coat of cinders that window had extinguished itself in the larger darkness which wrapped our troubled arc of the globe, as if a burning heart of flame, held in being by its fragile shell of ash, were to collapse inward, as it consumed itself, to emptiness and night.

Some such collapse, like that of a hive abruptly deserted by its queen, gripped us, as we cowered in that cellar's blackness, feeling the distant thuds of falling bombs and artillery shake the foundations of the City that was being rubbled above us, choking us with dirt torn from the very anatomy which protected us, breathing raggedly together as if to form, with our divided selves, a greater and more intensely living being; and as I reflected on the bad dream that History had become—the fantasy of some demon that was assimilating us with its tremendous acids and antinomies to its fundamental madness—I wondered whether modern civilization was, indeed, a conspiracy of the subconscious, a seminal illusion imposed upon us by beings greater than ourselves for an unknown purpose. After all the evolution we had, metamorphosing ourselves, passed through, our own verse, our subtle colour and nervous rhythm, and that unity of being where all the nature murmurs in response if but a single note be touched; after the world we had richly imagined together, with all the stately design and embroidery of some ancient tapestry that, stirring, gives shape to the unseen wind; after the breathing into life of a beauty that was not ours, what more was possible? After us the Savage God.

22

deals of beauty and bellicosity rise and fall; but a constant inheres through the most climatic change, as I have had cause to note: an original from which all the others derive. Thus to one obsessed with certain key images what is strange is not that they should recur, but that they should recur in so many different guises; that the smallest of stray perceptions—a wisp of mist, the sun releasing a blade of grass from its crystal sheath—should contain, hidden in flesh, in bone, or even in the angle at which velvet skin absorbs light, the single stamp with which, as it seems, his vision is informed. Even at night, I have found, even in the most abrupt and abysmal blackout, these images persist, floating against the buzzing blankness; and sounds . . . yes, those same sounds in the sudden emptiness, the rustling of restless paper, creaking of furniture as bodies shift, settle, the hiss of ragged respiration, sighs, belches, hum of conversation too low to be comprehended; the long interminable waiting, as for a dark and blank screen to liven, take on colours, the rosy unbelievable flush of yet another dawn; and those mysterious activities in the background, the soft regular flap-flapping as of tape being wound, things being resolved, sucked back, rearranged in an unknown alembic. One waits, one does not know; and one has the sense, although there is, of course, no way to ascertain this, that one is not alone: others are waiting as well. The very night is pregnant with other forms, anticipating that unreal dawn when they will be given another existence; and if this insight remains veiled in a cloud of unknowing, one is nevertheless convinced that such blindness is voluntary and resides with oneself—a matter of the correct way of looking through the crystal of one's eyes, not the crystal of the atmosphere. It is thus with a sense of dislocation that the world returns, changed in some indefinable respect, with the first slow stroking of those reborn rays. One has the feeling, as I did, of a tremendous reversal, as if the flood of radiation that the sun unceasingly produces were to be withdrawn, in long burning ribbons, to its source, there to be absorbed and kindled into yet another chain of luminosity.

It was, at any rate, with such a feeling of reversal, of being absorbed into a cocoon of darkness and emerging into a world created by a different spectrum of light, that I found myself after the blindness caused by the flash of her departure in the winter of 1906. The City seemed radically changed as I groped my way out of the deserted theatre; the light fell dryly through the suddenly, strangely mild air, illuminating rooftop and cornice and fluted gable with hopeless clarity, and the River, released from its stranglehold of ice, babbled senselessly to itself as it released its imprisoned current, like a sentence dissolving into meaninglessness in a mouth given speech after long silence. Imagine some anomalous mutant, or theoretical creature at any rate, of composite structure, uniting in itself a dual nature, with all the internal organs multiplied in perfect symmetry, in a perfect balance of nurture and growth; then imagine that exactly half of this creature is subtracted (not obliterated: transformed into a different mode of being, but one wholly inaccessible to the remainder), and you will have some small inkling of the feeling that gripped me as I walked through a suddenly desolated City, one identical in every respect to the one I had known, but changed as unnoticeably and utterly as if it had passed through the deadly invisible skin of a mirror.

The years that followed between her vanishing and my own violent precipitation from both the City and the land of my birth were occupied increasingly with a series of paper skirmishes against a ragged group of Puritan pamphliteers. These had originated in the late years of the last century under the common nomination of the Martin Marprelate controversy, and before that with the studiously clever diatribe by the former actor (and Oxonian) Stephen Gosson in 1879. The players, of course, were not slow in responding to these fanatical fulminations, and found eloquent inkwells in Greene (*Francescoes Fortunes*, 1890) and Nashe (*The Anatomy of Absurdity*, 1889, and *Pierce Penniless*, 1892). By the time I entered the fray it had been balanced heavily in our favour by the patronage of the ruling house itself; but its acrimony was, for all of that, intensified into a bitter undercurrent, with personal vilifications and allusions being constantly inserted into now this play, now that sermon, until the secular and divine discourses virtually ceased to exist in their own right, and became but empty mediums or vehicles for the invective of the moment. And that, indeed, is how I came to view it: in the tremendous space left by her departure another body was secreted and grown, another city erected on the smoking and vacant foundations, yes, another language spun to replace that fertile original; and if I threw myself so energetically and mindlessly into this arena of false trumped-up activity, it was only because its true object had vanished, leaving the irresistible draw of a vacuum to distort the heart—that organ by which the imagination perceives—into alien and unnatural shapes.

Often, to garner material for these satiric inclusions, one or another of our Company would attend the sermons which were the other main form of popular entertainment of the time, there to absorb whatever venom was being squirted in the guise of moral edification; and it is, indeed, not strange to me now, to consider that just as our theatre was to provide the Seed-Bed for the great flowering of Poesy, so the Pulpit was to act as one for that of Prose—not the journalistic periods of our Grub-Street novelists, of course, but the nobler and more sonorous rhythms indigenous to English syntax which were to find their natural culmination in the translation, under the auspices of the benevolent and learned James, of the Bible into the vernacular in 1911 (just, in fact, before the outbreak of the first European conflict). I can yet recall, casual believer though I am, attending these great congregations of the literate and the barely-literate; and although it may seem incredible to those raised in a different clime and time, to whom the notion of "sermon" connotes drowsy visions of Sabbath slumber and stultification, yet, to these largely unlettered church-goers, the sermon provided an exhaustless source of genuine entertainment, one which a mere printed text is powerless to convey: an emotional range which depended on the dramatic delivery no less than the rhetoric of its compositon for its effect. Of all the many churches and chapels scattered throughout the greater London area none had attained the fame and influence of St. Paul's; and it was to this venerable pile that I invariably found my way, leaving the smaller chapels, with their ranting Dissenters and Presbyters, for the more satiric-minded members of our Company, notably Sly and Burbage, in the latter of whose speeches the more theatrical of their absurdities would invariably surface at the next, usually Court, performance. I, however, drawn despite myself by the powerful tropism of that vowel-honey, in company with the sweet-tongued clown Robert Armin or one of the younger members of our Company, would seat nearest that voice and lose myself for some hours in those tralatitious periods.

The chief vitalizing impulse in that pulpit came from the figure who was to become its Dean for many long years, a former scribbler, it was noised in educated circles, of secular love-songs and lewd lyrics, and who was to bring to his divine calling much of the fire and fury of his ardour; toward the end of his life, wasted by a debilitating nervous disease, he had taken to appearing in the pulpit clad only in his ghastly trailing shroud; and I have conversed with men, old now but children at the time, who yet awake in the depth of night shaken out of their wits by that still-vital nightmare figure who would, as he did then, lecture learnedly and horribly on the putrescence and decomposition of his own body: indeed, to anyone who has looked within the prison of his own corpus, into the capacity of the ventricle, the stomach, and the receipt of all the receptacles of blood, and all the other conduits and cisterns of the body, and viewed the infinite hive of honey, the insatiable whirlpool of covetousness mewed within, will not indeed be loth to break that gaol, and to gladly note the manner of its breaking, of our awaking. For we are all conceived in close prison; in our mothers' wombs, we are close prisoners all; when we are born, we are born but to the liberty of the house; prisoners still, though within larger walls; and then all our life is but a going out to the place of execution, to death. Now was there ever any man seen to sleep in the Cart, between Newgate and Tyborne? between the Prison and the place of Execution does any man sleep? And we sleep all the way; from the womb to the grave we are never thoroughly awake, but pass on with such dreams and such imaginings as trouble the lightest and most fever-tossing sleeper, even the slumber of those famous Seven of Ephesus, till the dream is broken in death. As he spoke hollowly, projecting his voice into the huge concave of the cathedral, it was not difficult to imagine that he was even then immured within a giant's burying vault; and, indeed, as the months lengthened into years, and the cathedral gained a veritable transpontine fame, those figures fattened themselves upon the marrow of his rhetoric, gained tremendously in inflorescence and creeper-like complexity, and his metaphors sprouted and shot out rank luxuriant hair, like that of a corpse long after its bodily death, gleaming with false vitality in the white of a sepulchral gloom. As I look back on the monstrous mutations that his rhetoric was to take, as if under the black radiation of a baleful star, I think of the inevitable cycles that all living things take, from lymph to languages, from stars to infusoria; and that the seeds which fertilize their growth and dissemination also contain their rich decay and death—leaving way for a host of parasitic micro-organisms to fester and breed in that once radiant anatomy; and that these cycles no less guide and define the growth and decay of styles, for it was to take less than a generation for the stately organ tone which resounded in that stony vault to lose its passion and its capacity to move men deeply and decline, as if it were being emptied of its living flame, to the vapid decoratism and lifeless, though magnificent, mausoleums of Sir Thomas Browne; hence rapidly to the Gothic posturing of the "Graveyard School" of poetic composition, which quickly transformed itself into the surrealist nonsense that characterizes so-called "serious" poems in these barbarian times. Again, in their spawning and myriad evolution, one breed may clear a living space—only to unaccountably become extinct, leaving the way open for other completely alien organisms, ones that greedily grow in the plots thus prepared by their unknown benefactors; as this antique form, that appears to the modern mind (or non-mind) as incomprehensible as a fossil sculpted in limestone, was soon to atrophy, its exquisite foliature and powerful intertwining vines and vessels withering in the rays of a hostile sun, to leave way for the uniform monotonous vegetation, "suburban lawns" indeed, of the journalistic novel and the contemporary novel of manners (read Defoe and Orwell for the first, Austen and Waugh for the second).

At his prime, though, what a powerful, what an unencumbered figure he was, how he seemed to lash the elements together with the scourge of his almost biblical rhetoric, how the congregations trembled and quailed under the measured fury of his delivery! And yet he seemed but the merest gaol-keeper after all and we, the prisoners of his words, looking out through their luridly stained panes onto a brilliant, barren, inaccessible world drifting dreamily without. The entire City seemed, during those years ('06-'09), to have become an immense prison, a sterile, though fabulously appointed structure, with tiers rising cell-block upon cell-block into one's rarefied consciousness, a kind of elaborate Marshalsea of the mind, bounded at the nether terminus of one's awareness by the embracing sentence-like River, with its turreted watchful bridge, as if, in an elaborate conceit, one were to limit existence to what a line, though theoretically infinite, described; and, looking over all, the gargoyle-encrusted bulk of the Tower, whose battlements were often decorated with the heads of political miscalculators, its blank eyes gazing impassively out, its walls stained with the blood of centuries. As I became increasingly embroiled in these disputes, which oftentimes skirted dangerously close to the wide drifting territory of illegality, I became more aware of how deceptively simple it was to transform the boundless extent of the world into a single narrow cell; and often, falling into troubled sleep as evening drew its long grey textured shadows together, after a day of bitter debate in one or another of the taverns or coffee-houses, I would rouse to half-consciousness to find, sketched lightly over the dim ceiling, the cradle-like loops of distended chains, or, against the single, rather high shadowy window, the slightly darker shadows of bars or grille; and, at the dim border of awareness, the regular footfalls of some invisible warder, his heavy keys jingling faintly, musically, as he made his rounds.

Our chief leader in these arguments was the golden-haired playwright who had revolutionalized the English stage, as well as English poetry, through his innovative use of blank verse, and gained a different kind of notoriety among the middle-class citizenry as exemplar of a dissolute and atheistic way of life; and as the years narrowed toward their terminal point, nightfall found us unvaryingly at one or another of the coffee-houses or taverns in Southwark—the Upstart Crow, the Crossed Rapiers, the Lion and Unicorn, O'Rourke's (with its portraits of prominent Irish artists)—toward the smoky rear, around a large table that often served as a debating platform, with members of either faction packed closely together in heated discourse; while, isolated as distinctly as a ray of pure yellow sunlight on an afternoon of threatening gloom, our embattled advocate would stand, head thrown back, hair falling in aureate waves to his shoulders, smiling as the satiric din deflected off his bright wit, his eyes, I can see now in retrospect, clear sparks of light, as though our star itself had deigned to touch them with its unveiled and unbearable fire (though, now that I look more closely, one eye dims unaccountably, threatens to transform, by a mechanism I am unable to perceive as yet, into a blind pool of viscous ink or some other dark fluid). As the argument would rise and subside, with lulls during which the buzzing sound of the crowd would drift through, I began to notice, off in one corner, a solitary figure that recurred erratically from place to place, yet with a curious persistence withal, drinking long and steadily through the evening, his attention, I could see, plainly elsewhere; and it was only after diligent inquiries that I was able to unmask something of his mystery and create for him more than a mere outline. He was, it seems, an indigent writer and contriver of impractical inventions (windup armies, entire villages that carried on their ethereal activity with the barely audible hum of well-oiled clockwork, miniature theatres with delicately-jointed actors) who was infatuated with a peripatetic barmaid and waitress plying her trade at now this, now that tavern or coffee-house; and as he sat in his corner, watching her as she flew lightly here and there, his attention invariably on other parts of the room, he would slowly drink himself into oblivion (the saucers piling precariously upward as in the story by Hemingway). As the months eroded into years his disintegration grew more and more obvious; often, passing through the streets in early morning on the way to a rehearsal, or to watch the silver dusk returning with a young appreciative friend, I would view, through a misty window, that familiar figure in patched black beginning a long day's solitary drinking; and if I entered to wish him good day, remark on the early hour, or gently remonstrate with him, he would apologize quite automatically, his eyes elsewhere, muttering over and over like a litany, "My first of the day, my first of the day." At one or another gathering of friends and intimates he would be found, occupying a habitual corner with his habitual shadow; and no one would realize what condition he had gotten himself into until, at the end of the evening, the room thinned out into oases of smoky emptiness, he would attempt to rise, and have to be caught before he fell full length on the carpet. His poetry has always seemed to me, such of it as I read, indued with certain qualities of beauty, certain forms of sensuous loveliness, that were separated from all the general purposes of life; such a movement of our thought, unformulated till he took it up, that has more and more separated certain images and regions of the mind, images that grow in beauty as they grow in sterility. Perhaps it was this beauty, cut off from the fertile impulses of life, that he sought for in embracing Catholicism, or at least the rich glitter of its ritual, its formalized pageant. If it is true, as Arthur Symons, his very close friend, has written, that he loved the restaurant-keeper's daughter for her youth, one may be almost certain that he sought from religion some similar quality, something of that which the angels find who move perpetually, as Swedenborg has said, toward "the day-spring of their youth." And if, draining continually in the opposite direction, he wasted himself in his cups and a disorderly way of life, it was because the artist can only have that portion in the world, as one who has awakened from the common dream, of dissipation and despair.

I was only to hear of his ignoble death some years later, in 1916, after his release from gaol, when, slipping easily back into his old habits, and obsessed by the image he could no longer attain (even merely to look upon), he subsided rapidly to his terminal illness, brought on by a last drinking bout with two fellow-poets and bibbers, Drayton and Jonson; and gazing on that microscopic bit of print in the obituary columns of the *San Francisco Chronicle* which listed, in a highly skeletized form, his life and achievements, I seemed to see before me anew the horribly regular monochrome prison walls (he died, I have been told, in a sparsely-furnished hotel room not unlike, in shape and shading, the cell he had been wont to inhabit), the high inaccessible windows that showed the merest sliver of sky, the bowed heads revolving on their circuit in the high-walled prison yard, taking their daily exercise, the sun that sets at two o'clock, the winter chill, the rough garb. A common friend I saw many years after reported a story, perhaps apocryphal, about a "coming-out" party thrown to celebrate his release that, growing inebriated and rowdy, pooled their resources to purchase for him the services of a not particularly appetizing young harlot; and when, after an appropriate length of time had elapsed, he emerged from the rented room, whispered to an intimate, "My first in these ten years, and it will be my last: it was like cold mutton"—then, in a louder sibilant: "But tell them in England" (he was in northern France at the time)—"it will entirely restore my character." At the time I read of it, though, I was unaware of the comic-burlesque nature of his demise, and could remember only his fruitless ceaseless waiting for a light that never glimmered in his dark recess, chock-full with the shadows of his isolation. How strange it is to me, too, that I was to learn of these sombre circumstances in such totally different surroundings, ones that, as it were, bloomed from the tiny bitter seed which that announcement inserted there! Most of the winter of that year I had travelled west from Chicago (where, for seven fruitless years that belong in no way to this account, I had been lodging, under the marquée of an ancient movie house devoted periodically to the screening of old plays and even older historical pageants). Across a continent troubled with rumours of imminent war I wound my devious way, stopping at now this, now that half-deserted prairie town to recoup my energy, the few dim streets blurred with blowing grit or hard-driven fine granules of greyish snow, the odd sign creaking in the wind, its lettering rubbed away with the years, the pool-hall-cum-bar-cum-gas-station empty except for the attendant and one or two others standing shadowy around a rectangular pool of green felt lit up ghostlike by a low-wattage bulb, the traffic infrequent, drifting past with lowered headlamps. I was driving one of the early Cadillac limousines, a vehicle remarkable for stability and ease of operation, and the way that the vast plains lying between the outskirts of Chicago and Denver rushed up and sank behind my wake gave me the eerie impression of devouring the entire continent piecemeal. The regular demarcations of varied crops flowed past as if I were driving through a map of the region rather than the country itself. Slowly, Iowa gave way to Nebraska, and the great territory of grasslands began, a sea of darkly luminous green that rippled to the horizon whence a cold white light exuded. All across that state a huge storm was building, and it was an eerie sight to view, against the immense ink-black thunderheads, heavy with unreleased electricity, those rustling endless grasses lit up as if from within as I sped through their midst. As the plains began to rise in their approach toward Denver, the storm broke behind me, and swept with violence to the north and south, cutting a swath over the ground as with a giant's sickle of ice and snow. Ahead, however, the weather was clearing, and a pool of hard clear blue widened before me as I rose into the foothills toward Denver and the Rocky Mountains that lie behind.

This respite, however, proved short-lived. To the west of the mile-high city great masses of granite and fir reared themselves, blotting the sky with their unruly bulk; and among their huge bases the highway I was travelling, U.S. 40, inserted itself uncertainly and began to be inexorably lifted on their broad backs. A lurid light bled from the sky, a dark ozone heavy with unreleased crystal; and the snow of the preceding winter hung precariously here and there, among fir trees, loose boulders, a ghostly dirty white, crumbling and rotten. As the elevation increased the atmosphere grew more rarefied, and both I and my labouring machine breathed with difficulty, felt the troubled pounding of our hearts. Gradually there crept upon me a sense of intolerable oppression, as though I were being buried under masses of unliving stone; and the trees crept closer with an uneasy crepitation, blurred and baleful. Under overhanging cliffs I passed slowly, downshifting as I wound agonizing hairpin turns, and occasionally loose cascades of gravel, ice and rock would rattle nervously around me, as if a giant were stirring in his sleep, disturbed by some recurrent nightmare or delirium; indeed, as unnatural early twilight and dusk rose ominously around me, the impression grew that I was being involved unwittingly in some greater being's madness, the mammoth derangement of some cosmological monster. Infrequently, I passed through tiny settlements of a dozen or so dwellings, with perhaps a filling station and a general store, that huddled beneath the peaks expectantly, their few lights glimmering fitfully. After gathering momently, blackness fell abruptly; and as I crept through and left behind the lofty hamlet of Climax, Colorado, through its breathing bulk white whorls of flakes began to drift, polished to dazzling incandescence by the cone of my powerful headlamps.

The hours I spent in struggling over those misshapen peaks, those mountains of madness, have since taken on a nightmare tinge. As I crept up those treacherous inclines the snow fell thicker, in impenetrable masses of white clinging wool, against which the windshield wipers swept with increasing futility; and slowly falling temperatures froze the drifting wet stuff into slick patches my tires skidded over heart-lurchingly, only stopping that slow sickening drift toward the edge, where a white-infested abyss of blackness loomed, when the treads found bare road to cling to. My pace fell to fifteen miles an hour, then ten, then eight, then a crawling six. I admired with a kind of nauseated fascination those arrogantly certain truck and bus drivers who boomed past me, long veterans of each twist and nerve-like involution, their swaying bulks outlined by green and red lights, throwing up tall crystal curtains in their wake. Other less confident voyagers were not so fortunate; these were stranded in soft amorphous ditches, nose down, tail pipes fuming, snow drifting against their helplessly trembling sides. Infrequent snow-plows would thunder past, their shoveled snouts curling a white breaking lip that gradually formed an icy wall on each side of the road; these, however, had little real effect on the passability of the thoroughfare, and it was only due to the heavy construction of my machine, I believe, that it not only held to the road but managed to break its way through these frozen barriers. When I look back on that monumental traversion—much as one imagines an insect at one instar pausing to look back at his form at a previous ecdysis—I wonder not merely that I survived the exposure to the wrath of the unliving elements, but that I managed to keep my sanity, my identity, intact through that bitter passage; for even now, separated by a deceptively comfortable pad of years, I can yet surround myself with those peaks poking random fingers into emptiness, I am once more surrounded by glassy humps wherein my slowly passing reflection, lit by the ghostly luminence of the snow, is caught and coagulated, and on all sides, real or imagined, precipices, cliffs of fall leap away into unplumbed abysses below as into uncharted portions of the mind, or areas of brain wasted by lesion or aphasia. For hours into that interminable night I pressed, frozen into one agonizing block of awareness, keeping consciousness by sheer act of will (or the will of something harder and imperishable in me), the curvature of the spine imitating, I imagined, the terminal death-convulsion of a scorpion or armadillo, as fearful of resting in that snow, that drift, as a lunatic would be of falling into a snake pit in some medieval asylum. I had to creep at a snail's pace merely to keep the road; and when, as happened occasionally, the weather cleared to a few nervous flurries, and I tentatively increased speed, to ten, to fifteen, then to a seemingly headlong twenty miles an hour, I would inevitably hit an icy stretch just as I settled down to some real progress, and begin a slow tail-waggling skid that only ended when I managed miraculously to steer out of it; and then the shroud of white blindness would descend again, slurring the sentence I laboriously drew in the waste, and I would fall back to my previous torturous pace. Out of the grey cerebral mass overhead the adhesive white stuff fell, and still I continued as by an internal mechanism, foot numb against the accelerator, leaning stiffly forward, until it seemed I was not I, but was inhabited by some cold crystal daimon of the indifferent mountains, mocking me in my efforts to move with my apparent motionlessness. As the night wore toward a barely-imagined dawn I had, without noticing it, begun an imperceptible descent; and it was only when, somnambulistic miles later, I saw a ghostly sign announcing entry into the State of Utah (which sounded then, in my condition, like passing into another state of being) that I realized deliverance was near. The blizzard whispered down into flurries, the flurries into individual drifting flakes, and the flakes into an icy stillness. I increased speed. The road was rock-solid under. I braked and swiftly slowed to a halt. I got out, stretched, felt the pavement. It was wet but bare of ice. Overhead the sky had cleared utterly save, to my rear, a white miasma yet shrouded the great convulsions of earth and stone that had, as it were, given birth to the being I now possessed. Below me a cold desert dawn breathed colour and line and mass to the expanse whence the road dipped. Rousing birds cried brokenly in the chill, the shiver of returning sensation, like the first fragmentary notations of consciousness being reborn. I breathed deeply and exhaled a fine white plume of vapour. Behind me the engine coughed once and then resumed its powerful hum.

23

People with preconceived or fixed notions of time and space never fail to amuse me—and especially if they are among groups that ought to know better: poets and physicists, who, with few exceptions, have garden ideas of these wild and unclassified blooms. It has always seemed to me that Time is a fabric stored, crumpled in our deepest interior cell (that room, minuscule as an indivisible softly pulsing cell, wherein the solar system is reproduced to scale), and that in the process of storing the impressions which form its weave they are inevitably, gratefully bent and beautified (as light is in a distortive glass or in the solid crystal glance of water); bent subtly to one side, that is, to form the shimmering cross-weave. Thus the solid flow of narrative that has come to be recognized as "novelistic" does not do justice to the true nature of the fluid medium, a river, like that of a sentence, that shapes itself as it goes, with many back-eddies and cross-currents, and water-falls tumbling in reverse, and those looping involutions, like the pseudopods of parentheses, that, intestine-like, bear their liquid life to discharge into a mother ocean; and thus it is not strange to me that I should view, through the prism, as it were, of an atmosphere purified and sweetened as by the lungs of one desired, the blurred and fragmented passage that bore me there, a passage consisting of snapshots arranged to be thumbed rapidly through to provide a sense of continuity (the light produced in recollection by the unhooded eye of a transcendental projector): the desert, the gigantic hollow hulks of sagebrush blown by the ceaseless wind, moving across the dusty waste like houses loosed from their foundations, or statues of beasts, of great antiquity, suddenly made peripatetic, the bulky brains of cosmic monsters searching for craniums to bed down in; the salt flats of Utah, white and almost living slime and crumbled crystal;

the purple scrub-riddled hunched shoulders of foothills that march west into the towering wall of the Sierra Nevadas (that make a fertile terrestrial paradise on one side, a parched moonscape on the other); the mountains themselves, forbidding guardians, tall mist-shrouded sentinels; a mountain lake resting in liquid jewelled brilliance amid curtains of fir, its blinding surface shifting to reveal incalculable spring-fed depths wherein a flash of white, as of an inhabiting spirit or nymph, lurked (thus does moonlight or starlight find a body at last to clothe its restless homelessness); and the air that flowed thence through those high remote passes seemed to me one blowing from a far country, a land of lost content; and those images, compressed into as little space as the dancing heart of an atomie, sped faster, faster, into lines of blurred colour, incredibly elongated nerve-synapses stretched virtually to invisibility, as I descended down those suddenly sunny slopes, glowing in early afternoon radiance, and saw it shining plain, the happy highways of my youth recreated for me in a landscape as labyrinthine and simple as that of the heart; indeed, as I drifted effortlessly downward, as if borne onward by the luminous atmosphere itself, it seemed to me, with absolute clarity, that here was the promise fulfilled of my early days, the "land of heart's desire" of which the Irish poets wrote. That mad acceleration of fragmented pictures suddenly ceased, and not only ceased, but eased into a delicious dream-slow medium, a medium as clear and undivided as molten crystal. Flowing rills spilled over the mossy crags their thousand dangling wreaths of watersmoke that threw up curtains of incandescent vapour through which, miraculously, a gleaming valley could be glimpsed, with its settlement of tiny red-roofed houses and garden-plots rich with strange vegetation, that appeared magnified as by the concave lens those droplets formed. And on every side stately, bowed groves of chestnut trees spread their laden arms, weighted down with pyramids of white trembling blossoms, beneath which, over the fertile swells of earth as far as the glutted eye could see, clumps of tall wildflowers nodded, their corollas of petals stained with an unearthly spectrum of vibrant gold, cobalt, pulse-bright scarlet.

I had booked rooms earlier at the Hotel Regent on Sutter

Street (named after the prospector on whose plot undreamt-of gold lay buried) and, after a much-needed bath and shave, issued out into the mellow radiance of full afternoon. Flower-vendors were situated on the corners of the central district, their stalls overflowing with riotous blooms, and itinerant musicians filled the streets with the strains of antique instruments. A cable-car clanged down the hill to my left, painted a bright red, filled with a gregarious buzzing crowd. To the left of its luxurious, insect-slow progress, a block-square garden unfolded, planted with palm trees, their fronds shiny green, and banks of oriental flowers arranged to spell, in rainbow fashion, its name. As one rose, let us say, on one of these open cars, other hills would slide into view, or withdraw behind still other inclines, down which might straggle a motley array of ornate, sometimes Oriental apartment buildings, giving a breathtaking sense of distance and proximity, an entirely new organ, as it were, with which to perceive: the teeming sprawl of Chinatown would unwind its golden, red-diamonded dragon length to the right as one rose and dipped toward the Bay, suddenly revealed in its scaled glitter at the balanced top of one hill, where myriad fishing vessels were tethered to scrubbed gleaming wharfs. Cries rose distantly from the market that stretched around the waterfront, and the smell of fish and salt freshened as the air chilled one's face in an abruptly accelerated descent. This city, indeed, that had become in the space of a few years a metropolis vying with those of Europe in elegance and culture, spread itself precariously and picturesquely over a series of dramatic dipping hills that were inundated, in almost Venetian fashion, by the misty silver-skinned flood of San Francisco Bay over which the great sustained leap of the Golden Gate Bridge arched, a web-like creation of gossamer flutes and cables which appeared, from the bow, say, of the hourly ferry that plied these gentle waters, as the fragile yet prehensilely strong strands and links of an interconnecting sentence, that now, the sun firing to deep ruddy blood-vermilion, I swept gracefully across, the rounded green hills on the other side waiting softly to receive me. The car I was now in, a yellow convertible of Japanese make, had the top down, and the salty air tingled my skin as I accelerated effortlessly, the tall supporting pyllions, rising and dipping toward and away from the massive columns sunk into the bed of the Bay some eighty feet below, fluttering past me in stately undulations. The road rose slightly and curved into those hills to the right, entering and slipping away from the huge soft shadows they cast, almost verdurous from their graceful garments of vegetation. A brief tunnel enclosed us as we shot into the heart of one of these hills, its oval entrance on each side painted in a spectrum rising from blue to green to yellow to red. Then we came out the other side together, into a slow crystalline explosion of light. Light, indeed, lay over all the land as clearly and calmly as a mantle; and the smoky haze that hung around the distant edges, far from obscuring its far-reaching radiance, actually magnified and diffused it manifoldly.

In Sausalito, at a bar built over the lapping waters of the Bay and surrounded by the swoop and dip of sea-gulls, we found a table by the edge where the sun fell directly, on rough-hewn boards beneath which mingling waves whispered intimately. Flowers were planted in pots along the railing, a wild western species I was not familiar with (powder yellow, eyes of brilliant piercing blue). In the restaurant to our rear, amid flowering hair-like vegetation, two lovebirds sang a lilting duet; while the murmur of the crowd moved behind their scintillating counterpoint like the bass strings of some ponderously graceful symphony. To our right, across the smoky fire of the waters, the City we had driven from rose distantly, amorously. And the gulls and the salt and the sun and the overwhelming sense of fluidity, of liquid motion, converged together into a single unbearable impression, one I find it difficult to convey; a sense of deliverance into a world ontologically different from the one I had till then inhabited, a world with laws utterly unlike those of our mundane sphere, laws formed, with flexibility and rigidity, around the bone and beauty and symmetry I had only conceived hints of till then. A waitress, with long corn-yellow hair combed by the breeze and slender flamingo-like legs, brought us wine and cheese and fruit, and the crusty thickly-textured sourdough bread for which the region was famous. A paper hung loosely over the railing to my left offered a list of the day's dead (including a lurid photo of the bloody outcome of one of the *sales histoires* which this state seems to specialize in—the redlaced corpse lying in a bed of blooms in elegant Golden Gate Park). A tugboat entered our field of vision from the right, a brightly-dancing speck of ruby-red. By the time it had drawn across forty-five degrees of the limpidly curved horizon the wine and the sun had ignited their mutual fires, and we were laughing softly at something one or the other of us said. My eyes ran from the salt and wind, and my nose, filled with the rich ripened scent of a pervasive perfume, Golden Autumn, drank deeply of the scent and sweetness and mild aromatic sweat. The sun gradually lowered behind the restaurant's roof, but still struck the distant country across the waters with its mild flood. I was pouring wine from a second carafe—those rubies pendant at the lip, those globes expanding slowly in their dual crystals—when a single vagrant beam smote the water and the wine simultaneously. I reached across the table; it abruptly dissolved in a tongue of pure yellow flame, a yellow so pure it was almost white.

24

Of my other activity in the so-called "Golden State"—my collaboration on the runaway bestseller *Heywood in Hollywood*, the anonymous ghosting of the script *Poison Girls* for another, more famous name, and the tongue-in-cheek minor classic *Adventures of An Eye* (based on the popular triple punning and dead-panning, made possible by the orthography of the time, between *eye*, *I*, and *aye*)—this account does not, happily, deal with; after all, any burrowing ferret of a researcher (I can see the black lightless buttons of his eyes from any part of the room) can, if he so pleases, come up with the appropriate scraps of information in the reference libraries of Los Angeles or Santa Barbara or San Inferno gripped firmly in his worrying jaws. My pilgrimage there, despite many detours, was prompted by no other motive than the single one of contemplation at beauty's seat; and the long fertile sweep of the 400-mile valley that stretched between San Francisco and San Diego, the most bountiful agricultural womb the world has known, rich with musk-melons, clusters of variegated swollen grapes, plump nuts, the glowing ore of oranges, was indeed a fit setting for the elusive object of my quest. That object was the monastery, seated on the rocky coast between Carmel and Big Sur, modelled on an original in Italy nestled among the hills that surround Florence and overlook the peaceful flood of the Arno, in which was renewed, as the earlier institution had, the philosophy of being which originated in Greece and was brought to full fruition in the philosophic poem of an immortal Tuscan some centuries later. Well do I recall—as a reflection recalls the mirror in which it had its being—my slow measured approach along the gracefully curving coast highway, in the full flood of midsummer radiance, shadowed by gnarled cypress trees that centuries of wind and ocean had carved into a twisted beauty, the forests of huge fir and sequoia gradually lifting their massive presences on my left—massive but with a sense of light aery shadow, a floating feathery gloom—and the great stumbling breakers on the other side, falling to their glassy-green watery knees after a journey of untold leagues east: a recollection from which I imagine all else flowing inexhaustibly as, from the continuous explosion of solar energy, flow all the images we conceive. Toward evening we had come through the fishing village of Monterey to Carmel, a tiny hamlet of artists and the retired wealthy, just as the end of a pellucid sapphire day purified, as it were, by salt and ceaseless wind, lengthened its shapely shadows over the rolling green expanse of a meticulously tended golf links. As we descended gently into its hollow, now filled with clinging blue shade, the lights began to twinkle from the rocks above, while, to the east, the slow moon climbed, and the deep moaned round with many voices. Above, the great inverted dome of the heavens deepened majestically to royal shades of peacock green and amber and gold, and those inky layers of solid gloom beyond; while, in the afterglow, just above a tangled mass of dark and stirring cypresses, the star of even began to glow, as solid as a fist of garnet or heart of beating crystal. Slowly the shadows widened and broadened from mossy rounded roofs and dipping gables like long unfolding rolls of ribbons, in which the terrestrial stars of shops and dwellings began to gleam secretively, promisingly.

We booked rooms at a little hostel on a side-street, that wound from the main thoroughfare into a green streetlamp-shot tunnel of dense foliage, called Casa Verde; and after brief ablutions, issued out into the spacious well-lit sensuous gloom of early dusk, inundated by the afterglow of the long day that had soaked into the fabric of earth and heaven and now seeped richly down, oozed richly up. The main artery of this tiny jewel-like hamlet, whose many facets were beginning to twinkle in the dark-blue gloaming, connected some few hundred yards west with the lifting maternal billow of the Pacific; and all through the long winding corridor of night, that lengthened amorously toward a yet-unimagined dawn, we could hear, as now, from a cobblestone bend in a lane where we paused under a dark and summer tree, its crown lit up greenly from within by the radiating nucleus of the streetlamp, her slow stumbling gravelly voice, low and muted and powerful, straining against the shore of the continent like a mother to her restless child. At a small restaurant encircled with lilac and flowering dog-wood, through the crystal of whose leaded windows the light and warmth of the interior beckoned, we had, on snowy linen and crystal and tinkling silver, a substantial repast of fresh seafood and dry white wine. The voices of other couples rose round us in a gentle murmur—the friendly anonymous whisper of liquid sounding in a shell or empty ear. Through one leaded wave of glass we could see, outside, the garnet glow of a bull's-eye lantern trembling in almost visible gusts. Later, walking through empty streets, solid with the rush of wind and the distant boom of the Pacific, alive with dancing shades and verdurous gleams of half-extinguished light as now one, now another swaying tree, struck by a billow of air, threw a leafy arm against the glow of an overhanging lamp, we paused for a moment on the tiny arching back of a bridge under which an invisible creek trickled musically over wet stones, felt in the blood, and felt along the heart, combing the hair of roots and shrubs and other ravine-vegetation on its journey to the ocean below; and it seemed to me that all these sounds—the distant wavespeech, the vibrating thread of stream, the rustling restless voice of the wind pouring through the chords of innumerable trees—surrounded us as with the living layers of an immense and nourishing body. As we reached our abode for the night, it seemed that all the various flows of many-streamed Time by which, unwittingly, I had been borne, converged here, at the nethermost verge of this continent, where East rushed to meet West, and embraced in the white nacreous foam that bled from their encounter. And later still—and then even later—as the violet gloom deepened sensuously toward dawn, we lay together on our naked bed, the latticed windows open to the cool night air that yet burned on our skins, and to the whisper of the surf, the unclothed radiance of a white and trembling moon, and a whole crowd of stars rubbling the bow of the heavens with their bright and milky stones. It was no dream: I lay broad waking. The velvet sky paled, all the morning stars turned brilliant above the black ridges of rolling hills to the east, a horse coughed in the leafy lane outside, the roof above our heads creaked under the departing weight of night; the long withdrawing arterial flood grew brighter; the breathing rose, subsided; a beat, a pause; a beat.

25

ut no one can really prove, to himself or any other, that the tenuous necklace of beats he picks up upon awaking, fondles briefly, familiarly, and resumes with as little effort as he discarded it, follows the same unbroken strand; and, as day whitens his windowpane, it seems to him as though his interval of oblivion has been the means by which unknown powers have reduced him to his constituent parts and then rearranged them into an entirely different being altogether: he looks into his bare mirror as a child would who has been wasted with long fever, as though viewing himself for the first time in his brief moment of consciousness. And though the mind, like a thirsty sponge, sighs and unfolds and begins to drink in great masses of fluid detail (drink, desert-wanderer, from these springs), yet it will seem to him that something lurks at the tight kernel-hard root of the mass of petals we call the brain, something molded into a strange fashion of forsaking. Did I dream it? No. And if I did (I remember saying to myself) I must, I will make that dream part of the fabric of the world: something to be touched, fondled, caressed, dwelt upon, even dreamt upon; but not to fade into the common light of day.

As I spun down the coast highway from Carmel, after a reminiscent breakfast of scones, marmelade, and tea at a little outdoor teashop near the heart of town (a fine mist blew over the stone wall of the garden, causing the ginkgos and junipers to tremble and drench themselves with a shimmering array of morning jewelry), this was indeed my growing sense—that I was unfolding a fabric, of myriad and disparate weave, to reveal the reigning centre of its design (repeated, in glimpses and gaps, through the rest of that billowing garment), and, as I drew nigh it, and the Byzantine gables of that famous edifice lifted slowly and gently and inevitably out of the bosom of the surrounding hills, it seemed as though the threads of that fabric became more condensed, more tightly woven, more susceptible of varying angles of perception, and yet at the same time aerier, lighter, shot through with strands of dripping fire; and at the centre (that shifting elusive nucleus) the great unveiled eye of the sun.

That sun now balanced above the steepest and glossiest of the roofs that rose fountainlike to a single point which pierced the creamy blue, and fired it to the brightest band of the spectrum, one which I descended easily into the wide Spanish courtyard. Here, as elsewhere, was evident the pervasive hand of early missionaries from the Iberian peninsula, who carried the fiery silver of their cross into the furthest reaches of the continent; all around me arches of creamy brown and earthy white adobe outlined the brilliant depths of the morning sky; a single unbroken open corridor bent around the central courtyard, which was planted with trailing silver moss, wild roses, sweet basil and pungent thyme, and, at the centre, in a scalloped basin, the graceful feathery plume of a fountain lifted and fell against a cluster of wet submerged pebbles arranged in the shape of a corolla of rose-petals. From the central oval structure, that swung its ellipsis around under a curve of red-tiled roofs and gables that was almost Oriental in its effect, and in the angles of which might be seen rooks and swallows and an occasional heavy-winged cormorant roosting, exfoliated the petular protrusions of corridors and meditative enclosed tiled walks, in the shady recesses of which fountains and plants proliferated, and, on the inner walls, stained-glass windows set deep into the cool thickness of the adobe flooded, at certain hours of the day, their shadows with a pure rose light. The entire dwelling, as I began, slowly and haltingly, to see, my old habits of vision yet clinging and hindering my pure perception, was woven in the shape of a single garland of repose, a sacred plant pollenated by some ethereal impulse (for do not, indeed, the gods that mortal beauty chase end their pursuit clasped to the green flesh of a living tree?) Or imagine (I said to myself) the great loop of the solar system as the corolla of some cosmic rose, with the sun as its immense headed stamen, thrusting out to fertilize the solid space with the purity of its aureole, breaking in full crimson and unfolding and fading to palest rose, petal by petal and leaf of light by leaf of light, deepening outward in soft blushes on heaven's cheek: that image seemed to be realized here or, rather, sprang unbidden out of the depths into which I now gazed, depths untroubled by any clinging image of self, save the cellular surface of eye with which I gazed. And here, too, on the slopes of the hills surrounding that bloom, were planted fertile vineyards in which an occasional cultivator might be seen tying a branch back or aerating the soil with a prong or lifting a vine, heavy with luscious bloodripe clusters, from the warm and grainy loam.

I had made arrangements for this retreat some time earlier, and confirmed them only the night before, so my arrival was indeed anticipated: a tall, ascetic, classically-garbed figure waited for me in a pool of aery floating shadow, and when he spoke to me, the timbre was both hollow and piercing, as though he had grown voiceless from long lack of speech; and, extending his hand into the light, he drew me into the other path, through the shade into illumination and knowledge. He spoke as we went, through a corridor whose winding gloom was yet filled with floods of pure radiance; and as he did, it seemed that we were transported, on the backs of his muscular symmetrical sentences, to an antique time, an age of which the classical poets sang, and chief among them that Mantuan whose skill in sonorous verse kept green on earth a fame that shall not end while motion rolls the turning spheres along. While I cannot recall his exact words, they nevertheless evoked instantly for me a potent and beckoning figure of triform countenance, yet with but the single blinding face of the sun; a figure called up not merely to the deceived and deceiving visual faculty, but as a mental word is born to the rational soul, that was yet moved by all the ardor of love of one that dwelt in bliss: and it was this image, this mask transformed by its presence, that, as I thought, spoke to me throughout.

Beauty was, indeed, the one object of contemplation in that place, "id quod visum placet," that which, being seen, delights: but one which is the result of an inner rather than an outer act of perception, an act of knowledge or identification with the plenitude of being contemplated rather than mere aesthetic appreciation, passive enjoyment. Intelligence, then, is the proper perceiving power, the sense of the beautiful, the organ or inlet through which it floods inward. If beauty delights the intellect, it is because there is an excellence in the proportion of things to the intellect. Hence the three elements they sought for in beauty and its perception: *integritas*, because the intellect is pleased in fullness of being; *consonantia*, because the intellect is pleased in the relation of parts to whole, of disparate elements to their master design; and *claritas*, because the intellect is pleased in light—that which, emanating and overflowing from things, causes intelligence to see. That light, it seemed, was apparent all about us as we walked on our long looping path, imitating the horizon in our movement, or the passage of the sun from one season to the next as it rolled and balanced around our circular perception; it dripped in smoky cascades from meadow, grove and stream, falling with tiny explosions and magnifications upon the shiny surfaces of cypress leaves, it lay in splendour upon the glowing pelt of grass; and although his voice spoke as it were from the very heart of shadow, yet it seemed to me that those shadowy recollections formed the fountain-light of all our day, a master-light of all our seeing. But as the sun which oppresses our sight veils its own form by excess of being, so did I, blinded, not see directly, but through the guide appointed me in that place, who acted as our preconscious memory does, recalling the seed of light from which we flow.

The image I retain of that time—augmented and enhanced by the season which was then attaining its fullness—is that of a gradual yet continued ascent, the light increasing as we wound our way up a mount of revelation to some yet-unimagined apex of understanding. Slowly, as the days advanced, and the sun edged toward its meridian point (I was there a total of three months of thirty-three days each, plus one day I have not been able to account for), it seemed as though the unbroken spinning thread to which I was bound, up whose ribbon I flowed through a spectrum of ever-lightening colours, wound tighter and more closely in upon itself, wound into the blinding outline of a petular face, round which the other spheres were moved as by the magnetism of love.

That face, I clearly saw, I had seen but glimpses of till then, in the shifting arrangements of lower creation that, brokenly, reflected this unimpeded radiance, which now informed my understanding with its burning stamp; the same that, divided among the stars and lesser luminaries, showered upon each seed, great and small, its quickening influence. It had no sex; or, rather, as my vision, clarified by the reasonable discourse of my guide, strengthened, I saw that it partook of two natures, and that both male and female were united in the slow and solemn breaking of that smile: monstrous, surely, but only to our divided human natures which trembled at the vision of that resplendent and unimagined unity. Now more refulgently and with slower steps does the sun hold the meridian in the celestial vault of my memory, and more slowly do my words, those tiny bearers of a sweet and divine burden, hover, like miniature planets around the object of their contemplation. At the closest point of their orbit, the perihelion of their arc, they tremble as with one wave of light, turning their clear windows to the source of their life. Then their dance swings them out again, like bees around a hive of incandescent honey, to burn against the blackness of the emptiness beyond.

26

hat year (1916) saw the first rich flourishing of the cinematic art, as it were from the almost tropical atmosphere of the San Fernando Valley which was to produce so many strange offshoots and mutations; and as summer began to wane and slant dryly toward a mild autumn, and I made my way down a coast overflowing with the tremendously varied progeny the season had, labouring, produced, I saw, as I drew near the great film capital which was to hold sway over the imaginations of Western men for more than a half-century, numerous movie houses surrounded with insect-like swarms attracted by the powerful tropism generated from within, filling the early lilac gloaming of twilight with a low concentrated murmur of anticipation. Many of the small towns I passed through, although I knew it not then, were mere sets for the filming of huge spectaculars; and I cannot tell you the eerie feeling of wind and waste, of creaking props and a rustling whispering life going on behind totally unconnected with the shell facing the main thoroughfare, as I passed the saloons, the general stores, the stables of now this, now that deserted village, their dessicated fronts showing as drained as if they had been wrung of all their more potent images. All the types of the contemporary world were here gathered with a lavish hand, from Renaissance town, with its pennants and pageants, to industrial megalopolis, humming with trade and factories. There was in one a meticulous reproduction of the London Bridge of the time, with its shops and market-stalls; and one did not need an excess of imagination to be able to see, in the mind's illuminated eye, a royal progress making its measured way over its length weighted down with an adulant populace, heralded by fanfares of trumpets and hautboys. There were even, God help me, models of mock movie houses, perfectly functionless save as a backdrop for an audience of illusive movie-goers gathering under a ghostly marquée, the wind scouring the sky to blackness as night dropped its curtain. Seen from a distance, as one would descend from the vantage point of a gently sloping hill, they looked like nothing so much as the miniature toy towns of some demented inventor who had all space and time to play with; and it was only as one gradually approached that their true scale was revealed, and their character of mere props for a flawed imagination, the hastily-assembled palette for the spectrum of the mind's searching beam.

As my winding progress took me further south even more elaborate sets and backdrops cluttered the landscape. There was the gigantic spiderwebbed armature lifting twenty stories into the milky haze—the illusive support for a mammoth three-stage rocket to which it was tethered; this, as I discovered, acted as the central arena for a space epic being filmed at the time; and I can yet see the attendants running up and down ladders in their white smocks, the catwalks being balanced, the rocketmen, in their clumsy space garb, walking stiffly around like automata, a sailor in an odd corner shuffling a jig, and the director, grey hair blowing in a dry wind, dancing and waving his arms as he orchestrated this seeming chaos. The distant needle of the nose caught the blurred sun in a single blinding thrust: it appeared to be aimed directly at the heart of the oily disc that represented its ghostly presence. It seemed to tremble with uncontrollable energy about to be released—as if the earth, in an excess of ardour, were gathering its force to fling off a fragment of itself and inscribe, in a long glowing sentence against the abyss, its arc toward the mother body. And a little deeper into that lush valley a model "bioscape" was engendered—a controlled environment extending over nearly a thousand acres, in which were represented the basic varieties of terrains inhabited by living organisms (desert, rain forest, hardwood forest, etc.), and created, paradoxically, by a cartoonist and cinematographer of genius whose creatures, unfortunately, have only lately been banalized by the tremendous success which those early sketches wrought. These were the living backdrops for the deservedly popular series of revolutionary nature films he pioneered, films that utilized new discoveries in the realm of slow-motion and microscopic photography to vividly show marvels hitherto hidden to the impoverished human eye—the unfolding of a petal, the ecdysis of an insect metamorphosing from one instar to the next, a root's pale progress as it curls around a grain of nitrogen-rich soil, the feather-pattern of a hummingbird suspended in flight. And here and there, in oddly isolated corners and canyons, were the frozen lunar settings for the filming of pornographic fantasies: opulent rooms whose entire interiors were carapaced with shimmering mirrorskins, immense circular beds upon which were scattered the implements of some madman's torture chamber (and, I can see it clearly now, a woman's discarded shift and underthings, hatched with intricately erotic stitching in rose or vermilion, the signature of some bleeding monster of bliss), and exercise-rooms for sexual gymnasts (trapezes, bars, bar-bells, blue balls, etc.) These began to increase in number as I approached Los Angeles proper, coagulated under its canopy of vapour and vacuum, as if, in nearing the centre of some huge brain, some fabulously rich hive of consciousness, the humming cells, the insects of images that made up its varied life, were to increase in intensity and density to a scarcely conceivable degree.

These lifeless sets, indeed, were to remind me of nothing so much as the stage after the last act has rung the curtain down, and left the artifacts that had been animated so briefly frozen awkwardly in incomprehensible attitudes (yawns stiffened into death-grins, kisses into the final stages of rigor mortis), and I tried, with some scant success, to populate them with shades of my own fashioning (but that, as I have noted elsewhere, is reserved for another account entirely). And drifting through those maimed and mutated props as evanescently as a glimmer of light in some cosmic glass—they merged palpably and imperceptibly with those of the natural landscape to a vertiginous degree—I reflected, or would, that all human endeavor, futile from its conception, depends, helplessly and childishly, on an observer: some master-seer who, by the mere act of perception, revives, restores, indeed causes to exist, on a richer and more remote plane, the inscriptions and involutions of that minute insect activity. And as slowly and inexorably does one's fleeting sense of self erode (that reflection in other mirrors which are always moving away—a kind of microcosm for an "expanding universe" theory), as, one by one, like stars flickering out, the limited number of observers in one's limited cosmos vanish beyond the edge of one's awareness, or turn their beam of perception in an unknown direction entirely. Thus the child in his sick-room, wasted by some unknown disease (perhaps the one incurred by the very act of gratuitous existence itself), being slowly resolved into the tiny seed of his genesis (as though a film were suddenly and sickeningly to reverse itself), poised before that tiny black hole whence he, unasking, issued (and that will close seamlessly and soundlessly upon the wake of his passage), yet is held up and sustained as on a liquid billow by the mere presence of his mother sitting invisibly outside the isolating sheet of his tent: the breathing outline, the merest intimation of substance, the rippling reflection of colour and shape, the sweet odour of powder and purity, the affectionate invisible vigil, are more immediate and moving to him than the malady inexorably erasing him. So should we be sustained in our brief flicker of consciousness. The entire world, it seemed, was here represented as on a stage; and it was with the ease of old habit that I became, once more, a player among those other shades.

Shades press around me, even as I draw these varied threads into some semblance of the unity shadowed here. I am sitting, that fateful year, at a table in a vacant lot along Sunset Boulevard (that glassy thoroughfare which imitates the hazy horizon falling into the ocean leagues west). A dry wind flaps unceasingly the pennants strung overhead (there are used car lots on either side and, further down, a gun shop I will visit before the day is out). Strings of light bulbs also creak overhead: that they are lit is impossible to discern against the blinding greyness of the thickly textured sky. A battered loudspeaker trembling against a hollow flagpole plays a scratchy record over and over, a dreary and haunting monody popular at the time: *je t'aime, je t'aime*, whispered over and over, against a background of moans and heavy aspirations. A stack of magazines, weighted down with a crumbling yellow brick, flutters at one edge of the circular table. The title of the top one is visible (*The Silver Screen*) plus a third of a starlet's glossy face (a crescent moon in stony flotation). A backdrop may be glimpsed behind her, one of those portable affairs erected to give an illusion of location (London, Chicago, Hollywood) to otherwise bare and banal sets. Each tabloid seems well-thumbed; and thus (one imagines) is the silvery trail of a lone star traced over the restless void above, as bright and dreary as a photographed tear sliding, with infinite arrest, down the outline of a curved cheek. A shadow, barely distinct due to the extremely diffuse illumination seeping from the milky concave overhead, on which are painted slightly darker cloud-puffs, falls on the white table-top to my right. It trembles at the edges as if it wished to be absorbed into the viscous atmosphere. A golden wave of hair ripples in the constant current of wind. Traffic roars beyond a wire fence, releasing clouds of blue exhaust into the air.

The "true" version of every fiction, every dream, secretes its diamond-hard point somewhere under the shifting rainbow skin of illusion and resists, with its impenetrability, the transformations all around it, that seek to assimilate all reality (all versions of reality) into their mysterious processes—just as a being who aspires to become a god begins by attempting to include the entire universe within his body (or within his imagination's body). But something hard and opaque remains that cannot be absorbed or excreted, a point of irritation from which the metamorphoses, rippling uncontrollably, flow. Thus in that stack of yellowed tabloids we might read of the melodramatic parabola of one or another "star" (whose lustre and magnitude are composed wholly of their reflections in their gazers' eyes). Here she is, red-eyed in a blue bassinet (the colour of her irises when opened). Her mother is a rosy flush above. Next we see her at a party of her elders, peeping down the stairs in a white smock (she always was, and would be, a shy child, even at the height of her later excesses). Riding her father's horse barebacked. Sleeping in her attic room, the window wide, the starlight flooding in and filling her partly-opened eyes with liquid crystal. A first prom (orchids and organdy, the beau as yet a mere blur in the dim background). Summer nights in a convertible, the top down, hair blown in the sensuous dark wind, radio-music whipped back to the wake frothing behind. A full young throat bared to the golden radiance of midsummer. In the spacious park at the rear of her family's suburban home (wood and shaded water, sunny meadow), her yellow dress spread over her legs onto the swelling turf. The bees that hum, hypnotized, around this luminous blur, attracted by its imaginary pollen and fragrance. Growth, budding. Beauty. The pages crackle as they turn. The wind blows.

After the death of her mother, a great and flamboyant beauty in her own day, her European trip, her father's remarriage (and here the reel spins faster), the melodrama begins to cloud over, darken. Figures appear in the background. She deliberately takes a series of menial jobs. She surrounds herself with jackals and buffoons, satyrs and grobians. And abruptly, one dark morning at the end of a bleak November, she deserts the city of her birth (that feminine seat of all the fertile passions) and begins a rootless continent-wide series of deviations—best described by the correspondent as a "postcard trail"—which is to return, again and again, to the sun-infested film capital where, consummated over and over like a religious ritual, she is involved in a classic triangle of jealousy: the wronged lover, the brutal beau, and—the focal point where the blinding energies intersect—the "star" who catalyzes the event, celebrated in tabloids, enacted in the blood-red, blood-bright dream or drama that every man has in common.

All along the flat reaches of this blurred landscape, dominated by the dim silhouettes of mountains to the east, misshapen forms bulk up dreamily and are dissolved in the hazy wake of one's passage: immense cartoon figures, mice with the ears of mastodons, ducks with dinner-plates for bills, pirates, princes, and gigantic caricatures of historical personages. The colours blur and run together. One's eyes smart. The leathery wings of artificial pterodactyls darken the terrain with their shadows. The hiss of sprinklers is heard everywhere—without which this valley would be an uninhabitable desert. In this light pervasive haze the motions of objects are fragmented into barely-linked series, as if the film of light that winds through one's seeing faculty were being turned by a faulty stuttering mechanism. One has the sense, indeed, of being in a very early, very primitive film: the jerky movements of pedestrians and automobiles (with their headlamps that look so much like half-lidded cartoon eyes), the lightly sketched-in fronts of buildings leaning and swaying in an endless desert wind, the distended vertical pipes dangling above an uncompleted basement like the bleeding stumps of a double amputee, the hiss of wind in one's ears like that of the tape in some decrepit machine, all conspire to place one on the other, reversed, side of a pervasive and invisible veil of illusion, a skin or screen whereon dance the coloured motes or images that make up one's perception of the world (pictures painted to elude the abyss which lies beyond), till all that is left for one is the numbering of beloved images dissolving helplessly into others and those into blackness; to sit in an emptying theatre after the curtains have dropped for the night; to adumbrate the links of one's loss, tell the endless rosary of one's deprivation—the very lack, however, out of which one conceives a world. This entire sub-continent, it seemed, and the globe of which it formed the model, was reduced and compressed into the form of a theatre, a skull-shaped edifice on whose interior surface insubstantial pictures played; and as I settled down easily as into a comfortable well-worn seat, I reflected that all the movement of our art till then, from the first crude bombast and clumsy moralities to the aery fabrications of our later period, had but refined itself to this, purged itself of its grosser elements to fly, released, into the light which had, after all, been its ultimate source of being. The ceilings of a whole chain of rococco theatres that proliferated through the Valley were made of the texture and consistency of the sky itself, when it is just deepening into the imperial purple of evening; and scattered in their illusive depths were tiny stellar chips which winked and twinkled in a kind of glittering code. The shell of the interior was fronted with a second, false, dermal layer, which gave the effect of a Spanish villa, with its turrets and towers, and casements, and windows glowing with unnatural light. A cracked record might be playing some ditty, as it usually does during such moments of pre-dawn darkness—changed, invariably, into a dirge because of the frayed belt driving the mechanism. There is a rustling stir around one, an anticipatory breathing. One waits as one imagines a window or picture waiting for a luminous pencil to draw it into life, give it colour and depth and dimension. And speaking of pictures or windows (those "living pictures" composed by an unknown artist): how maddening it is that one cannot widen the frame according to one's focus or preoccupation, draw, with a palette extracted from one's bloodstream, the figures one imagines moving and merging invisibly beyond that impenetrable margin! One is sitting, for example, at a table in an outdoor café. Saucers slowly accumulate by your elbow. The boulevard is filled with the anonymous murmur of traffic. The waitress you wish to focus on darts here and there, a mere blur outside your fixed field of vision. As the afternoon wanes she grows less and less distinct. You long to turn, to seize that image with one decisive pounce, but find, for some unknown reason, that you cannot. The pile of saucers grows higher. There is nothing else, really, for you to do. Wind flutters leathery leaves or tiny plastic pennants with a dry susurration. Wires vibrate overhead. It grows darker. Or else (changing the picture with a sudden blinding flash) the unrelieved tedium of a gaol cell, pierced only by a high inaccessible slit of a window (the building narrowing its hooded eyes); the sweating bricks, the stench of urine, the murmur of other inmates, the clanking of warders making their interminable rounds, the invisible tower that strikes the interminable quarters, the dawn that brings with it another death, all constrain you to look out the only aperture letting out into a larger world, through which, however, nothing whatsoever can be seen save, occasionally, the blur of a darting bird, or a cloud languidly dissolving into the implacable azure. And then the iron and brick reassert their primal rights. The picture changes, changes relentlessly. You might be in a coffee-house or tavern (and here your heart disturbs you with desperate gigantic thuds, the blows of a lunatic attempting to get out of his cell); angry voices surround you with their aroused buzz; you are at the point of extricating yourself from the scene as imperceptibly as an image on a film suddenly overexposed when a pistol or rapier materializes before you; and there is that wrenching transforming gasp or explosion of light you have come to dread and know so well. Oh, there are other images, other pictures blooming out of the abyss. One goes past the stage where one can control them at will. Sitting at a shaky desk, in one of a number of interchangeable rooms (high smoky ceiling, pool of prisoned light), inscribing an interminable history, a history with no visible beginning or end—a history with all the privacy and impenetrability of a poem translated from a foreign language. The night stirs without. The sheets whisper. A wind breathes maternally, amorously. The lamp abruptly goes out. The montages come more and more rapidly. One's sense of location is slowly being eroded, together with a fix in the temporal flux, without which there is only the drift into the indeterminateness of death—which might be defined as the simultaneous acquisition of all points of view. Before the lighted windows at dusk, watching her undress before a dazzling mirror. A bulky shadow always intervenes at the crucial moment. Praying before an austere image in a museum or chapel. The guide or priest at one's side. The toy villages of one's childhood. The miniaturization of your gaze as you bend down lower, lower, to fit into a tiny domicile, slip under a microscopic lintel. Your childhood bed, your childhood sickness. The images are shrinking, shrinking, with an incredible sense of breathlessness. Your genesis: the star that accompanies the birth of awareness. Then it flickers out, a film run sickeningly in reverse, and all is emptiness and blackness, as it was in the beginning.

Oh, one might, I have discovered, one might imagine anything! One might imagine a solipsist who has not learned to love anything, except the pictures that chase each other, and coalesce, and split, in the private projection-room of his mania. One might imagine a lunatic who imagines himself to be a dead and immortal poet—and to substantiate his fantasy rearranges time and space and all of human history, from whose low eminence one might, at least, glimpse from afar the towers of the true City; or who imagines that in the cell of his dementia is contained the body of all the poetry of the past. But whatever I, or you, or anyone imagines, one image always recurs, as inevitably as the sun reborn each day at the centre of our long elliptical orbit: in a field of flowers, in a park of rich shade and light, in a glade of sensuous shadow and luminous blooms, a graceful figure, in vibrant yellow, reclines; a yellow so pure and pale it is just the hue of honey in the waxen interior of a cell, when the sunlight falls and filters through from the outside; or the shade of gold that freshly reaped wheat takes to those harvesters who have been long without bread; and round its illusive fragrance, its fantasy of perfume and pollen, dance, to measure, decoratively emblazoned bees, not landing, but maddening themselves with the scent and vision of so much sweetness and passion. The glass you hold is filled with the wine of the region, a sun-warmed musty fluid that tickles your tongue and palate; the remains of a picnic are scattered on the lush grass. Sunlight falls smokily through the tops of the attendant trees, dripping from the canopy of brilliantly-veined leaves and delicately-articulated twigs down the sheen of the tender-skinned bark, to heap upon the springy turf in medallions of soft refractive glass. It is golden autumn; all things throughout the fertile countryside are poised for winnowing; the solar radiance and clear glassy atmosphere strike all fruit with ripeness to the core. You turn to look full upon that revealed face, your mouth still drenched with the wine, your face burning, just as apples do when touched with Ceres' departing wand. At that moment a shadow intervenes. He stands somewhere behind and to the left. He is dressed in black silks and a Spanish sombrero which completely hides his face. He holds something metallic in his left hand. You are about to speak, to rise, to do anything to shake this dread paralysis, when a flame splits the shadow, a flame drawn from the whitest and most intense portion of the solar spectrum. There is another flame, then a third, each encompassing the other in its mortal stab. A great withdrawing whoosh of breath —then emptiness, a luminously humming void in the contemplation of which, however, you, or another, might hear odd unaccountable noises, the crackling of paper, a cough, someone clearing his throat, the murmur of muted conversation too low to be distinguished, a hammering at innumerable doors (or at the valves and portals of your heart).

27

he members of our Company have now been scattered to the round earth's imagined corners; yes, into the very elements from which, unwitting, they were composed; some in Europe, some in Afrique or Asia, some in the bowels of the earth, another in a hidden ventricle of the sea, and yet another shivered into the very air; and still, still God knows in what cabinet every seed-pearl lies, in what part of the world every grain of every man's dust lies; for though the body may not be resuscitated and reassembled after being dispersed so utterly, yet it may be augmented in the body of a more varied, more elevated being. Thus in a colony or hive of insects: the extinction of one or another member of the swarm means little in the rhythm of its daily existence, for each individual is, essentially, replaceable; it matters not at all who bears the pollen, the nectar, or who engages in mortal copulation with his queen; the basic unit is the hive, not the discrete insect, who has no meaning apart from the swarm and, as a matter of fact, dies shortly when isolated from the colony to which he belongs. The only irreplaceable member is, of course, the queen, who acts as the social and reproductive nucleus of the larger, more varied, and shifting corpus.

And so I am not indulging in hyperbole when I say that, as far as the work our Company, in its brief association, engaged in, it made little difference whether (for example) one was gaoled, another murdered in a low tavern brawl, a third succumbed to alcohol, a fourth to a virulent strain of botulism, a fifth to the plague, a sixth to the languishments of lunacy (or any other mixture of melodrama you care to concoct); for the corporation, the collaboration in which we were engaged, not only was larger than but actually was independent of its feeble individual members. The work that these words will form a meager contribution to is not merely a greater entity; it includes and sustains those among us who have perished or come to naught; these are not my words but might be anybody's; the light that strikes across the void to stroke to life the details woven here might have fallen upon anyone's helpless eyes; but that one's is closed in sleep, another's in death or blindness, you, or anybody, might be the lens through which this vision is cast; I am not I; or, another is I.

It is thus futile to ask who composed what in any given writer's canon. A biographical dictionary is the most absurd thing in the world, unless you want to call a biography that. The problems of attribution and bibliography which have plagued grubbing scholars for centuries have as little chance for solution as a child's attempts to classify the wind that strips a tree of its burning hair, yes, bares it to all the brilliant and heartless heavens. The history of poetry is not the history of a number of individual writers and their individual works; it is, more correctly, the germination and growth, through countless metamorphoses, of an increasingly larger, more varied, and symmetrical body; it is an immense collaboration of poetical workers (who exist, in terms of their work, outside the time-stream) in the eduction of that body, for the contemplation of all men. Other labourers will come, I know, to reflect their minuscule portion of light into the blinding mirror that holds her monstrous beauty (and which is always betrayed by alien shadows); the same that, tilting now as the earth tilts toward autumn, reflects her flaming mane, the glory of her loosened hair as it drifts and floats and ignites the various portions of her swelling and symmetrical body, till nothing but an outline of fire can be seen there.

Autumn already. From this vantage-point I can see both fore and aft, and all around me the countryside described in these pages smokes in beauteous desolation. In the future, I see nothing but war and the elevation of an iron peace; in the past, an irretrievable landscape; in the circumscribed present, the pursued image that, even now, slips out of its captive glass. Autumn. But why regret an eternal sun if we are embarked on the discovery of divine light—far from those who fret over the turning seasons.

Sometimes in the sky, or in the blank oval that passes for the sky, I see endless beaches covered with white nations full of joy. I, who created all dramas, all deliriums, who fashioned new flowers, new tongues, new flesh, must now content himself (or his fading reflection of a self) with a mirror desolated of its image. The night is falling, the night when no man works.

Meanwhile this is the vigil. The labour continues, though I myself am nothing, a bit of glass that caught, for a moment, a drop of hidden fire. Before I move toward that larger, silvery skin (disguised as death), to be absorbed utterly into its luminous void, I pause, I float suspended in the large aery theatre of the mind, to recreate the movement of that labour, extended over the triangle formed by the three points of the English capital and the two major coastal cities of California (with Chicago at its imaginary centre): the toil in the great libraries of London to formulate a poetic theory and practise; the composition in innumerable rented rooms, bare of the presence they were dedicated to, of a poem-series in an antique measure; and the tracing, in countless theatres, always moving west into the final cradle of illusion, of the image it has been my part to reflect.

That image now retreats into her glass, yes, retreats and trembles like a tree about to be ignited by the first frost of the year. I rise to follow. Around me darkness presses implacably. There is a buzzing in my ears. She is sitting at her dressing table, she is taking off her jewels after the masque, she is combing out her long dazzling waterfall of hair. A sudden constriction of breath, as if my chest were squeezed by a giant. She puts down her tortoise-shell comb, she tilts the mirror. For one split moment she looks at me directly and smiles. A needle of light thrusts across an interval of darkness into an open eye.

This is the first of a four-part work.